MW00878204

THE WEIRD ADVENTURES
OF THE BLOND ADDER

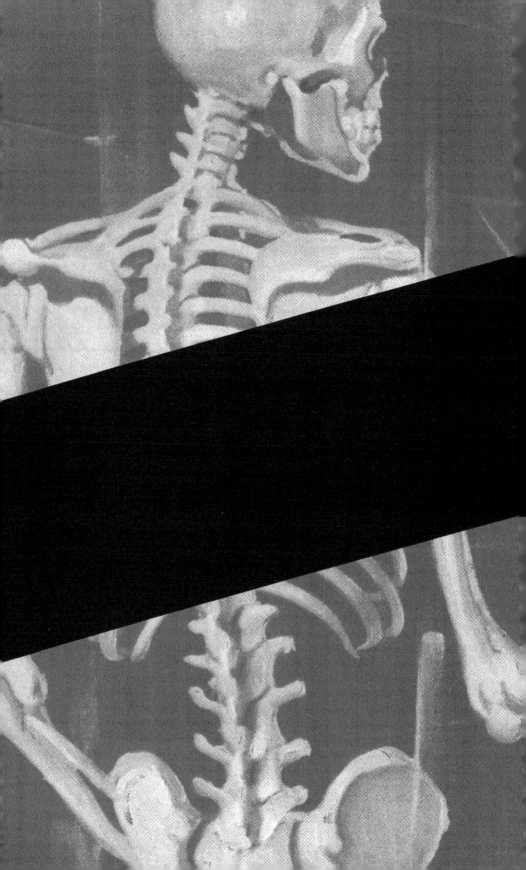

THE WEIRD ADVENTURES OF THE
BLOND ADDER
The Complete Cases of DETECTIVE LEE NACE
LESTER DENT

ALTUS PRESS

BOSTON • 2010

First Edition — 2010

EDITED AND DESIGNED BY

Matthew Moring

COVER BY

George Rozen

SPECIAL THANKS TO

Will Murray, Ray Riethmeier and William Stolz & the Western Historical Manuscript Collection at the University of Missouri, Columbia

PUBLISHING HISTORY

THE DEATH BLAST originally appeared in the July 1933 issue of *Ten Detective Aces* magazine. This version copyright © 2010 the Estate of Norma Dent.

THE SKELETON'S CLUTCH originally appeared in the August 1933 issue of *Ten Detective Aces* magazine. This version copyright © 2010 the Estate of Norma Dent.

THE DIVING DEAD originally appeared in the September 1933 issue of *Ten Detective Aces* magazine. This version copyright © 2010 the Estate of Norma Dent.

THE TANK OF TERROR originally appeared in the October 1933 issue of *Ten Detective Aces* magazine. This version copyright © 2010 the Estate of Norma Dent.

THE FLAMING MASK originally appeared in the December 1933 issue of *Ten Detective Aces* magazine. This version copyright © 2010 the Estate of Norma Dent.

LEE NACE: HIS CHARACTER TRAITS copyright © 2010 the Estate of Norma Dent.

HOT OIL copyright © 2010 the Estate of Norma Dent.

Published by arrangement with the Estate of Norma Dent.

Printed in the United States of America

Set in Caslon.

TABLE OF

Contents

Will Murray

LESTER DENT USED to boast that his true claim to fame rested not as the creator of Doc Savage, but in the fact that he had scored nineteen consecutive cover stories in *Ten Detective Aces*. Strictly speaking, this is a wild exaggeration. The number was closer to ten. But looking at the record, it's understandable why Dent would remember it that way.

Ten Detective Aces started off as an early Harold Hersey gangster pulp, *The Dragnet Magazine*. It debuted in 1928. Two years later, gangster stories were on the way out, and the traditional detective tale of clues and ratiocination was considered old-fashioned. Action and melodrama were what readers craved. So in 1930 the title became *Detective-Dragnet* and metamorphosed into *Ten Detective Aces* in 1933.

By this time, the publisher was Aron A. Wyn, later to start Ace Books. The A. A. Wyn school of pulp writing was a revival of the 1920s melodrama which had just begun to cool in its literary grave before it was exhumed and made to dance, like a captive puppet, on new strings.

Dent came in early in '32 and bowed out at the end of 1933, missing only one issue in a run of fourteen. So he dominated the magazine for two solid years, scoring most covers and seeing his name almost always cover-featured, even when the cover painting was not reflective of one of his stories.

Dent's debut in that magazine was "The Sinister Ray," a novelette starring a scientific detective in the mold of Arthur

B. Reeve's Craig Kennedy, the so-called American Sherlock Holmes who was such a huge hit in *The American Magazine* and hardcover books. Lynn Lash only appeared one more time, but in between Dent put other scientific sleuths through their paces in electrifying tales like "The Invisible Horde" and "Terror, Inc."

When *Detective-Dragnet* retooled as *Ten Detective Aces* with the March 1933 issue, Paul Chadwick's criminologist of the weird, Wade Hammond, was carried over, but not much else. That issue shows signs of hasty remaking. The running heads on each page said simply "Detective"—suggesting that it had been made up as an issue of *Detective-Dragnet* and partially replated.

New characters soon began sprouting up—Frederick C. Davis' memorable Moon Man and Norvell W. Page's Ken Carter both debuted in the May issue. Others, like Richard B. Sale's The Cobra and Emile C. Tepperman's Marty Quade, followed in short order. As Carl McK. Saunders, author Philip Ketchum revived his dormant series starring Captain John Murdock of the Central City police.

As the apparent star contributor to *Detective-Dragnet*, Lester Dent made the transition easily, scoring most of the 1933 covers, as he had many of the 1932 covers. He contributed a trio of interesting weird stories about random agency detectives, but initially offered no new fresh character of his own. But *10DA*—as it is sometimes styled—was becoming a vehicle for series heroes and having just started writing Doc Savage, Dent was evidently asked to create one by editor Harry Widmer—or perhaps it was Wyn himself, who remarked in print that sometimes series just "happen." He advised contributors thusly: "The best way for an author to break in with a series character is not to submit three or four stories of the series at the start, as so many do, but rather to allow the editor to discover the series—particularly if the writer is a new contributor."

Lee Courtney Nace, AKA the Blond Adder, debuted in

"The Death Blast," July, 1933. Dressed like a priest and sporting an angry serpentine scar on his forehead (evidently inspired by Tarzan of the Apes), Nace took on the creepiest cases this side of Wade Hammond—who was rarely cover-featured. Four more stories followed. Dent started writing the series in May, 1933, which makes it contemporary with the classic first-year Doc Savage adventures, *Brand of the Werewolf, Meteor Menace* and *The Monsters*. Lester was hot that year!

It's not too much of a stretch to imagine Lee Nace as an ego projection of Les Dent. Like Lester, Nace was born in Missouri, and possessed many other Dentian traits, including a habit of eating in different restaurants every day. The author gave his new hero a wildly-varied background to justify his many skills, rather like Dent's own. Having been a stage magician, an acrobat, cowboy, chemist and dabbling in other exotic fields, the Blond Adder was equal to almost any challenge. His bag of tricks was virtually limitless. Many future Doc Savage gadgets were first fielded in the Nace stories. The character was one of those who paved the way for James Bonds' reliance on unusual weapons and scientific devices.

The Nace series was an interesting blend of science detection, the action-detective story, and a new sub-genre some editors called the "menace" story. Other names were coined. Sometimes it was "mystery-horror," or "ultra-mystery." The formal weird menace sub-genre would grow out of this emerging trend, later filling the pages of Popular Publications' *Dime Mystery Magazine, Terror Tales, Horror Stories* and many others. But in *Ten Detective Aces* it was still in its nascent stages.

For *Writer's Digest,* literary agent Lurton Blassingame described this type of pulp tale as it was in 1933:

> There is an unusually good market today for the well-written story of menace. If this word does not give you a clear picture of the type of fiction desired, I suggest that you read *The Phantom of the Opera* and the adventure of Sherlock Holmes in which he uncovers *The Hound of the Baskervilles.* Then to

get a little closer to the present, reread Sax Rohmer's *Fu Manchu* and you will be ready to read current magazines with a full understanding of what editors mean when they speak of "menace." In this type of story some person or thing hangs a veil of horror over the characters in the story; we never know when this "menace" will strike, but we do know it will continue to commit depredations until the hero does his stuff and overcomes it in the final climax. *Dracula* was a menace play.

Blassingame went on:

These two stories represent the two tendencies in the "menace" fiction being published today. In *The Hound of the Baskervilles* we do not know who is committing the crimes or why; so in addition to the menace there is also a mystery. Sax Rohmer, however, lets us know the identity of his criminal, but the monster Fu Manchu is too clever to be captured and continues to commit his crimes despite all the efforts of the police to apprehend him.

So was Mary Reinhardt Roberts' popular play turned film, *The Bat*, which was certainly another major influence on this type of tale. As were other 1920s stage dramas such as *The Cat and the Canary* and *The Monster*. This trend also seized Hollywood, carrying clear into the 1930s. And where Hollywood ventured, the pulps inevitably followed.

Most of *10DA's* star series characters delved into menace cases, but as Wyn explained to *Writer's Digest* in 1934, he wanted to see more than what he called "menace-action" manuscripts:

The one feature on which we do insist is that all of our stories must be fast-moving and develop plenty of suspense. The menace-action type story is one of the best for us, but it has unlimited possibilities of variety, and variety is what we are seeking. For example, in *Ten Detective Aces* we use stories showing the human side of life; stories of the hard-boiled detective presenting life in stark reality; horror stories, stories from the murderer's point of view, stories with or without romance or woman interest. Our detective stories are usually against an American background, but occasionally a good yarn featuring an American hero against a foreign setting will also fit into our scheme. And we use an occasional humorous detective yarn. In fact, our policy is so elastic that even a good action-detective story against an underworld background or in which underworld characters are featured, has a chance with us although we emphatically do not want the straight gang-mob yarn. The typical straight deductive story has no place in our lineup—but in a short-short, for example, if it has enough suspense and a really clever surprise twist, we might make an exception. Or in a story where deduction plays an important part but which is worked out through action.

The latter variation was a Lester Dent specialty. In his article, "Why Aren't Your Detective Stories Selling?" Blassingame singled out Dent's first Lee Nace exploit as an exemplary example of the menace plot:

> In the current issue of *Ten Detective Aces* Lester Dent has a mystery-menace story where the criminal does not disguise himself as something fantastic, but succeeds in spreading terror and death through his cleverness. At the end he is revealed by the hero as [DELETED], who decided that he would kill off all the persons concerned and keep the wealth for himself. It doesn't make any difference to the editors whether you use a disguised menace or not; your menace must be kept logical whether he uses a disguise or whether he simply gets by in his own character and dress.

The Nace series is doubly fascinating because it ran parallel with the first year of *Doc Savage Magazine*. Gadgets that first appeared in Nace became standard Doc Savage equipment. Some of these plots and locales were revisited in Doc Savage as well. "The Diving Dead" anticipates *The Annihilist*. "The Tank of Terror" prefigures the Oklahoma oil backdrop of *The Derrick Devil*. That story's colorful outlaw, Robin Hood Lloyd, is based upon Oklahoma bad boy, Pretty Boy Floyd, who was still alive and robbing banks at that time. He would be gunned down the following year. The 1933 Chicago Exposition site of "The Flaming Mask" reads as a dry run for 1939's *World's Fair Goblin*. Dent probably visited the Exposition before writing this tale.

And if there is any proof that Dent, not his Street & Smith editors, introduced Patricia Savage into the series, it is the appearance and development of Lee Nace's equally resourceful cousin, Julia Nace, who first pops up in "The Diving Dead" and soon becomes a full partner in his agency—something Pat Savage never succeeded in doing with Doc Savage.

Nace's nemesis, Sergeant Gooch of Homicide, is also introduced in "The Diving Dead." He was evidently meant to be a continuing foil, but the locales of the follow-up stories precluded a second appearance. Gooch was to have debuted in "The Skeleton's Clutch," but was written out of the final draft. As originally conceived, the character had a broad Irish accent.

Earlier drafts of "The Skeleton's Clutch" have Lee Nace carrying an automatic. His character trait of not carrying a weapon began with this story, and runs parallel to Doc Savage's identical no-pistols policy early in his adventures.

Most of Dent's titles were changed. "The Death Blast" was originally "The Hoader Horrors." "The Skeleton's Clutch" was "The Green Skeleton Kills." "Hot Oil" became "The Tank of Terror," and "The Flaming Mask" had been "The Hell Heat." Only "The Diving Dead" stood unchanged. All but one rated a cover illustration.

The Lee Nace series ended abruptly, and circumstantial evidence indicates that a combination of overwork and nervous exhaustion led to its discontinuance. Dent had wanted to keep his byline alive and before the public while ghosting the monthly Doc Savage novels under the house name of Kenneth Robeson. It proved to be too Herculean a task for the former brass-pounder from Tulsa. After skipping the November 1933 issue, Lee Nace made his final bow.

The ending of Lee Nace's brief but colorful career was not

the last of this type of character. In 1934, Dent moved over to Dell's *All Detective Magazine* and offered another reformulation for editor Carson W. Mowre. Foster Fade, the Crime Spectacularist, ran only three installments, alas. In 1937, this concept achieved its ultimate expression with Click Rush, the Gadget Man, who ran in Street & Smith's *Crime Busters* from 1937-39. Running for 19 episodes, it was the longest and most successful of Lester Dent's many gadget detectives.

While all but two of the Lee Nace stories have been reprinted over the last 30 years, their appearances were widely scattered. This Altus Press edition marks the first time all five of the bizarre quintet have been collected in a single volume. We've gone back to the surviving manuscripts and reedited and restored all but one. As a bonus, included also is Lester Dent's previously-unpublished biographical background profile of Lee Nace.

And now, it's time to meet the enigmatic and resourceful Blond Adder as he takes on some of the most diabolical fiends in pulp history...

The Death Blast

Thunder and lightning gashed the sky
over the mountain lake shore. But a
more sinister, more diabolical thunder
rocked the earth. And a more lethal
lightning flared on the ground. It
illuminated the grisly horror of man-
made death. Fighting through this maze
of murder was Lee Nace, ace detective.
And with him was a redheaded beauty—
who led the way to a terror trap!

CHAPTER I

The Hoarder Horrors

THE RED-HEADED GIRL had a pistol hidden under the newspaper she was pretending to read. She trained it on Lee Nace the instant he stepped out of the hotel elevator.

Nace walked on across the lobby, stride normal. The gun was an automatic. Chances were she couldn't hit him, shooting from her lap.

Anyway, why should she shoot? He had never seen the girl before. He passed outdoors. Reflection in the swinging door told him the red-head had arisen, was following. She had wrapped the gun in the newspaper.

The street was warmly murky, no one in sight. Mountain Town was an upstate New York summer resort, and the season had not yet started.

Nace waited, thumbing tobacco into his stubby pipe. He stroked a match flame over the bowl, drew in fragrant smoke.

The red-head crowded her gun muzzle into the small of his back.

"Your hat needs straightening!" she said. Her voice was hurried, husky.

Nace lifted both hands and made motions of adjusting his Panama.

Nace was a tall man, so gaunt he had a hungry look. His face was angular, solemn, almost puritanical. His attire was dark, very plain. He might have been mistaken for a young minister.

"I'm going to turn around," Nace said. Then he wheeled slowly.

He got his first close look at the girl. She made his head swim. Maybe it was her form. Or maybe it was her face, or red hair. Or her clothes; he couldn't tell. In Broadway par-

lance, she had what it takes.

"You sold out to them!" Her husky voice was bitter. "I want to know who paid you. You can be a nice boy and talk here, or you can act stubborn and force me to use measures."

Nace pulled smoke out of his pipe.

"It'd be easy to be nice to a baby like you." He made it sound like an insult.

She bored the gun muzzle into his breast bone, said scathingly, "The great Lee Nace! The famous private detective Scotland Yard kept in England a year, on a fabulous salary, to study

Lee Nace took a chance—and walloped!

his methods! What a bust you turned out to be!"

"So you know me?" Nace mixed smoke with his words.

"That surprised you, did it?" she clipped. "I've seen your pictures. I've read some of the ballyhoo about you. That's what led me to wire for you."

Nace chewed his pipe slowly until it was half turned over in his teeth. "What's your name?"

"Benna Franks. You saw it on the telegram."

"I got no telegram from you."

She didn't believe him. "So that's your story?"

Nace still held his Panama brim with both hands. "Believe it or not, Benna."

"Are you going to tell me who bribed you not to work for me?" She gored him with the gun muzzle.

"Where'd you get the bribe idea, Benna?" His pipe turned the rest of the way over and was now upside down.

"You've been in town since noon. You didn't call me, as my wire directed. It's plain they bought you off."

"Who's *they?*"

Her gun gouged. "Quit stalling! Either you tell me who it was, or—!"

Nace blew through his pipe, suddenly and hard. Sparks spurted out, fell on the girl's hand.

She gasped. Instinctively, her hand jerked back.

Nace's hands left his hat brim with a speed that dazzled the eye. They reached the girl's gun. A twist, and he had the weapon.

BENNA FRANKS looked at her slender, tanned hands. The sparks had not burned them in the slightest. She slapped Nace—one, two, right hand, left hand.

Nace dropped his pipe. His ears rang as though full of sleigh bells. Rage smoked his pale eyes. He bent over and got his pipe, and when he straightened, the rage had subsided.

The girl whirled and ran. Nace grabbed, got her arm. He pulled her back hard enough to slam her against his chest. She opened her mouth to shriek. He cupped a hand over it. She bit his palm, but he stopped that by crowding a thumb hard against her nose.

He carried her down the street a few yards, so no one in the hotel would see them. She hissed, struggled, kicked. The perfume she used eddied faintly in his nostrils.

When she showed no sign of ceasing her exertions, he growled, "Lay off, Benna, or I'll have to smack you down!"

The girl went on scuffling. Nace, watching her eyes, discovered she was looking behind him. He twisted hurriedly. He was just a fraction too late.

A man had glided up behind Nace and the girl. He gripped a wrench. It was all of iron, the sort of wrench which comes as factory equipment with most moderate-priced cars. He slammed it on top of Nace's head.

Nace dropped.

The girl recoiled, unconsciously straightening her hair, saying hoarsely, "Fred! Fred! You didn't hit hard enough to kill him?"

"Small loss if I did!" grated Fred.

Fred was almost as tall as Nace. He was thick in shoulders and neck. His face was handsome in a jaw-heavy sort of way.

"Go get in the car, honey," Fred said. "I'll bring this bum."

He stopped to pick Nace up. He was entirely off guard.

Nace hung a beautiful right-hand jab on the point of Fred's ample jaw. Stunned, Fred piled down on the detective. But he must have done some boxing in his time—he had sense enough to hold Nace's arms.

Nace banged the top of his head against Fred's head.

A strange wig of a contraption Nace wore was dislodged and fell off his head. The interesting part of this consisted of a steel skullcap, thin and light, but very stout. It bore thick blond hair and fitted over Nace's close-cropped natural hair, which was the same color. This had kept the wrench blow on the head from harming Nace to any degree.

The red-headed girl had started for a coupe parked nearby. She came running back and hunted frantically for the wrench, which Fred had dropped.

Nace rolled Fred over, hit him again, then a second time. Fred sighed loudly, became limp.

Nace leaped to his feet. He saw the girl pick up the wrench, and started for her.

Fifty feet distant, a man stepped from behind a building and began firing a revolver at Nace as rapidly as he could pull the trigger.

THE RAPIDITY of the man's shooting made his aim erratic. The first bullet passed Nace's head with a sucking smack of a sound. The second broke glass somewhere up the Mountain Town street.

Nace leaped sidewise, landed flat in the street gutter. He pulled himself along the gutter. A four-foot-wide park of grass lay between sidewalk and street pavement; a large maple tree grew out of this. Nace stood up behind this, drew the girl's gun, got a bead on the man trying to kill him and pulled the trigger.

The gun hammer slapped down with an empty click. Nace tried again. The cylinder made a complete revolution to the accompaniment of more clicks.

The girl had been using an empty gun to menace him.

The man shooting at Nace reloaded his revolver. He resumed his barrage. Bark flew off the tree. Glancing bullets squawled. More windows broke. The powder thunder rolled and boomed in the Mountain Town street.

The gunman ran forward a little to shoot better, and Nace got a good look at him.

The fellow was short, extremely fat. He wore a long tan topcoat, a black-banded black hat. A white handkerchief was tied over his face.

The red-headed girl had seized the unconscious Fred. She dragged him to the coupe. She tried to get him into the seat, but it was too much for her strength. She dumped him on the floorboards, climbed over him, took the wheel.

The coupe sped away with Fred's legs protruding from the door.

The masked gunman had made no effort to prevent her escape. He emptied his revolver again, and once more started to reload.

Nace flung the red-head's empty pistol. The gunman, busy reloading, failed to see it coming. It hit him in the face, knocked him down.

The man got up and ran, still reloading the revolver.

Nace ran the opposite direction, across the street. He dived between two buildings, circled around the block and joined some excited natives who were racing to the sound of the shots.

No one, it developed, had more than a hazy idea of what had happened.

"I seen 'em from my window!" excitedly shouted a man who lived up the street. "There was a whole gang of 'em! They drove off in a couple of big touring cars! They was city gangsters, I'm bettin'!"

"Where's Jan Hasser, the town constable?" somebody demanded.

"Here he comes."

Constable Hasser galloped up. He was a thin, wrinkled man. His age was probably forty, but a stringy white moustache made him look sixty. He wore a shiny blue coat. He chewed black, sweet tobacco which he took from a yellow paper package.

"Dern city gunsters shootin' each other up," was his verdict.

Nace picked up his pipe without being noticed. He loaded the bowl, put a match flame to it, and went into the hotel trailing fragrant smoke.

"You just missed the excitement, Mister Leeds," the sleek clerk told Lee Nace.

Nace had registered under the name of Jules Leeds.

"Yeah," Nace agreed without interest. "Say, who was the eyeful waitin' in here when I went out? The red-head."

"That one? Her name is Benna Franks. She runs a summer

camp on the lake—Camp Lakeside."

"On the make?"

"Not her! She's principal of the Sunday school."

"Yeah," said Nace, and went up to his room.

NACE OPENED his bag, took out a pair of black oxfords which were rather worn. He exchanged them for the low-cuts he was wearing. To his left arm, just below the elbow, he strapped a sheath which held a hammerless .38 revolver. The grip had been machined off the gun, and a wooden knob fitted directly back of the cylinder. The weapon fitted nicely up his sleeve.

The hotel room had a stone fireplace. In this, Nace burned a magazine which contained an article on criminology, written by himself. He tore the leaves off a few at a time, so they would burn thoroughly.

From a coat pocket, Nace produced a telegram. It was addressed to his New York office. It read:

GOT BIG JOB FOR YOU AND WILL MEET YOU AT SOUTH END OF MOUNTAIN TOWN LAKE AT TEN WEDNESDAY NIGHT AND YOU BETTER BE CAREFUL.

SOL RUBINOV

The message was sent Monday; Nace had received it on Tuesday. This was Wednesday. Nace eyed his watch.

The hands said twenty minutes until ten.

Nace folded the telegram and put it in a small, flat silk pack. The pack held other articles. It was half an inch thick, four wide, six long, and it tapered toward the edges. He stuck it on his back, just above the belt line, with adhesive tape.

He left the hotel and swung off across town, drawing briskly on his pipe. He watched his back trail. But no one followed him.

Nace thought a little about the telegram. He had never heard of the sender, Sol Rubinov. Judging from the composition of the message, Rubinov was a foreigner. Nace knew nothing more than the wire divulged.

A faint smile tickled Nace's solemn mouth. Ordinarily, he didn't take a case without knowing more about it than this. But he had intended coming up here for a short vacation, anyway.

Houses became scattering about Nace. Sidewalks gave out. He strode a path paralleling the paved road. The way dipped sharply.

Moist air off the lake pushed gently against his face.

The night was sultry. The moonbeams had a bilious yellow cast. Clouds were piled like black sponges around the horizon. Heat lightning jumped about in the clouds. Occasional thunder groaned and boomed.

Half a mile or so distant, a train clamored through the night. It began whistling for a crossing, and whistled perhaps twenty seconds. Then the train must have dived behind a hill, for its sound abruptly became fainter.

It was then that Nace heard a man gurgling and screaming faintly and crashing about in bushes near the lake shore.

CHAPTER II

The Man Who Blew Up

NACE HALTED. HE cupped both hands back of his ears.

The noises continued. The screams were stifled, as though the one who uttered them had a finger in his mouth. The brush fluttered; branches broke. It was as if a drunk was repeatedly falling down and getting up.

Nace slid a fountain-pen flashlight out of his vest and advanced. But he did not have to use the light. The man making the noises staggered out on the beach, where moonbeams bathed him.

It was the fat man who had tried to shoot Nace outside the hotel. His forehead bore a cut the exact shape of the trigger guard of the automatic with which Nace had hit him.

The man now wore a bathing suit, and nothing else. The suit was wet.

A wad of cloth was embedded between the fellow's pudgy jaws. A wire, tied tightly behind his head, held it there.

He was fighting wildly, desperately, to undo the wire. The effort had torn his fingertips until they were stringing scarlet.

"I'll take it off, buddy," Nace said, and stepped out into the moonlight.

The fat man ran toward Nace, still tearing at the wire.

Then he exploded.

Nothing else quite described what happened. The fat man simply blew up. A sheet of blue-hot flame burst open his bathing suit. His head and waving arms sprang fifteen feet in the air. What was left of his lower body slammed into the sand.

Nace reeled back. He clapped hands over his ears. The terrific report of the explosion had deafened him.

The upper portion of the fat man's body thudded into the sand. Gory fragments strewed about.

Nace shuddered, turned the pen light on himself. His clothing had not been soiled.

He stepped into the brush and crouched down, nursing his aching ears. He had never before heard such a sharp, deafening blast. It had been worse than a pistol discharge alongside his ears. The ringing in his head subsided. Hearing returned until he could detect the flutter of leaves in the faint breeze.

Waves made moist sucking sounds on the lake shore. Far away, thunder clapped and rumbled; lightning splattered the clouds with fitful red.

Running feet came *clap-clapping* down the paved road. One man! He turned off the road, came toward the lake.

"What're you doin'?" he yelled. "Dynamitin' fish in that lake, I'll bet! By crackey, that's agin the law!"

It was the Mountain Town constable, Jan Hasser. He came up, a big pistol in hand, his left cheek wadded out with chewing tobacco.

He saw the head and shoulders of the fat man. His mouth fell open. Tobacco juice spilled down his chin, unnoticed.

"Jumpin' snakes!" he gulped. "That's my deputy constable, Fatty Dell!"

NACE REACHED inside his coat.

"No you don't, by crackey!" yelled Constable Hasser. He leveled his big pistol at Nace. "Stand still, sonny!"

Nace scowled. "I wanted to show you my credentials. Get them—my inside pocket."

Hasser came over, making a hard mouth under his stringy white moustache. Gingerly, he withdrew Nace's papers. He read them, peered closely at Nace's face.

"Lee Nace, huh," he grunted. "Reckon that's right. I've seen yer picture in the New York papers. Well, what happened to Fatty?"

"He blew up."

"He what?"

Nace used his pen light. His solemn, puritanical face registered no horror at the scene.

"I don't see any sign of what caused it," he said. "The man simply exploded."

Hasser cleaned off his chin with his sleeve. "Poor Fatty! Who stuffed that rag in his mouth and tied the wire around his head?"

"Search me, Hasser. It was there when I saw him."

"What were you doin' around here?"

"I was out walking."

"That all?"

"It's enough for the time being, Hasser." Nace went over and played his thin flash beam along the water edge.

"Fatty Dell swam to this point," he said. "Here are his tracks leaving the water. Somebody met him. Whoever it was had his shoes wrapped in cloth so as not to leave a distinct footprint. Here are that fellow's tracks, too. It looks like they wrestled around in the sand some."

"Who was the other feller?"

"How the hell should I know?"

Nace raced his flash beam out over the water. He waded in, continued out until nearly waist deep. He dipped up a soggy bundle which had been floating on the surface.

"Here's the rags the other man had wrapped around his shoes. The piece between Fatty Dell's jaws was torn off these."

Nace studied the sodden cloth carefully.

"That ain't liable to help us much," mumbled Constable Hasser. "Or will it?"

"It's part of an old shirt," Nace said dryly. "Size seventeen.

That means the wearer was husky. There's several laundry marks, all the same. That makes it simple to trace the owner."

"By crackey!" grunted Hasser.

"The owner is not necessarily the man who seized Fatty Dell," Nace went on. "The fellow who had the rag tied around his feet wore black and white sport shoes. Some of the shoe polish and the white cleaner rubbed off on the cloth."

"Gimme," said Hasser, extending a hand. "That thing is a clue."

Nace passed it over. "Want me to call the medical examiner?"

"Yeah—sure. You'll find a house with a phone up the road about half a mile."

Nace swung off. But he didn't go far. When he judged Constable Hasser could no longer hear his footsteps, he wheeled and ran back silently.

CREEPING THROUGH the brush, Nace stared at the moon-bathed lake shore.

Nace was of the opinion Constable Hasser had appeared on the explosion scene a bit too early. Therefore, he was not greatly surprised at what he saw.

Constable Hasser stood knee deep in the lake. He was industriously washing the fragment of shirt—obviously to remove traces of the white and black shoe polish.

Hasser wrung the shirt out, then scrutinized it.

"That oughta put a crimp in the dang city feller!" His surly mutter reached Nace's ears.

Coming out of the water, Hasser stared at the fragments of Fatty Dell's body. He seemed extremely puzzled.

"But why kill Fatty?" he grumbled. "Fatty was goin' to croak this dang Nace. By crackey, maybe Nace done Fatty in!"

Hasser bit off a segment of plug tobacco, growled, "I gotta find out about this! Better spread a warnin' about them black and white sport shoes in case it wasn't Nace—!"

He moved off beyond earshot.

Nace trailed in grim silence. Hasser went to the road, followed it a short distance, then turned off on a path. The path was well made. It crossed gullies via rustic bridges, and was graveled in the low places.

The gravel prevented Nace getting close enough to Hasser to hear what he said, in case the man talked to himself again.

Trees interlaced above the path, making it a black tunnel. But the distant lightning reddened the tunnel occasionally, furnishing another reason for Nace remaining well to the rear.

A wooden bridge boomed under Hasser's feet. Far-off thunder rumbled a louder echo.

Nace listened carefully, heard Hasser crunching through gravel a hundred feet ahead, and thus relieved, ran lightly across the bridge.

At the farther end, he sprawled headlong over a taut wire.

A man hurtled from the darkness and landed upon him.

NACE TWISTED quickly upon his back, spun half around and kicked with both legs. His feet hit the attacker squarely. The assailant squawked surprise and pain. He was propelled backward. He made a loud crash in the trailside brush.

Then the man cut loose with a gun. The weapon made a nasty *chung-chung-chung* series of reports. It was silenced. The silencer swallowed nearly all the muzzle flame.

Nace was burned on the leg slightly. He got to his feet with a rolling convulsion. He jumped the direction which came handiest. It happened to be toward the bridge.

He jumped up and down on the planks, then swung over the rail and hung by his hands, as far under the bridge as he could get. Holding with one hand and a foot, he dug his gun out of the sleeve sheath.

Constable Hasser came charging back along the path, bellowing, "Hey! What the devil—?"

"Shut up!" barked Nace's attacker. "That damn New York

detective followed you!"

The shrillness of the man's voice, its strained quality, told Nace it was disguised.

Hasser began, "Oh, it's you, Mister—!"

"Hell!" ripped the other. "Don't speak my name! The dick is on the bridge somewhere. I tripped him with a wire, but he got away—!"

"Well, we'll get the gol-dinged—!"

"Nix. Come on!"

The two ran off rapidly. Before they were out of earshot, the shrill, disguised voice of Nace's assailant drifted back.

"My car is on the road. We'll leave Mister Detective a present there."

Nace swung back onto the bridge, wondering about that last remark. He ran to the end of the bridge, stopped there to yank the wire loose. He splashed his flashlight on it for a short instant.

The wire was the same type as the length which had been tied between unfortunate Fatty Dell's jaws. Nace felt certain that piece had been cut from this one.

Nace left the trail, then moved along a few yards from it. He was wary of another ambush. The remark about leaving a present at the road was still in his thoughts. He wondered what it meant.

He knew an instant later.

A jarring, smashing roar of sound caromed across the woods. A bluish flash, brief, brilliant, splashed on the treetops. Then a procession of echoes boomed from the surrounding hills.

The explosion had come from the left.

Nace discarded caution, sprinted for the spot. He could guess, now, what the present would be. Tree trunks and branches smashed his head, shoulders, arms. Brambles dug at his hide and picked small holes in his clothing. He sprawled into a gulch. After that, he used his flashlight.

Ahead, a car starter made a loud sawing noise; an engine blared up. The machine screamed away in second gear.

Nace reached the road too late to get even a glimpse of the fleeing vehicle. It had whirled around a curve in the highway.

Nace fanned his flash beam about.

Like a white string, the luminance crawled over what remained of Constable Hasser.

It wasn't much.

HASSER'S HEAD and torso were nearly intact, as were his legs. These two segments lay a full ten paces apart. The explosion which had demolished the man had been nearly fantastic in its violence.

Nace searched some minutes, seeking something which might tell him the nature of the explosion. He found nothing.

Using the flash, Nace hunted for footprints. The leaves were dry, the ground below arid enough to be solid. There had been no rain recently.

Thunder hooted from the horizon, as though in derisive laughter at his efforts. Lightning winked redly.

Nace kept at his search. Constable Hasser had been murdered so Nace could not get hold of him and pry out information. Hasser had obviously known a lot. And his murderer was the man who had also done in the deputy constable, Fatty Dell.

Nace growled sourly. Fatty Dell had been at the lake to kill him—Nace. Constable Hasser's mutterings had revealed that much. Nace could think of only one reason for their desiring his own end—to keep him from doing any investigating.

They obviously knew of the telegram he had received, signed by the name Sol Rubinov.

Nace doubled to study an object his flashlight had picked up. It was a mushroom, the type called a puffball because of the brownish powder it contains when mature. This one had been kicked and burst open, the brownish powder strewn about.

Nace went back and examined Hasser's shoes. They bore no

traces of the brown powder.

Next, Nace conducted an intensive hunt for the old shirt. It was nowhere to be found. Hasser's murderer had taken it.

Voices were to be heard, and running feet. Residents of the vicinity were coming to investigate the noise of the explosion.

Nace cut across the woods, making for Mountain Town. No one saw him. Once on the village sidewalks, he set a course for his hotel.

CHAPTER III

Deceit Trail

THE SLEEK HOTEL clerk was turning a telegram thought-fully in his hand when he came in.

"Danged if I know what to do with this wire," he told Nace in a mildly puzzled tone. "The thing came in this morning. It's addressed care of the Mountain House hotel, but we ain't got nobody named Lee Nace registered here."

Nace was holding his pipe. He made a mental note to see that his secretary got a ten per cent wage cut starting next pay day. She was always pulling stunts like this. He had told her distinctly he would be at the Mountain House, Mountain Town's largest hotel, under the name Jules Leeds.

"I'll take the wire," Nace said.

"But your name is Leeds, not—"

Nace proved who he was. Then he opened the telegram. It had been sent from Mountain Town to his New York office, and forwarded back.

WISH YOUR SERVICES IN URGENT MATTER
STOP REGISTER AT MOUNTAIN HOUSE THIS
CITY AND PHONE ME STOP WILL EXPECT YOU
UNLESS YOU WIRE OTHERWISE.
                              BENNA FRANKS

"So she was on the up and up," Nace murmured.

The clerk had an ear open. "What say?"

"Sounds like rain," Nace replied, after a couple of salvos of thunder had chased themselves across the countryside.

The clerk had been thinking. "Say, buddy, are you the Lee Nace the newspapers write about—the private detective? I read a story where it said people had tried to kill you more'n four hundred times. Tell me somethin', was that a damn lie?"

"Draw your own conclusions." Nace put his elbows on the desk and grew confidential. "What's the low-dirty on Constable Hasser and his deputy, Fatty Dell?"

The clerk's eyes saucered. "Cripes! You tryin' to get somethin' on 'em?"

"Just finding out what's what."

"You got a case here, Mister Nace?"

"Maybe."

"Well, I guess Hasser and Dell are all right," said the clerk. "There was some talk of them takin' money to let beer trucks pass through Mountain Town. Then there was some scandal last winter when a local judge got hell for issuin' pistol permits to some New York City gangsters. The judge claimed Hasser and Fell recommended the gangsters to him as honest citizens."

"That all?"

"Yeah—except Hasser and Dell knock off a crap game sometimes, and take pay for lettin' the boys go."

Nace smiled wryly. "What you mean is that Hasser and Dell are all right, except they're a pair of cheap crooks. That right?"

"Oh, hell! This is just gossip!"

"Sure." Nace smiled knowingly.

A CAR drove up and two tourists, man and woman, came in and registered.

It was sultry in the lobby. Flies buzzed. A loose window somewhere rattled every time it thundered.

Nace waited until the clerk was free again. "Where is Camp Lakeside?"

"Red-headed Benna Franks' place?"

"It's up the west side of the lake about two miles."

Nace spilled smoke from both nostrils. It was up the west side of the lake that Constable Hasser had been killed by the strange explosion.

"Much of a place?"

"The camp—yeah, it's quite a layout. Of course, it ain't opened up yet. But Benna Franks takes in plenty of jack later in the summer, when the season opens up."

"Where can I rent a car?"

"Down the street a block. You goin' up to Camp Lakeside?"

"Keep it under your hat," Nace warned with an exaggerated air of mystery.

"I sure will. And if there's anything else—"

Nace left the sleek youth declaring his willingness to be of assistance. The fellow was a good sort; his type had given detectives tips that had broken many a case.

The car-renting concern was a branch of a nation-wide chain. Nace had a card which the chain issued to reliable customers. It enabled him to rent a machine without the formality of putting up a deposit.

The machine was an eight-cylinder green roadster, the fastest heap in the place, Nace believed. It was a two-year-old model. A carbon knock tinkled under the hood as he drove out.

He glanced at the hotel in passing. What he saw made him stamp the brake until all four wheels slid. He burst out of the car, flung across the street, took the hotel stairs with a single vault.

The hotel clerk was draped like a rag across his desk. Crimson ran in a squirming red cord from his nostrils.

NACE TURNED the clerk on the desk, hunting wounds. He found none, unless a smashed nose counted. The clerk's face had banged the desk. There was a knot like half a walnut on his head.

The hotel elevator clanked open. Nace watched it, right hand on the ball-gripped gun in his left sleeve. Only the colored operator was in the cage.

Nace flipped a hand at the clerk. "When did that happen?"

"Lan' sakes, Mistah, ah don' know!" gurgled the boy. "Dat hadn't happened to 'im when ah took de ice watah up a minute ago."

"Who'd you take the ice water to?"

"Old lady in four-ten. Evah night at dis time, she has me fetch her ice water—!"

Nace shoved the elevator operator for the door. "Run out in the street and yell bloody murder!"

"Lawsy, Mistah, I don' know what to holler—"

"Yell that there's a murdered man in here!"

The colored boy must have taken Nace's words to mean the clerk had been murdered. He ran squawling into the street.

Nace whirled out through the back door. He waited in the darkness, one eye on the fire escape, the other on the exit. Seconds dragged and pulled minutes after them.

The hotel filled with excited citizens.

Nace was disgusted. It had been his guess that someone had visited the hotel bent on taking his life, and that the person would flee when the alarm was given. The guess had been bad somewhere.

He walked around and entered the hotel. Several persons had formed a sort of volunteer bucket brigade to relay ice water from the cooler to douse the unconscious clerk. The fellow stirred finally, sat up. He saw Nace and made a wry grin.

"Did you get a look at whoever hit you?" Nace questioned.

"Nix. I was dozin' with my face in my hands."

Nace slid a tenspot across the desk. "Buy yourself some aspirin with that."

The clerk blinked. "You think they came in here huntin' you?"

"You're a good guesser, boy."

Nace kindled his pipe, listening to the remarks of curious

citizens who had been drawn by the colored boy's yells. If the nearly-destroyed body of Constable Hasser, or that of Fatty Dell, had been found, the news was not yet in town.

Turning away, Nace saw something that nearly made him swallow his pipe.

It was Fred—the thick-necked, jaw-heavy young man who had helped the red-headed Benna Franks.

Fred had been working furtively toward the door. He saw he had been observed. He ducked outside.

Nace ran to the door, popped through, rattled his feet down the steps. Fred was diving into a car. It was the same coupe in which the red-head had driven him away from this spot earlier in the night.

The coupe lunged into movement.

Nace's gun came out of his sleeve, banged once.

The coupe engine died. Nace knew exactly where to shoot to hit the distributor under the hood.

Not aiming his gun at Fred, Nace ran to the machine.

Fred had an automatic in his hands. His arms were steady, but he made no effort to use the gun. He laid it on the cushions.

"Hell!" he said thickly. "I guess I ain't got no guts to kill a man."

Nace reached over Fred's lap for the gun on the cushions. Fred grabbed at Nace's head.

Nace chopped his hard hand, edgewise, to the man's temple. Fred moaned and fell over.

Nace got the gun. Then he reached further and plucked a rag off the coupe floorboards. It was the rag the murderer of Fatty Dell had used to wrap around his shoes.

Fred wore black and white sport shoes.

NACE POCKETED gun and rag, then hauled Fred out of the coupe and carried him to the rented roadster.

An excited crowd had poured out of the hotel. A beefy, red-necked man ran at Nace, cursing and brandishing a nickeled revolver. He demanded that Nace throw up his hands. Nace showed his agency card and his license.

"Anybody can steal them things and you look like a damn crook to me," snarled the nasty-tempered man. He added a string of insults.

Nace caught the smell of alcohol on the man's breath. Pointing behind the fellow, Nace said, "That man will identify me!"

The drunk turned. Nace knocked him down, grabbed the nickeled revolver, unloaded it and smashed it on the concrete pavement. The cylinder was broken off its pin, ruining the weapon.

"Who is this palooka?" Nace demanded of the crowd.

"A railroad dick," said the hotel clerk, who had weaved out with the crowd. "He always was too free with that gun."

"He's too free with his mouth," Nace growled, some of his anger departing.

He clambered in the roadster. Fred was awake. He said nothing. Nace drove off.

A lightning flash blazed like blood in the street, and afterward darkness came black and muggy. Nace thumbed the lights on. He glanced sidewise and saw Fred gathering himself in the seat.

"The next time I hit you, they'll need a doctor to wake you up!" Nace warned grimly.

Fred relaxed. "What are you going to do?"

Nace gave him silence for an answer.

The plunging roadster left Mountain Town behind. It banked around a curve, tires squealing in a slight skid, then straightened out.

The headlights picked up clustered cars and people alongside to the road.

"Know what that is?" Nace asked.

Fred muttered, "I stopped long enough to ask when I came in town."

Nace slowed up until he was through the jam. On the right side of the pavement, a crowd jostled each other to see the remnants of Constable Hasser's body.

The roadster increased speed, as though trying to catch its headlights. Thunder clapped and gobbled over the engine moan. A sign, white lettered in black, appeared. It said:

CAMP LAKESIDE

Nace jockeyed the roadster into the grounds. Lighted windows glowed in a rather pretentious two-story log building. Nace braked to a stop before it, looked at Fred.

The jaw-heavy young man was pale, trembling. His fists clenched and unclenched.

"Damn you!" he said thickly. "If you lay a hand on Benna, I'll break your neck!"

"Boo!" Nace said amiably. "Get out and let's go in."

Fred quitted the car as if afflicted with a stiffness of the joints. They put feet on a slab porch.

The door opened. Benna Franks stood there. Nace knew positively he had never seen a girl more beautiful. Standing in the light behind her, she looked like an angel with a halo.

She didn't see Nace at first.

"Fred!" she cried. "I've been worried about you."

"I'm all right, sis," said Fred.

Nace grinned. So these were brother and sister!

The Third Man-Blast

NACE FELT UNREASONABLY good over his discovery for some seconds. It gave him a feeling of elation out of all proportion to its importance in the trend of the case. He was not too dumb to realize why it tickled him, either. It was the red-head, of course. She was getting to him. He'd have to watch his step.

The red-head discovered him. She looked like she'd found a snake.

"What are you doing here?"

"Freddy brought me along," Nace said, face solemn.

"He's a liar!" Freddy yelled. "He shot into my car downtown and killed the engine, then knocked me senseless and brought me here."

Nace's voice rapped out before anyone else could speak.

"Maybe you'd like to tell what you were doing downtown, Freddy!"

Fred looked like he was been choked. He swallowed twice, made no answer.

"Why did you go downtown, Fred?" the red-head asked.

The jaw-heavy young man swallowed twice more. "To get some cigarettes."

Nace could see past the girl into the large front room of the log building. It was a small general store, selling everything from groceries to Indian curios.

Cigarettes were prominently displayed.

"Tsk, tsk," Nace chuckled. But his solemn face showed no levity.

"What was your purpose in coming here?" Benna Franks asked Nace angrily.

Nace, debating his answer, chanced to drop his eyes to her shoes. They were black-and-white sports.

Nace suddenly felt as if the air had frozen around him. It wasn't so much the shoes—almost all women wore them now. But it was the memory of that shrill voice which had cried out to unlucky Constable Hasser. Nace had taken for granted that it was a man's.

It could have been a woman's.

There was something else, too—the red-head's shoes bore a few brownish smudges that looked powder-like.

Nace thought of the puffball mushroom which had been broken by Constable Hasser's companion. The puffball had contained a powder this color.

"Where did you get that brown stain on your shoes?" he asked.

"Are you crazy?" the girl snapped.

Nace's voice turned hard. "Answer the question!"

"It's cinnamon," said the girl, startled out of her anger by his tone. "I dropped the cinnamon box in the kitchen."

"All right," Nace told her mildly. "Let's go in and talk."

"I don't want you in here."

"What you want don't cut much ice." He gave Fred a shove. "Get inside, you!"

Fred acted for an instant as if he were going to take a swing at Nace. But he reconsidered, felt of his temple, then stumbled inside.

The girl eyed her brother, seemingly surprised at his meek-ness. Then she followed him in.

Nace stepped across the threshold after them.

He knew instantly that he should have been more careful. But it was too late then.

A gun was shoving a cold round nose to his temple.

"Stand still, shamus!" gritted a harsh voice.

NACE STOOD still. He rolled his eyes sidewise enough, though, to see the man who held the weapon.

The fellow was blond, slender, snappily dressed. He was very handsome—if one liked features so fine they were almost feminine. In age, he was probably thirty-five.

Nace's scrutiny took in the blond man's hands. They were strong, manicured, with the nails so healthily pink as to lend a suspicion of artificial tint. But it was the many small pits in the skin that Nace gave particular attention. Nace didn't think they were disease pits—they looked more like the result of a spray of hot metal. Yet they weren't ordinary heat burns.

The blond young man's gun cocked with a noisy click.

"Spencer!" the red-head shrilled. "Don't shoot him!"

Her shriek rang out so sharply it startled the blond man. His gun muzzle jiggled, moved upward perhaps three inches. It now rested against the top of Nace's head, which was protected by the steel helmet-wig.

Nace took a chance. He hit Spencer in the midriff—just about as hard as he could. The blond man made a horrible face and fell to the floor. There, he had convulsions. His first twitch flung his gun skating across the floor.

The girl pounced on the weapon, pointed it at Nace.

Nace shrugged. "All right. Just so somebody's got it who doesn't want to shoot me."

Then he remembered the brown smudge on her shoes and nearly shuddered.

Fred growled, "Gimme that gun, sis!"

"You do, and somebody is liable to get killed!" Nace warned her.

"Get out!" she hissed.

"In my coat pocket in a telegram," Nace told her. "It's the one you sent to me in New York. It was forwarded here, and because I had registered at the hotel under a fake name, I didn't get it until less than an hour ago."

The red-head eyed him steadily, considering this. She looked like a flame-haired Madonna with the lights playing on her features.

Thunder bawled over the log house roof. Blond Spencer twisted and moaned on the floor.

The girl said jerkily, "I wonder—if—if I've had you all wrong?"

"I hope so." Nace pointed at Spencer. "Who's this?"

"Spencer—Jim Spencer. He is athletic director here at Camp Lakeside."

Fred Franks came over and gingerly extracted the telegram from Nace's coat pocket. He eyed it.

"Forwarded back here from New York City, all right," he admitted.

Nace picked the suffering Spencer up, dumped him in a chair. Then he seated himself with a flourish, took out his pipe, gorged it with tobacco and applied a match.

"Let's get to the bottom of this!" he said briskly. "Who's Sol Rubinov?"

"He is—was the caretaker and man-of-all-work here at Camp Lakeside," said the girl.

"It was in answer to a telegram signed by Sol Rubinov that I came here. As I told you, I didn't get your wire until tonight."

"Oh! Then Rubinov sent for you! That explains it!"

Nace looked at blond Spencer's shoes. They were plain black.

"GET RUBINOV," Nace suggested. "He may want to be in on this."

The red-head became pale, somewhat rigid. "I can't. I don't know where he is. I think—he has been murdered."

Fred Franks gave his sister a dramatic stare.

"I know he was murdered, sis!" he rapped. "I saw something on my way to town tonight which makes me sure of it. There was an explosion, just like we heard here night before last, and afterward, at the scene of the blast, the mangled body of Constable Jan Hasser was found."

The girl shuddered and sank into a chair made out of branches with the bark still attached.

"There was a terrific blast here at Camp Lakeside night before last," she told Nace swiftly. "Fred and I hunted around several minutes before we found the exact spot. There we discovered—!" Her mouth closed so tightly little muscles bunched around it, and her face looked as if it had been whitewashed.

"We found pieces of flesh and blood scattered around," finished Fred. "But we couldn't tell whether it was human. There wasn't no sign of a body."

"This happened the night after Rubinov sent me the telegram," Nace pointed out.

"Constable Hasser chanced to be passing and he laughed at our idea of calling in the state police," the girl said, voice strained.

"He would!" A fog of pipe smoke was growing in the sultry air over Nace's head.

Blond Spencer pusher himself out of his chair. He rolled his eyes at Nace, keeping both hands over his middle.

"I'm goin' to the kitchen an' wash my face!" he said hoarsely. "Maybe cold water will make me feel better."

He staggered into the kitchen, leaving the door open. Nace, looking through the gaping door, could see a second door across the kitchen, evidently leading outdoors.

"There just the one kitchen door going outside?" he asked.

The red-head nodded.

Nace sat where he was. Spencer turned on a water faucet in the kitchen. The splashing, mingling as it did with the thunder outdoors, made it seem as though it had started to rain. Nace kept his ears cocked, just on the chance Spencer might try to get out of the kitchen by a window.

"What's behind all this?" he questioned.

"To make you understand, I'll have to tell you Sol Rubinov's history," Benna Franks said, plainly glad to get away from the explosion subject. "He was born in Russia. His father was a successful shopkeeper, but rather ignorant. He trusted no one. He would not put his money in the banks, but hoarded it always in metal coins. He had a large hoard of coins when he died.

"Sol Rubinov, his son, had the same mania for hoarding. When he came to America, he brought a small fortune in coins gathered by his father. He never made a large salary here, but he saved nearly all of it. And every dollar of it, he changed into gold or silver and added to his secret hoard."

"He was sure inviting trouble," grunted Nace. He could hear Spencer splashing in the kitchen.

"Two days ago—the same day he wired you—Rubinov came to me and told me where his hoard was hidden," continued the girl. "He told me, that in the event of his death, I was to have his money."

Nace shut his eyes tightly and thought of the shrill voice in the night-ridden woods, of the brown powder on the girl's sport shoes. He thought also of what a jury would say when they heard Rubinov's death meant the girl was to have the old Russian's gold hoard. His forehead felt clammy.

"We looked for the hoarded money, Fred and I," said the girl. "It was gone, except for one coin wedged in a crack."

SPENCER CAME weaving out of the kitchen, blond hair touseled, wiping his hands in a towel. The washing had made the strange little pits on his hands stand out more noticeably.

"The hoard was supposed to be in a box under the floor of Rubinov's cabin," Benna Franks continued. "This is the single coin we found."

She arose, extracted a coin from a brown leather bag, passed it over.

At first glance, it looked like silver. But it bore an unusual face design. Nace bounced it on the table. He bit it. He eyed it closely.

"Bless us!" he ejaculated.

"What is it?" questioned the red-head.

"This one coin is worth a small fortune," he explained. "In the old days, Russia made a little money out of platinum. That was in the days before platinum became so valuable. This is one of those coins. But it has a worth greatly beyond the platinum content as a collector's piece."

Nace clattered dottle out of his pipe in a hammered iron stand, reloaded it, asked, "Did Rubinov seem worried when he told you where his hoard was hidden?"

The red-head nodded. "He did."

Nace blew smoke and followed the squirming gray cloud with his eyes. "How about two or three months ago—when the U. S. government began raising cain with gold hoarders? You know—when the banks all closed for a while."

The girl gave a slight start. "Why—Rubinov was worried by that! I remember now. He came to me several times and wanted to know all about what it meant. If a man had been getting gold coins and keeping them, could the government take them away from him? That was his question."

"And you told him?"

"I gave him to understand the government might confiscate his gold as a penalty. That, you recall, was the talk at the time."

Nace frowned through his smoke fog. "Want to hear me do some guessing?"

They all three nodded.

"Here is what I think happened," Nace said briskly. "Rubinov got scared and decided to turn his hoarded money into the bank. He wanted a guard while he did it, so he went to Constable Hasser and Deputy Constable Fatty Dell. But Hasser and Dell persuaded him not to turn it in, probably lying to him and telling him it was all right to keep the money.

"Hasser and Dell got someone else to help them—somebody who kills with that infernal explosive. They watched Rubinov and found out where the hoard was hidden. But Rubinov got wise and sent for me. Then they killed Rubinov and stole his hoard.

"The third person, the real murderer, killed Hasser and Dell so as to have the loot for himself. Now he's trying to kill me so I can't do any investigating."

The girl stood up. "Do you want to see the spot where the hoard was hidden?"

"Yeah." Nace looked at her shoes. "But first, I'd like to see where you spilled that cinnamon on your shoes."

She turned toward the kitchen. "I can show you the partly emptied box." Her voice was shrill.

She entered the kitchen, looked at a shelf.

"The cinnamon box is gone!" she gasped.

CHAPTER V

Prowler

THE RED-HEADED GIRL pressed hands tightly to her cheeks. Her eyes acquired a sheen of moisture. She looked very scared.

"Does this—throw suspicion on me?" she choked.

Nace swung over, put a long arm about her shoulders. This seemed to the thing he most wanted to do at the moment.

"Somebody may be trying to frame you, Benna," he said.

He felt her shiver, could feel her heart trip-hammering.

The blond Spencer, walking in a half crouch because of the agony in his middle, shuffled into the kitchen. He eyed the shelf at which Benna Franks pointed, then squinted at the window.

The window was near the shelf—an easy arm reach. The sash was up.

"That window was closed when I washed my face a few moments ago!" Spencer barked. "Somebody has opened it since then!"

Nace grunted, herded them all back in the big room, and swung grimly for the door.

"Stay here!" he commanded. "I'm going to browse a little!"

The night outside had turned several degrees blacker. It was hotter. The breeze had died. The world was like the inside of a gigantic bomb, the only disturbance the less frequent bark of thunder and the crackling blaze of lightning.

Nace prowled. He did not use his pen flashlight. And after each gory burst of lightning, he made a wild jump eight or ten feet in the most convenient direction. He was taking no chances of a skulker pot-shooting him.

Camp Lakeside consisted of long lines of attractive three- and four-room log cabins, connected by graveled drives. Boat-houses, bathhouses and a sanded beach were down on the lake shore.

Nace weaved among the cabins, covering a few yards, then stopping to listen. He worked down toward the lake. The air here had a faint tang of fish. It wasn't unpleasant.

At some farmhouse in the distance, a dog howled. The animal was some breed of hound—its howl was long and quavering and eerie, like the wail of an ogre spawned out of the rumbling, flaming night.

Nace wrinkled his sensitive nostrils. He had caught an alien odor, very vague. He advanced a few silent paces. The odor became stronger. He identified it.

Whiskey!

The lightning gushed a white-hot blaze.

Nace jumped a foot—a hulking figure of a man stood almost against his nose. His back was to Nace.

Nace smacked a fist into the fellow's back. The skulker barked hoarsely in surprise and pain. He folded forward on his knees. Nace pounced on him, fists bludgeoning. He hit the man in the nape, the temple. He reached around to slug him in the jaw—and got kicked in the back of the head.

Nace felt for a moment as if he were a big comet smashing through a galaxy of stars. The kick had been a complete surprise. He was half stunned.

The other man was bigger, heavier. He crawled atop Nace. If the fellow had used his fists then, Nace would have been finished. Instead, he tore at a revolver in his coat pocket.

Nace got his knob-gripped gun out of his sleeve and kissed the top of his opponent's head with it. The man shrieked. The revolver he was getting out of his pocket exploded under his convulsive fingers.

The bullet clouted harmlessly into the ground; the cloth of the coat pocket began to glow and smoke.

Nace hit him again. The man fell over senseless.

Arising, Nace used his flashlight.

It was the beefy, red-necked drunk who had menaced Nace with the nickeled revolver in front of the hotel.

NACE HAULED him down to the lake, threw him in, then pulled him out again. That revived the fellow.

The man began snarling, "What the hell do you mean by—?"

"Going to pull an injured innocence act, huh?" gritted Nace. He stung his knuckles on the man's jaw, and the beefy hulk lay stupefied for half a minute.

During that interval, Nace searched him. He found money, cigarettes, a silver flask entirely empty, and letters addressed to Alva Coogan, railroad detective, in Mountain Town.

"Why were you nosing around here, Coogan?" Nace demanded, after making sure the letters were nothing but advertisements.

Coogan started cursing. A close look at Nace's knobby fist shut him up.

"Aw—I came up to get even with you for knockin' me down!" he growled.

"How'd you know where to come?"

Coogan slapped a moist tongue over puffy lips. "They told me downtown that you had come up to Camp Lakeside."

"You're a black-faced liar, Coogan. Nobody knew I was headed for this place."

"I ain't a liar!" rumbled Coogan. "To hell with what you think!"

Nace laughed nastily and kicked the man to his feet. "A pal of Constable Hasser and Fatty Dell, aren't you?"

"Quit kickin' me!"

Nace booted him again. "Pal of Hasser and Dell, huh?"

"What if I was? They were a couple of all-right guys."

"Were! Were! How'd you know Fatty Dell is dead? I don't think anybody has found his body yet."

Coogan shut up.

Nace propelled him toward the house, growling, "You're in this over your ears, my friend!"

To the unholy tune of bumping thunder and jagging lightning, they strode the graveled walks. The two-story log main building hove in sight.

Nace rapped out a violent grunt. The structure was now dark!

Running the stubborn Coogan ahead of him, Nace clattered onto the porch. Coogan was seized with a shaking as they came near the door. He knew any bullets from inside would hit him. He tried to break away.

Nace struck him, and the man fell.

Letting him lay, Nace reached in, found the light switch and tweaked it. The room glared.

The red-head was tied to a chair. A cloth was tied between her jaws, another over her eyes.

Fred Franks and Spencer were nowhere to be seen.

COOGAN HAD been feigning a knockout. He leaped to his feet suddenly and ran.

Nace yelled at him. Coogan only ran the faster. Nace shot past the man's head. Coogan put on still more speed. Nace aimed at the runner's back, but reconsidered. He holstered the gun in his sleeve with an angry growl.

He flung to the girl. She was tied with tent ropes. He wrenched them off and plucked the cloth from her jaws and her eyes.

"I didn't see who it was," she begun. "I was struck and stunned a minute after Fred and Spencer heard a shot down by the lake and ran out. Then—"

"Was anything shoved down your throat?"

"Why—what—?"

"Your throat—could they have pushed anything down it?"

"No—I don't think so!"

He shoved her to the nearest door. "Get in there! Take off your clothes! Every stitch! Throw them out to me!"

"What—?"

"Damnation!" he bellowed. "Strip, or I'll take 'em off for you! Quick!"

She ran into another room, closed the door.

"Hurry!" Nace rasped through the door. "They may have planted their infernal explosive somewhere in your clothing! Throw the stuff out here."

The red-head lost no time. The door opened a crack. A frock came sailing through, then underthings, shoes. Nace balled each garment as it arrived and relayed it outdoors with all his speed.

"That's all," called the red-head.

Nace eyed the door. "Anything in there you can put on?"

"Yes."

Nace waited. He did not have the slightest proof that explosive was in the girl's clothing. He was just playing safe. Perspiration crawled on his forehead. He wondered if the explosion, should one come from her clothing, would be sufficient to blow the log house down. He made no move to go out and carry her garments further away.

He shifted his feet nervously. His eyes roved, passed over the floor.

A small fold of paper lay at his feet. Obviously, it had fallen from the red-head's garments.

He picked it up, read it.

MISS BENNA—I PUT IT IN THE REFRIGERATOR.
HASSER

He pocketed the paper hastily, for the girl was coming out of the other room.

She had put on one of the Indian suits she kept for sale to the summer resort trade. Buckskin blouse and trousers were beaded and fringed, as were the moccasins. It was a very nice fit. In the rig, she looked more entrancing than ever.

She stared at her discarded garments, visible in the light which slanted through the open front door.

"I make quite a few mistakes," Nace told her dryly. "This may be one of them. Let's get out of here—the back way."

They entered the kitchen, crossed it.

Nace noted a large hotel-type electric refrigerator against one wall.

The night wrapped them with sultry gloom when they stepped out into it.

"My brother and Spencer—where did they go?" the redhead whispered anxiously. "Maybe we'd better call them."

"No. That lunk, Coogan, may be hanging around. He'd love to cut down on me in the dark with a club. Take me to the cabin Rubinov occupied."

THE SEPIA sky blazed with electric fire at intervals of a minute or so. Far away, the hound still howled. Such sounds as their feet made seemed magnified a thousand times in volume.

"What a night!" Nace muttered.

"It's horrible! Fighting and killing and attacks—"

"I meant the weather."

"Oh, that. It's just a thunderstorm. You don't notice such things in the city. Out here, well, we get used to it."

"You like the country?"

"So-so."

"Rather live in the city, huh?"

"Why so curious?"

"Can't I talk?" Nace demanded in a hurt tone. He had been wondering how she'd like his apartment on upper Fifth Avenue. She ought to like it. The lease was costing him enough. He was just realizing what was wrong with the joint. It needed somebody like this red-head in it.

He'd better forget such thoughts—at least until he found out who she'd killed, or who she hadn't.

Rubinov's cabin was on the lake shore. It had a rear porch which extended out over the water.

"He liked to fish," explained Benna Franks.

They entered. The place was fitted with electric lights. The girl clicked these on. Then she skidded a bearskin rug aside. Nace's experienced eye did not detect the trapdoor until she lifted it, so cleverly was it made.

Below was a concrete box. This seemed solid. Benna pressed a hidden button and the entire box lifted steadily on a rusty piston until it was waist-high above the cabin floor. Below was visible the lid of a stout wooden chest.

Nace started to reach in. The girl grasped his arm.

"Wait!" she rapped. "Rubinov fixed a death trap! If you touch the chest lid without adjusting another concealed button, the concrete box will fall on you!"

Nace felt a pleasant warmth. She wasn't trying to do him in. The note addressed to her and signed with Constable Hasser's name seemed to become a red-hot iron in his pocket.

Benna made the button adjustment, lifted the chest lid and disclosed its empty interior.

"We'll hunt fingerprints later," Nace told her. "Where was the explosion which you think killed Rubinov?"

"Just outside this cabin."

They closed the empty treasure vault, then went outdoors. Nace listened a while, trying to ascertain if anyone was near, then used his pen flash.

Signs of the explosion were profuse. The ground was torn, and swept bare of leaves, branches, even grass, for some feet around.

The red-head shuddered, pointed. "Throw your light on the cabin wall."

Nace did so. Bloodstains were there, brown and dry.

THE GIRL began to breathe jerkily and make faint noises in her throat. Nace, realizing the murder scene was undermining her nerve, escorted her back toward the two-story cabin.

The front room was as they had left it—no sign of Fred or Spencer, or even the red-necked railway detective, Coogan.

Nace turned out the lights. "Just to play safe. Now I'll call the state police and have them watch for Coogan, in case he really left this neighborhood."

He picked up the phone in careless fashion, then stiffened alertly. No line sing came from the instrument.

"Wires out," he said dryly, and tossed the receiver onto its hook.

"Who could have done that?"

"Search me." Nace planted his flash beam on her face. "Now let's look at the refrigerator."

He could detect no flicker of alarm in her features.

They entered the kitchen, moved to the refrigerator.

"Read this," Nace said, and gave her the folded paper he had found on the floor.

She glanced over it. "I never saw this before."

"It dropped out of your clothing."

"So that was why you had me change—"

"Oh, no, it wasn't. I was really afraid there was explosive in your garments. I was mistaken. I found this note by accident."

"I don't know—what to think of it!" She sounded scared.

"The bird who tied you up might have left it—trying to frame you," Nace said, then wondered why he was suggesting alibis to her.

"That must have been it." A shudder quavered in her voice. "The disappearance of that cinnamon can! Yes—that's it! Somebody is trying to frame me."

"Have you looked in the icebox recently?"

"No. We don't use it until the summer guests come. It's too

big and expensive to run."

Nace used his handkerchief to lift the refrigerator catch. He yanked the door open.

Benna Franks screamed shrilly, horribly. She whirled from the awful sight in the white refrigerator interior. Wildly, she stumbled from the door.

Nace overhauled her. She fought him in her hysterical horror, scratched his face. After ten or fifteen seconds, he succeeded in trapping her arms.

Then he went back and closed the refrigerator door. It took a lot to get under Nace's skin. But even he didn't care for the grisly sight of Rubinov's remains piled in the refrigerator.

CHAPTER VI

Another Man-Blast

NACE SEARCHED AND found a quart bottle of applejack in the kitchen cupboard. He administered a shot of the colorless liquid dynamite to the red-head. He was forced to hold her to do it.

Four or five minutes later, she was normal again, except for a nervous rasp in her breathing.

"I'm sorry—that I fought you," she said huskily. "I didn't know what I was doing. It seems like everything went to pieces for a minute."

Nace tried to make his laugh hearty. "That's all right, Benna."

"Nace, everything depends on you. Any jury in the country would convict me of these murders on the evidence you've uncovered. You've got to find out who did it! You've simply got—oh, my—!" She was going haywire again.

"Cut it out!" Nace said grumpily, and reached for the apple-jack bottle.

The lightning flamed outside, and Nace's eyes instinctively sought the front door. The sky fire danced and flickered several seconds—long enough to let Nace get a good look at blond Spencer.

The man was laboriously hopping toward the log house. His pitted hands were bound before him, his ankles tied, and a handkerchief stoppered his mouth.

Nace played his flashlight outdoors, wary of a trap. Then he ran out, dragged Spencer in, and untied him.

"I was struck down!" Spencer moaned. "I ran out when I heard that shot down by the lake! Then somebody jumped me."

"Where's Fred?" Benna shrilled.

"I don't know," grunted Spencer.

Nace became hard-eyed. "Did Fred run out of this room ahead of you or behind you when the shot sounded?"

"I went first. I don't know whether Fred went out at all or not."

The red-head cried angrily, "Listen, you! Fred is not involved in these killings—"

"Dry up, Benna," Nace snapped.

She spun on him in a frightened rage. "You've got more evidence against me than against my brother! Fred didn't—"

Nace held up the applejack bottle. "I guess you need more of this to make you see straight."

She subsided. "I'm sorry."

Spencer grabbed the applejack, lowered its level an inch and a half and immediately seemed to feel better.

"You can go to the nearest phone and call the coroner and the state police," Nace told him. "The state troopers especially. I can stand some help around here."

"Shall I use your car?"

"Use your feet. I may need that car."

Spencer peered out into the thunder-and-lightning infested night, shivered as though he didn't like the prospects, then glided out. He made remarkably little noise.

Nace turned the pen light on his face so the red-head could see his amiable grin. "I wish you'd quit throwing fits around here. The tantrums don't do anybody any good, not even you. They're hard on your nerves—"

He swallowed the rest. Someone had stepped into the room. Nace slid the knob-gripped gun out of his sleeve and pointed it at the spot where he judged the newcomer stood.

Fred Franks' voice, hoarse with emotion, cried, "Benna! Nace! You here?"

"Present," Nace admitted.

"Fred!" Benna's one word was a relieved sob.

Her brother ignored her. "Nace! I've got the whole thing solved! I followed the devil to your hotel when he went there to kill you. That's how I happened to be there.

"A few minutes ago, I saw him tie up Benna and blindfold her and thrust a note in the fold of her dress. Then I followed him and he got the parts of Rubinov's body and put them in the refrigerator in the kitchen. I saw him throw something in the lake—I think it was that cinnamon box he lifted out of the kitchen!"

"Who is it?" Nace snapped.

"Wait until I tell you the rest! I think I know where old Rubinov's hoard of money is—"

Flame, blue, sheeting, sprayed in the doorway. In the midst of the horrible blaze, Fred's body seemed to fall apart. Then the blue glare extinguished and the explosion cracked.

So tremendous was the blast that Nace suddenly stopped hearing things. He was slapped backward as if by a great fist. The floor jumped up, split. The logs of the front wall fell outward, carrying the porch crashing down. The ceiling of the room above fell in.

Nace found a quivering form with his hands—the girl. He rushed her back into the kitchen, then outdoors, thinking the whole house was coming down.

But the building stood.

He cradled the girl in his arms. "You hurt?"

"Fred!" she screamed. "Fred! Fred!"

Nace carried her and ran around to the front of the house. He was afraid she would dash in and be hit by falling logs.

"Quiet!" he hissed in her ear. "The killer is around here somewhere!"

He lowered her to the ground. She lay there, stiffly inert, not even sobbing. She understood the need of silence.

Nace moved a dozen paces to one side and used his flash-light recklessly. The thin beam spiked right, left, straight ahead, behind him. It disclosed no one.

A log fell noisily in the wrecked part of the house. A nail pulled out of a board with a shrill squawling noise. Overhead, thunder chased lightning flashes across the sky.

Nace ran swiftly back to the girl, scooped her up, raced her to his rented roadster and deposited her on the cushions. The starter clashed, the motor gave a surprised moan, under his madly stamping feet. The car jumped ahead as though a giant had kicked it.

"Fred!" Benna Franks moaned. "We can't leave him—!"

Nace replied nothing. They could not help Fred. His body probably reposed in a hundred places in the wreckage.

The roadster tires threw gravel all the way to the concrete road, then rubber shrieked in a skid as Nace straightened out on the highway. The speedometer needle climbed past thirty, forty and fifty. The headlights bloomed brilliantly ahead.

The girl sat white, trembling and wordless in the deep leather seat.

They wheeled into Mountain Town. The windows of Nace's hotel appeared.

"We'll look through your brother's car, first thing," Nace said.

He braked to a stop before the hotel, then looked around narrowly.

Fred Franks' coupe was in sight.

THEY ENTERED the hotel. The dapper clerk grinned at Nace, came forward. He seemed to have something to say. But he didn't have time.

"Wait here," Nace told Benna Franks.

He boxed himself in a phone booth, got long-distance to New York City. He talked at length with the man in charge of the identification bureau. The conversation ran ten minutes, fifteen. Phone operators broke in on them twice.

Nace left the booth bright-eyed with satisfaction.

"It was a good hunch," he told the red-head. "The New York police had his picture and his record. He got out of Sing Sing in a prison break four years ago."

"You mean the—"

"The murderer. All I've got to do now is grab him, and find the money they stole from Rubinov." Nace said the last wryly, conveying by his tone that quite a bit still lay ahead.

"Mister Nace," said the hotel clerk tentatively.

"Yeah?"

"I hired a taxi driver to pull Fred Franks' car around behind the hotel. I thought you might want to look it over, seein' as how you left here in such a hurry."

"Great!" Nace told him briskly. "Show me to it!"

The clerk didn't stir. He looked uncomfortable. "I tried to do a little detective work myself. I hope it won't make you mad."

"Moving the car was swell stuff. It kept people from crawling around over it."

"I done more than move the car. The rumble seat was locked, but I pried it open. Here's what I found."

Reaching under the desk, the clerk produced a pair of black-and-white sport shoes. The toes were smeared with brown powder from a matured puffball mushroom.

"I hope you ain't mad that I done this."

"Mad!" Nace grinned. "Kid, those are the murderer's shoes. The New York police just told me there's a thousand dollars reward for the guy. Consider the thousand your own."

The clerk appeared relieved. "I'm glad it's all right, because I found some other stuff that kinda had me worried."

With that, he pulled four canvas bags from under the desk. They clanked loudly when he deposited them on the desk top.

"Take a look," he said. "There's money enough in there to stock a mint."

Nace jerked the drawstring of one bag, got it loose. He

dipped a hand in and ladled up a palm full of silver and gold coins. Some few were of U. S. mintage. The majority were Russian coins of the old Imperial days.

Nace saw dozens minted from platinum.

The clerk scraped sweat off his brow. "There must be a hundred grand in them bags—if those funny looking shekels ain't phony."

"I'm betting a million will come closer to it," Nace muttered. "This is Rubinov's hoard, all right."

Thunder laughed noisily over the hotel.

"But how did the money and the shoes get in my brother's car?" Benna Franks asked hoarsely.

"Remember when you first met me tonight, and we had the merry-go-round outside the hotel?" Nace countered.

"Of course."

"You drove straight home to Camp Lakeside, didn't you?"

"Yes."

"The murderer borrowed your car right after that, got the coin hoard from where they had hidden it after stealing it, and set out to systematically kill the rest of his gang, so he wouldn't have to divvy. After he did for Constable Hasser and Fatty Dell, he left the car at your place, because he was afraid I'd seen it. He found the puffball dust on his shoes and left them in the machine."

"It was Spencer who borrowed the car!" the red-head gasped.

"SPENCER ISN'T his only name," Nace said dryly. "He's got a string of aliases the read like the telephone directory. The New York police recognized his description, especially the part about his pitted hands. He got those pocks on his hands when powerful acids splashed on them. He was once a chemist—a chemist specializing in explosives. He later became one of the most efficient safe blowers in the business. He was caught and escaped from Sing Sing four years ago and—!"

"He has been right here in Mountain Town every time since!" cracked a harsh voice.

Nace made a mental note that whatever happened to him, he had it coming for his carelessness—he could have kept a closer watch. Then he turned around.

Spencer stood just inside the door, a pistol in each pocked hand.

The red-necked railroad detective was a little back of him, with a revolver.

CHAPTER VII

Death Shoe

THE STREET OUTSIDE was vacated. No one else was in the hotel lobby. The hour was long past midnight. Mountain Town went to sleep with the chickens—which was one reason why it was so popular as a summer resort. The urban tranquility was good for city jitters.

Thunder bounced across the hotel roof, rumbled in the street, and when the clashing echoes subsided, Spencer snarled, "Don't move, anybody! How'd you get wise to me, shamus? I didn't make no slips."

"Just one," Nace said mildly.

"What?"

"You didn't wear gloves to cover those hands. The scars suggested acid, and that got me to thinking about how it must have taken an explosive chemist to make up those bombs—"

"I don't want to hear about it!" gritted Spencer. "Frisk 'em, Beef!"

Beef, the red-necked railroad detective, came forward. He knew how a search should be made. He missed little. He even tore off Nace's coat, ripped his shirt down the back and got the packet stuck to his back with adhesive tape.

"What's in that?" Spencer wanted to know.

"Knife, file, dooflicker to pick locks with, some yaller stuff that looks like sulphur," Beef enumerated the packet contents.

"The last must be stuff that makes tear gas when burned," Spencer grunted. "Throw it away! Finish friskin' 'em!"

Beef completed the search.

"I'll eat anything they got left on 'em!" he grinned.

"Tie 'em! Use this!" Spencer flung Beef a roll of wire—the same sort of wire with which Nace had been tripped earlier in the night. "Just tie their hands for the time being."

Beef did the tying, showing gusto for the job.

Spencer nodded at the money on the desk. "Take it to the car!"

Beef carried the four bags outdoors, making two trips to complete the job. The bags were extremely heavy.

"Now you go out!" Spencer pointed his guns successively at Nace, the red-head, the hotel clerk.

"What are you gonna do?" the hotel clerk demanded.

"Can the chatter!" rapped Spencer.

"Yeah—can it," Nace said dryly. "Do you want to start the crackpot shooting in here?"

Spencer snarled and kicked Nace in the leg. "Call me a crackpot, will you!"

They all moved outdoors, where the lightning spurted gory luminance upon them.

A sedan was parked at the curb. It had a very long wheel-base. Nace, the girl, the clerk, all sat on the rear cushions. Spencer watched Beef tie their feet with wire, then occupied the drop-seat in front of them.

"To the circus, James," he told Beef. Both he and Beef laughed at their joke.

THE SEDAN rode rough on over-pressured tires, out of town and past where the explosion had killed Constable Hasser. The headlamps whitened the sign of Lakeside Camp. Several cars and a few people were there, evidently drawn by the blast noise. They were working in the log house wreckage, a grimly silent group, assembling the remnants of Fred Franks' body.

The red-head began to sob steadily.

The sedan pitched ahead at increased speed. The hard tires

sucked noisily at the pavement. Tools banged together under the front seat every time they went over a bump.

Spencer smiled sardonically and watched the sobbing girl.

The car angled off the road, ran a hundred feet up a lane and stopped. Beef said, "This is as good a place as any, Spence."

Then Beef got out of the driving seat. Spencer also got out.

With a quick move, Spencer put his right-hand gun against Beef's head and pulled the trigger.

Beef fell, his head horribly mutilated.

Sneering, Spencer wiped the grip of the gun with which he had killed Beef. Satisfied it was free of fingerprints, he threw it into the surrounding woods.

"The goop thought I'd split with 'im!" he growled, referring to Beef. "Maybe he knows better now."

He scowled into the car at Nace. "What's the matter with you, shamus?"

Nace was doubled over, wired hands hanging close to his feet. His face was strange.

"What you just done made me sick," Nace said.

"You'll feel worse before I'm done," Spencer promised. He reached into the sedan front seat, brought out a tin box shaped like a tobacco tin, but somewhat larger.

He opened this. It apparently had a double wall. Pale grayish, steam-like vapor swirled out of the box mouth.

Spencer upended the box, shook it. A piece of dry-ice fell out. It was this which was making the vapor.

"My pocket refrigerator," Spencer leered. "It keeps these babies cool!"

He shook from the box four metallic balls about the size of grapes.

NACE WAS still doubled over, wired arms hanging down. The fingers of one hand toyed absently with his right shoe. But his eyes were on the killer.

"So those are your bombs?" he grunted.

"There ain't a more powerful explosive in the world," Spencer declared with an insane pride. "I made Fatty Dell swallow two of 'em, an' tied his mouth so he couldn't get 'em up. I only had to use one each on Rubinov an' Hasser, droppin' em in their pockets. But I tossed three in the log house, close to Fred Franks' feet. I wasn't takin' no chances on him."

The girl gave no sign that she had heard.

"So they explode automatically after they've been exposed to normal temperatures a while," Nace grunted.

"After about three minutes, shamus," Spencer agrees. "Each one has a tiny detonator of two acids which explode when they get together. They're held apart by a little wall of a gelatin solution. When it warms up, the gelatin turns to a liquid and lets the acids mix. Then—whango!"

Spencer put the metallic balls back in the can, replaced the dry ice, clamped the lid down and pocketed the container.

"I ain't quite ready to use 'em. I'll have to tie all of you more solid. Then I'll drop a ball in each of your pockets, tie the pockets shut so you can't shake 'em out, and go off and listen to the fireworks."

He reached into the car to drag the prisoners out. The dome light, slanting downward on his face, made it a countenance of limitless evil.

He saw Nace was now fumbling with the heel of his shoe. He cursed sharply. "Hey, shamus, what—!"

A crack of a report answered him. The heel of Nace's right shoe seemed to spit a two-inch tongue of flame.

Spencer jerked convulsively, reeled back out of the sedan. He turned around twice and fell heavily on his back. A sluggish fountain of crimson played on his chest, above the heart, subsided quickly and became a grisly trickle of crimson.

Nace patted the heel of his shoe as though it had done good work. These were the shoes he had donned at his hotel when the trouble first started.

"Short barrel holding a single .32 bullet built into the heel," he told the open-mouthed hotel clerk. "Fired from a lever inside the shoe."

They worked on the wires holding each other, and were no more than two minutes getting free.

Nace led the girl away, down the lane toward the road. She'd seen enough hell for one night. His arm was around her shoulders.

The hotel clerk remained behind a while. He took the tin box out of dead Spencer's pocket, ran into the woods a couple of rods, pulled the lid off the box, and dropped it. Then he broke a dash record leaving the vicinity.

The explosion as the metal balls detonated exceeded for violence anything the clerk had ever heard.

To Nace's sharp yell, he said he was all right. Then he hurried to overtake Nace and the girl.

"About that gun in your shoe heel," he called. "How's it rigged so it won't go off when you ain't expectin' it?"

No answer.

A convenient lightning flash sprayed the scene with brilliance. The clerk saw Nace and the red-head. He had gone a dozen feet past them, and they were pretty well blended in each other's arms.

The clerk could take a hint. He ambled on down the lane, an appraising eye cocked on the noisy heavens.

"Danged if I believe it's gonna storm after all," he grinned.

The Skeleton's Clutch

Lee Nace had seen many men die, their
going was a thing to chill the heart. But
he had never seen a man dragged into
the grave by a grisly, bony skeleton's
hand. And he had never felt the power
of the Green Skull. But then Lee Nace
had never met Baron von Auster before.
The baron had many ghastly surprises
up the sleeve of his natty jacket.

CHAPTER I

The Treacherous Baron

LEE NACE, A tall and big-boned man in a baseball uniform, leaned a hard shoulder against the partly opened bungalow door.

Nace's bony jaw was out angrily; his cheeks were craggy with drawn muscle. His pale eyes threatened.

"A woman—a scared woman!" he said vehemently. "She buzzed me from a phone that traced to this address!"

The man inside the bungalow glowered and pushed harder against the door, trying to keep Nace out. The man was plump. His cheeks glowed pink, as if recently slapped. He looked very natty in summer evening dress, with a white monkey jacket.

In a vacant lot on the corner of the block, small boys were playing baseball—a batter had just popped their ball into a weed patch and they were all hunting it. Inside the bungalow, a radio droned big league scores for the day.

"*Nein!*" he gritted, lifting his voice over the radio. "*Das ist unrecht!*"

Lee Nace, gaunt and disheveled in the ball uniform, did not look like a scholar. Nevertheless, he could converse fluently in more languages than he could number on his combined fingers.

He had been advised in German, that he did not know what he was talking about.

Speaking German through his teeth, he said: "The woman no more than got hold of me before she started yelling! She was screeching like a calliope when somebody cut her off!"

The pinkish man blinked rapidly. His surprise showed he

had used his mother tongue unwittingly in the excitement, and was a bit taken aback that Nace had understood it.

"I tell you there is no woman here!" he hissed in excellent English. He was forced to lift his voice over the rattle of baseball scores from the radio.

Nace was extremely tall, only a little under seven feet. His big-boned frame had a knobby, clumsy aspect. His long, solemn face was reddish with sunburn. His dark suit was dusty, wrinkled, and his white Panama possessed little shape.

On Nace's forehead, anger was bringing out a strange, flushed design in scarlet—the mark of an old scar. More and

*The baron switched on
the light, came in.*

more distinctly, the scar burned as he shoved at the door. It
assumed a definite design—the likeness of a coiled serpent.

Nace had once been hit in the forehead with the hilt of a
knife that bore a serpentine carving, and the design was destined to remain forever imprinted upon his head. It gave him
a sinister look when he was enraged.

"I'm coming in there, brother!" he grated.

He put more weight upon the door. The Teutonic man's black *kummerbund* burst with the effort of shoving from the other side, uncovering the stiff white front of his dress shirt.

"*Gehen!*" puffed the dark man. "Begone!"

Then a veiled, wily look entered his sea-blue eyes. He sprang suddenly backward, wrenching the door wide open.

Nace had been around enough not to be caught by that one. He did not fall headlong across the threshold. He did not cross the threshold at all. Instead, he leaped to one side.

Ten feet distant was a window. It gaped open, but was fitted with a screen. Nace shoved head and shoulders through the screen as if it had not been there.

In the middle of the room stood the dapper man who spoke *Deutsche* when excited. He had a shiny, small-calibre revolver trained on the open front door.

THE RIPPING as Nace tore through the screen brought the man half around. There was a rigidly set expression in his face—the grimace of a man who has steeled himself to shoot.

Immediately before the window stood a light table. It had two modernistic metal vases. Nace hit the table with both palms—hit it hard!

The table jumped end over end. The pinkish man, very agile, bounded to one side. But he had no time to shoot.

Nace, wriggling over the windowsill, grabbed one of the metal vases which had fallen to the floor. He threw it with a wrist-snap. It seemed to half-bury itself in the plump man's middle. He dropped his gun; his eyes popped, and he folded in agony.

Lunging forward gauntly, Nace seized the revolver, unloaded it, then threw it through the hole in the screen. It sailed far away in the night.

Sitting on the squirming prisoner, Nace searched. He found a roll of bills containing more than two thousand dollars. There was nothing else, not even shells for the gun.

Nace flipped open the white monkey jacket. It was obviously quite new. He read the label.

THE PLAZA SHOPPE

The ruddy man still writhed from the pain in his middle. Nace tangled thick, bony fingers in the fellow's luxuriant hair and lifted. The man forgot the ache in his ample middle for the new agony in his scalp. He came to his feet, spluttering.

"For laying hands on the Baron Marz von Auster, you shall—"

The serpentine scar on Nace's forehead seemed to come and go with his pulse. He shook the man. "Is that what you call yourself?"

"I am the Baron Marz von Auster!" snarled the other. "The title of baron is genuine, I might add!"

"That's two strikes on you—I don't like titles!" Nace, flushed and hard looking, shook the man again. "Where's the woman?"

The baron licked his lips. "You are wrong! There is no woman here!"

Still gripping a fistful of black hair, Nace straight-armed the baron out ahead of him.

"We're going to look this dump over!" he advised.

The living room of the bungalow was paneled, and beamed in natural wood. The furniture was natural wood and red leather. The Aubusson underfoot looked expensive. A telephone stood to one side.

The radio droned away noisily beside the phone stand. It was a large set in a custom cabinet that matched the other furniture.

Nace glanced at the kilocycle number at which the dial was set.

"The *Morning Tribune* station," he murmured, and listened to the Yankees-Red Sox score. The Yanks had won.

"Did you come in to get baseball scores?" snarled Baron Marz von Auster.

Nace kicked open the handiest door. It gave into a study. He glanced in, whistled shrilly.

Almost every piece of furniture in the study was torn to bits. Stuffing, springs, upholstery leather, strewed the floor. The search had even progressed to splitting the table legs.

Nace's shaggy brows snuggled together. He asked:

"Is this your house, baron?"

"Yes!"

"You're a liar! The phone book and the city directory both said a guy named Jimmy Offitt lived here!"

Baron von Auster knotted his fists so tightly his pursy arms trembled.

"I do not know who you are, or what brought you here!" he snarled. "But I do know this—you had better go! Go! Go—before something happens to you!"

"Don't get sassy!" Nace nodded at the mutilated study. "Hunting something, eh?"

Baron von Auster answered with stiff silence.

"Hadn't got this far with your search, eh?"

"I was not searching!" Baron von Auster clipped. "What happened here was my own affair! Now, if you do not leave at once, I am going to have you arrested. I am wealthy, and I will use my money to see that you rot before you get out of jail!"

"You talk as big as that robber of an umpire the cops rung into our ball game!" Nace jeered.

SNORTING CHEERFULLY, Nace shoved his prisoner for another door. His cleated baseball shoes left big, unlovely scars on the varnished hall floor.

He found a bedroom. It was a wreck. The dressing table had been taken apart, paper scraped off the walls, the mattress ripped open. Nace tried a second bedroom, a kitchen, the bath, pantry. He looked in closets, cupboards, the refrigerator. He climbed into the attic and struck matches. He descended to the basement, peering into coal bins and the furnace.

He found no one. About half of the house had been torn up. They returned to the front room where the radio was mouthing ball scores.

There, Baron von Auster suddenly missed his two thousand dollar roll.

"Thief!" he wailed. "So that is it! You are one of the thieves who have torn my house up in this fashion! Not finding what you wanted, you came back to hunt!"

"To hunt for what?" Nace asked curiously. "What was I after?"

Baron von Auster swore, and spread his hands. "What do you thieves usually seek? Jewels—money—"

Nace scowled. His knobby face was red with fresh sunburn. And about his left eye, a bruise was growing. It had darkened perceptibly since he had entered the bungalow. Unmistakably, he had been in a fight before he arrived.

He grasped the baron's hands and turned them palm-up. Under the fingernails was a gray deposit of plaster and colored bits of wallpaper.

"I suppose your manicurist put that there?" he questioned dryly. "Of course, you couldn't have gotten it while pulling paper off the walls!"

Baron von Auster said a tight-lipped nothing.

Nace boxed the knuckles of a big fist and shook them under the pinkish man's nose. The movement caused dust to puff from his grimy baseball shirt. His cleated shoes had been leaving dust prints on the Aubusson.

"I asked you a question!" he rumbled. "What was the object of this search? What's going on here? Where's that woman? And who was she?"

Baron von Auster sucked in his stomach, pulled in his chin, as if to get them both away from that big, hard fist.

"By what right do you demand to know?" he wailed.

Frowning, Nace seemed to consider. The radio muttered on. It was giving the scores of commercial and sand lot teams of the city.

"Listen!" Nace said, and pointed at the apparatus.

The voice from the loud-speaker was saying: "The real fire-works of today's baseball came from a local diamond, where a game between the police nine and a team of private detectives ended in a free for all fight, with the score seven to nothing in the sixth inning;

"Lee Nace, probably the city's most astute private detective, and certainly the most widely known, was pitching. According to reports, he beaned a sergeant of police. The latter swung on Nace, with the result that it took three riot squads of policemen to save their own team from the embattled private operatives."

"HE FORGOT to say that bunch of cops rung a retired flatfoot in on us for an umpire!" Nace growled. Then, glowering at the baron, he indicated his own darkening left eye. "There's where that bum of a sergeant sockoed me!"

The rosy man wet his lips three times in quick succession. He ran a hand slowly across his hair where Nace had pulled it.

"You—are—Nace?" he muttered, as if repeating some very bad news.

"In person—not a pinch hitter!" Nace told him with a sort of fierce levity. "The cops chased us out of that ball park—the tramps—and we couldn't get our clothes out of the lockers. I went to my office. When I came in the door, the phone was ringing."

He shot his jaw forward belligerently. "It was that woman! She asked if I was Nace, speaking in a whisper. Behind her, I could hear a radio going. Then the woman began to yell. In a minute, she was cut off. But that radio—it was tuned to the *Morning Tribune* station. They were just starting the baseball scores. This set is tuned on that station!" He pointed at the radio.

Baron von Auster wet his lips several more times. He peered furtively at Nace, then away. He seemed fascinated by the weird serpentine scar on Nace's forehead, the scar that had become so brilliant it was almost like a design done in red ink.

"I don't know you!" he said thickly. "I do not know anything about what you have found here! *Nein!*"

Obviously, he was lying on both counts. He had heard of Nace. He couldn't have helped it, if he had read the recent newspapers. Nace—dubbed the "Blond Adder" because of his light hair and the serpentine scar on his forehead—had just returned from England, where he had spent some months as technical consultant at Scotland Yard.

Nace made good newspaper copy. He was tough. His language was picturesque and forceful. His methods were spectacular. He knew that newspaper publicity boomed his business, so he went out of his way to accommodate the news hawks. Occasionally, he wrote magazine features.

Nace blew on a fist. "For a little, I'd tap you a few times to see what would shake loose!"

The prisoner squirmed uneasily. Then there came into his azure eyes a foxy look akin to that which had first appeared there when he had leaped back from the front door to draw his gun.

"I am tired of your insults!" he snarled. "We are going straight to the nearest police station! You shall regret your high-handed behavior!"

Nace laughed noisily, angrily. "Yeah?"

Baron von Auster put up his hands and seemed to be having trouble with his chest. He questioned hoarsely, "You won't—go?"

"No!" Nace said cheerfully. "You won't, either! You and I are going to hunt that woman!"

The baron had more difficulty with his chest. A minor convulsion seemed to double him over. He sought to straighten.

"My—heart!" he croaked. "This excitement—"

Another paroxysm carried him to the floor. His pudgy hands fluttered, clenching over his heart. He opened his mouth wide and a strange gurgling noise came out. Then he lay motionless.

NACE LEAPED sidewise—did it as swiftly as he knew how. He crashed to his knees back of a chair, twisting as he did so. His suspicions were right!

Two men stood in the front door. One was round and oily, a small man. The other was a giant, modeled after the lines of a steamer trunk with arms and legs. They both held guns—black automatics.

The weapons were of foreign make, with barrels but little larger than pencils. And on each muzzle was a metal can of a silencer.

Nace whirled the chair toward them. Simultaneously, he plunged for the handiest door. It happened to be the one that led into the kitchen. One automatic made a *chung!* of a noise. He felt the bullet ridge the Aubusson under him.

Another bullet gouged a fistful of splinters out of the door-jamb as Nace went through. He dived down the hallway. These two behind were seeking to kill him. They had been loitering outside, of course, and had reached the baron with some signal. The baron had sought to draw Nace outdoors into their hands, then, that failing, had sought to keep his attention with a fake heart attack.

Nace sloped into the kitchen, the caulks of his baseball shoes scraping loudly on linoleum.

The cellar door gaped open at one side, a pantry door on the other.

Nace seized a chair, shied it down the cellar stairs—at the same time scuttling into the pantry. He was out of sight before the three men—Baron von Auster had leaped up and joined the other two—came charging in. They heard the clattering chair and were fooled.

"Good! The son of a dog went into the basement!" hissed Baron von Auster. "We will lock him in, then go away from this place! *Himmel!* I hate to lose my two thousand dollars, which he has!"

"But what about the green skull?" wailed the round, oily

little man. "That is worth a lot more than your two thousand!"

"*Nein!* Our necks are more precious!" the baron snapped. "This man is Detective Lee Nace, the Blond Adder! Have you not heard of him, Moe?"

"*Oi!* Just a private detective!" Moe looked at the giant who had accompanied him through the front door. "What about that, Heavy? You know New York. Is this Nace such a bad man that we should run away without finishing our search for the green skull?"

Heavy heaved a shoulder against the cellar door, slamming and locking it. "This Nace is worse than bad! He's hell on runners!"

"*Beeilen Lie sich!*" rapped Baron von Auster. "Come along! There may be windows to that cellar, although I do not recall seeing any. Let us depart while there is time! I will consider my two thousand dollars as lost!"

They ran out, Moe muttering, "*Oi!* I don't see why that Nace didn't use a gun—"

"He don't carry any!" Heavy snapped. "At least, no regular gun. Or so the newspapers say!"

Their voices faded into the raucous clamor of the radio.

Nace eased out of the pantry. He glided through the back door, out into the rear yard.

Twilight lay gloomily upon the rank shrubbery and clipped hedges. None of the neighboring dwellings could be seen.

Nace veered around the corner of the house, intent on following the three men who were behaving so viciously.

He stopped suddenly. His eyes, despite the gloom, had detected a path through the grass and shrubs. It looked like some heavy object had recently been dragged to cover.

With long strides, he followed the trail. It led into a bed of tall flowers. It ended at the body of a man.

Nace stared. At the same time, he absently brought his pipe out of his pocket. The pipe was stubby, with a rather new stem and an old, black bowl. He put it in his teeth. He liked to bite on something when he was bothered.

He bit on the stem now—so hard the bakelite broke like gravel in his mouth.

CHAPTER II

Violence Trail

THE BODY LAY face upwards. The fellow was tall, athletic. He had been rather handsome.

It was not the sight of the corpse that shocked Nace into chewing up his pipe stem. He had seen many of those. It was another thing, a horrible, grisly object—a thing that made the short blond hairs crawl on his nape. It made the weird scarlet serpent scar come out vividly on his forehead.

The arm of a green skeleton lay on the dead man's chest. The pointed finger bones were embedded in the fellow's throat, as though clutching. The bones were those of a right arm.

They were green as the leaves of the plants among which the body lay. The fingertips were stained brown. Some kind of poison!

Nace slowly took his pipe out of his teeth, lipped away pieces of the broken stem, cleared his throat softly.

Out in the street, an automobile engine had come to life. That would be the three men in flight.

Nace stooped over the corpse with the grisly green bones clutching its features. He slapped pockets. All but one were turned inside out. In that one, as if carelessly shunted there after a search, were all the man's belongings.

He examined them. Cards, some money, a billfold, speakeasy passes! The cards bore a name.

JIMMY OFFITT
Importer

They bore no address except that of this bungalow. This, then, was the owner of the place.

Nace ran to the street. The car was gone, except for a murmur in the distance.

Sprinting, Nace made for his own car. He had parked it around the corner. It was a roadster, big, quiet, expensive, but of a model five years old. It was somewhat battered.

In the rumble seat lay three baseballs, two bats, a pitcher's glove, and five New York Police Department badges. The badges were Nace's souvenirs of the fight that had terminated the afternoon's ball game.

The motor caught with the first stamp of the pedal. But the car bearing the three men was hopelessly gone.

Nace knew the machine; he had made a mental note of it when he entered the bungalow—a brand new sedan of inexpensive make.

He wheeled his car westward. He drove fast, using only one hand. With the other hand, he picked a flat case out of the door pocket. This held half a dozen extra stems to fit his pipe. He replaced the broken stem, stoked the pipe with tobacco from a bright silk pouch and, crouching low behind the windshield, fired the weed.

Ten minutes later, he came in sight of a sign that read: The Plaza.

The Plaza was a swanky apartment hotel on the shores of the Sound. It was big, new. It had everything the Park Avenue places boasted, as well as small, good shops downstairs. It had its own golf course, beach, and swimming pools.

Baron Marz von Auster's white monkey jacket had been labeled as coming from a shop in the Plaza.

The rush of night air—it was now fairly dark—had cooled Nace's forehead. The weird serpentine scar was gone, almost magically. His shaggy blond hair blew about like a plume. This uncovered the upper part of his left ear, disclosing a large notch—the mark of an old bullet. Nace wore his blond hair long to hide that scar.

He wheeled in to the curb, pipe smoke a fog about his bony face.

A brand new sedan of moderate price was pulling up before one of the numerous side entrances of the Plaza. Baron von Auster and the other two! Nace was sure of it—positive when, an instant later, he saw the trio hurry to the side door and fit a key in the lock.

Nace drew a bag from the roadster rumble. It was rather large, that bag, of canvas and closed with a zipper fastener. It was shabby, for it had seen use. Nace always carried it when he went on a case. It was his bag of tricks, and there were those who said it had no bottom.

His cleated baseball shoes gritted noisily on the curbing. He frowned down at them, then eased into nearby shrubbery. When he came out a little later, he had exchanged his baseball suit for a dark coat and trousers and soft-soled shoes. The dark clothes and sneakers had been in the zipper bag.

His baseball suit was rolled around the noisy shoes. He pegged the bundle into the roadster rumble. He ran to the apartment house. He had been in the Plaza when dallying with the idea of taking an apartment there. He liked the idea of those side entrances. He knew of no other place in town that was arranged just like this.

The entrances were fairly private—each admitted to a bank of automatic elevators serving the apartments immediately above. There was no bother of wandering through long halls and leaving and entering through a central lobby—unless one desired to do so.

THE DOOR was locked. Out of Nace's zipper bag came a bundle of master keys. These locks were usually not very complicated. This one was not—in twenty seconds, he was inside.

The elevator was still going up. Nace drew a slender steel rod from the bag and waited. The elevator cage stopped somewhere overhead.

Nace promptly inserted his rod in a small hole provided by the elevator manufacturer for just that purpose, and got the sliding doors open. This broke the electrical connection that permitted the lift to operate. The cage would remain where it was until the doors closed.

Nace propped them open by wedging half a dozen matches in the track. Then he ran up the stairs, hunting the cage.

The car had stopped on the top floor—the sixth. There were doors opening off a small corridor. All were closed. Five of them! His quarry might be behind any one.

Out of Nace's zipper bag came a can. It resembled a talcum powder container, even to the perforated top. He sprinkled a fine yellow powder over the handiest door knob, then brought his nostrils close to it and sniffed.

There was a pungent odor. But it was not strong.

Nace tried another knob—another. From the fourth, he got a very strong odor. He tried the last one. But only at the fourth was there a pronounced result.

This told him which apartment the men had entered. They had not worn gloves. The hand of one of them, in grasping the knob, had left an oily film—the same sort of a film that accounts for fingerprints. Nace's powder, a concoction of his own, produced an odor when it mingled with the oil. But so microscopic was the oily deposit that it would not react with the chemicals in the powder after being exposed to the air for some minutes.

Nace listened at the door. There was talk, but it came to his ears as a hollow, unintelligible murmur. The keyhole was not of a type that extended completely through the door. He tried the crack at the bottom. Nothing doing there, either. The crack would not have let a sheet of paper through.

Nace felt of the door, pushed gently. It was of metal, a thin sheet.

Out of Nace's zipper carry-all came a remarkable device. This consisted of a super-sensitive microphone that could be held to a flat surface with rubber vacuum cups of the type employed in sticking ashtrays on car windows. There was a powerful amplifier, utilizing vacuum tubes of small voltage, and a sensitive phone headset. All three were connected by wires.

Nace set his microphone against the door, donned the headset, and switched on the amplifier. He twirled the volume dials. The murmur of voices loudened rapidly. Somewhere downstairs, a door slammed and, so sensitive was the apparatus, it was like a thunderclap. A truck ran past in the street outside, and the phone diaphragms roared with vibration.

Voices finally became understandable.

"WHAT'S THE matter with leavin' the shade up an' watchin' from the darkened room?" Heavy was demanding.

"*Oi,* and why not?" Moe echoed.

"Does it not occur to you that Reel or Hoo Li, like ourselves, may possess binoculars?" Baron von Auster asked dryly. "They might catch the reflection of starlight upon our own glasses. We will cut small holes through the shades. *Ja!*"

"O.K.," Heavy agreed. "There ain't no sense in takin' chances, at that!"

There was a little stirring about in the room; a knife ripped noisily at a window shade.

Nace scowled, fingering absently at the sweat-shirt sleeves projecting from the short sleeves of his baseball blouse. These three were watching two men named Reel and Hoo Li. The latter name sounded Chinese. The other—English, probably.

"Hell—they're there now!" Heavy barked suddenly.

"*Nein!* I noticed nothing!" Baron von Auster snapped.

"That orange light—"

"That does not mean Reel or Hoo Li are present! Reel, I believe, keeps that light burning in his room at all hours, whether he is there or not. It is, I believe, a light made from one of Reel's green skulls."

"Green skulls—ugh!" Moe muttered. "I can't get it out of

my head how that Jimmy Offitt looked when we found him! Them green bones diggin' into his face!"

Nace was nothing if not surprised to hear this. He had mentally attributed the killing of Jimmy Offitt to these three. Now it seemed otherwise!

"We should've left the body of Offitt layin' where we found it," Heavy offered grouchily. "We left tracks draggin' it into them bushes from off the lawn."

"We could not leave it lying in plain view to be seen by any tramp who chanced to cross the yard!" sneered the baron, "Anyway, the tracks do not matter. That private detective, Nace, already has us connected with the affair. *Der Hund!*"

"We should have put the croak on that shamus!" Moe snarled.

Heavy gave vent to a big, uneasy rumble of a laugh. "We done the wise thing in beatin' it! This Nace is poison, I tell you!"

FOR FULLY four minutes, there was silence. Then Heavy made another of his nervous, grumbling mirth sounds.

"Why not go over an' be friskin' Reel's house for this green skull?" he demanded. "Then, when Reel and Hoo Li show up, we can grab 'em! I know ways of makin' 'em talk!"

"My friend, I also know ways of making men talk!" Baron von Auster said softly.

"Then why not go over?"

Baron von Auster let several seconds pass, then made a clicking sound with his tongue.

"*Himmel!* Have you ever been near that black house, my friend?"

"Hell, no! What's that got to do—"

"A great deal! That house is a place of peril! I am honest when I tell you I would not dare go there unless Reel and Hoo Li are on hand to welcome us. And you know I am no coward."

Nace considered this. They were watching a house—and they were afraid to go near it.

He took out his pipe, put it away again. He felt absently of the notch in his left ear. The apartment house was very silent, probably due to the soundproofed construction.

Nace fell to wondering about the mysterious woman who had called him. He did not know her name—knew nothing except that she had called him with an excited plea for aid.

He would, he was sure, recognize her voice if he heard it again.

Word of the girl suddenly came from within the room.

"That girl, what about her?" Moe asked abruptly.

Baron von Auster chuckled. "I should not be surprised to learn she is lying somewhere with a part of the green skeleton clutching her pretty face. No doubt she possesses dangerous knowledge. Reel and Hoo Li will not give her a chance to get to the police."

"Blazes!" Heavy grunted. "You say Reel is doin' the killin' with the green skeleton?"

"*Ich weiss nicht!*" snapped the baron, then translated into English. "I do not know—for sure! But who else could it be? Jimmy Offitt and the girl—Rosa Andricksen—were working together, against us. We all know that. *Ja!*"

A match scratched—evidently Baron von Auster lighting a cigarette.

"The green skull vanished!" he continued. "Who could have gotten it but Jimmy Offitt or Rosa Andricksen? It is obvious Reel and Hoo Li sought to recover it, just as we three are seeking it. *Ja!*"

"And they got it first!" Heavy growled. "They croaked Jimmy Offitt, after scarin' him into tellin' 'em where he had it hid! The girl was there, so they grabbed her, too. She got to the phone and squawked to this Nace guy. That's how it figures, huh?"

"That is how it figures, *mein Herren*. Reel and Hoo Li now have the green skull. As soon as they appear at Reel's black house, we shall go and have our try at getting it!"

Silence fell. One of the men coughed, and the concussion

in Nace's headset was ear-splitting. The trio seemed to have settled down to wait, binoculars glued on some neighboring dwelling. A black house where an orange light burned.

Nace detached his listening device and eased it into the zipper bag. He walked down the stairs, carrying the bag, released the elevator doors so the cage could operate and swung out into the night.

He was going to hunt that black house with an orange light. It looked as if the next developments would be there.

CHAPTER III

The Grasping Foot

LEE NACE MADE a tall, bony, somewhat incongruous figure in the pale night, dark clothing and sun-broiled features merging with the gloom. Removing his shapeless white
Panama, the only article of his attire which clashed with the
murk, he rolled it and shoved it inside his vest. At the end of
the apartment house, he stopped and let his gaze rove.

Before him lay the Plaza golf course. It sloped down to
the sea, spotted with trees, and with some carefully cultivat-
ed brush between the fairways. It had the name of being a
sporty course.

Beyond the golf links were scattered houses, great mansions. Nace knew the men upstairs must be watching one of
these—they were looking in that direction.

The moon had come out faintly, and was casting creamy
luminance. Two of the distant houses were very white. A third,
one nearest the water, was extremely dark—black and ominous as a coffin. An orange light glowed from a downstairs
window.

"That's it!" Nace decided, and set out.

He charged his short pipe, planted the cracked stem in his
teeth, and gnawed it as he strode along.

He swung in a wide circle, keeping out of sight of the three
sinister watchers in the Plaza, and reached the shore of Long
Island Sound. He followed the beach.

The golf course shrubbery now shielded him from the

watchers at the Plaza. He shook dottle out of his pipe, chewed it cold.

The black coffin of a house bulked bigger and bigger. Nace neared it from the rear. Bushes, small trees, dotted the grounds. A concrete drive down to the beach, walled with a low hedge. Moon shadow lurked in the lee of the hedge like shapeless black animals.

Nace drifted into the shadow, but did not go far. He crouched in the murk, drew softly on his unlighted pipe, and did some pointed wondering.

The trio at the Plaza had been afraid to venture near this place. They were not cowards—their attack on Nace at the bungalow showed that. Therefore, there must be deadly danger about this casket house.

Nace was going in. But he was going to use some care.

He retraced his steps to the beach. A rowboat was drawn up on the sand. It held oars. Nace got one.

Probing ahead with the oar, he advanced along the hedge, keeping low and out of sight. The black house grew even more in size as he came nearer. It was of some expensive dark brick, roofed with black tile. On one side was a garage large enough for four or five cars, and tool houses. On the other side lay a commodious swimming pool.

There was a macabre air about it, as if the place encased a gigantic, deadly corpse. Nace stopped suddenly.

He punched gently with the oar. It came again—the thing that had halted him. A sharp, ugly tap on the end of the oar!

From his bag, Nace produced a flashlight. This light was peculiar in that it threw a beam of unusual shape—a thin rod of light, no thicker through than a finger. He streaked the ray at the end of the oar.

His scalp crawled. *Cru-n-c-h!* went his teeth through the new pipe stem.

Before him, a loathsome cone of yellowish-brown coils glistened in the light, squirming and heaving. A hideous hood waved like a gently moving fan.

Nace had no trouble recognizing the species of the snake. It was the likeness of just such a reptile that he was doomed to wear to the grave as a sear upon his forehead. A scar, fortunately for his association with the rest of mankind, which only became visible when his skin flushed with anger—the scar which had given him his nickname of the Blond Adder.

The cobra was picketed with a small wire, tied tightly just below its hood and running to a steel peg thrust in the ground. Like a frightsome watchdog!

NACE STRUCK at the blunt, venomous head with the oar. The single blow put the thing out of commission, and without much noise.

He went ahead, somewhat more cautiously, leaving the reptile lifeless behind. It was not without reason that the three watchers in the Plaza had feared to come near this place, he reflected.

The sepulchral shadow of the vast black house enwrapped Nace. He kept probing with the oar, not knowing what other death traps might await.

Reaching a window without incident, he drew his listening device out of the canvas bag, stuck the microphone to the glass and clamped on the headset. Tiny sounds within the house assumed gigantic volume.

He could hear two or three clocks ticking, a radiator bubbling, and a drone that probably came from an electric refrigerator in the kitchen regions. If there was anyone in the house, they were keeping very quiet. Nace replaced his listening apparatus.

From the bag he took a bottle of chemical and a fine brush. Wetting the brush in the chemical, he ran it around the puttied edge of the window pane. Almost at once, the putty was softened to a paste.

Nace had put in many hours of experimenting in his own laboratory to perfect the ingredients in that chemical concoction. He pulled out small brads around the pane, using pliers.

Applying a rubber suction cup to the pane, he lifted it out.

But he did not go through. Instead, he daubed another chemical on a long, slender, stiff wire and passed it up and down and from side to side in the opening.

Nace knew burglar alarms utilizing a beam of invisible ultra-violet light impinging upon a photo-electric cell were in common use. Interrupting the unseen light beam operated the alarm. The chemical on Nace's wire was one that fluoresced, or glowed, when exposed to ultra-violet light. It did not glow now.

Apparently there was no unseen alarm. He entered.

The room, a parlor of some sort, smelled of an Oriental incense. His unaided ear could now detect the ticking of one clock. The gurgling radiator was in this room, also. Evidently the heat was on so as to dispel the cool dampness of the sea breeze.

Out of the capacious zipper carry-all, Nace picked a small cardboard carton. He strewed the contents of this on the rug behind him as he crossed the room. It was ordinary corn flakes, which would crackle loudly if stepped upon.

The darkness was intense; the overpowering strength of the incense made breathing unpleasant. Just as the exterior of the strange house was coffinlike, so was the interior like an Oriental sepulchre.

Nace calculated, decided the room where the orange light burned was to the right, and headed in that direction. He was resolved to wait there for the return of the mysterious Reel and Hoo Li. They seemed the only link to the woman—Rosa Andricksen.

He entered a hallway. Ahead, he discovered the light. A crack of it marked the lower edge of a door. He advanced, still strewing the corn flakes.

He was reaching for the knob when there came a faint crunching sound behind him. Some one stepping upon the corn flakes!

HE TWISTED the head of his flash, which prepared it for the throwing of a wide beam. He extended it. His thumb sought the button. But he did not press it.

Instead, he leaped high in the air.

The encounter with the cobra had sharpened his already keen alertness. He had heard a scraping noise underfoot—his first thought was to get somewhere else as soon as possible. It might be another snake.

An instant later he knew it was no reptile—the thing slapped noisily against a wall. A disgusted gasp followed.

Nace guessed that a loop of wire had been spread on the hallway floor. His jump had saved his ankles from being trapped.

He sprayed his flash beam. But he was off balance, and the light spouted in the wrong direction. It did disclose the wire loop, however, still squirming and dancing where it had fallen after being jerked. It was common wire clothesline.

Nace's flash splattered a door just as it was shutting. He caught no glimpse of the person who had gone through. A key rattled in the door lock.

Nace took two fast steps, a jump—hit the door feet first, legs stiff. There was a crack. The panel, shucking free of its hinges, lowered like a drawbridge—and carried Nace, sled-fashion, down a flight of stairs, finally dumping him on a cool concrete basement floor.

He had bargained on nothing like this—he only wanted the door open. He came to his feet like a sprinter, high-jumped the first six stairs of the flight down which he had slid, barked his shins, swore, and made the top in two more jumps.

Drawing a tear-gas gun, constructed to resemble a fountain pen, he fired it down into the basement.

Some of the gas was bound to swirl back into the hallway. He ran to the door behind which burned the orange light. Might as well take a look there while there was time!

He entered, blinking owlishly, eyes roving.

The place seemed a combination of a sleeping room and study. There were a desk, smoking stands, easy chairs, in addition to a bed. The bedstead was big, old-fashioned, a four-poster affair with a canopy.

On it lay a sheet-swathed form.

Nace advanced, saw a cane lying on the desk, picked it up and used it to lift an end of the sheet.

The body underneath was that of a man of rather stout build. He was perhaps fifty. His hair and close-clipped mustache were gray.

Upon the man's chest lay an assembly of green bones—the framework of a human leg. The tips of the toe bones, filed sharp, bore sticky brown smears. The points were not, however, embedded in the man's rather swarthy features.

Nace lifted the bones gingerly, using his handkerchief to keep his hand from contacting them. He sniffed of the brownish stains. There was an almond odor, very faint.

"Some poison with prussic acid in it," he decided. "Prussic is usually blue, but this is mixed with some brown stuff, maybe molasses."

Shuffling steps, a series of choking gasps, came from the hallway.

Nace, smiling fiercely, the adder scar on his forehead glowing red, fished a pair of handcuffs from a hip pocket. He was careful not to let the links chink together. The bracelets were the type that closed and locked automatically when slapped against a wrist.

He dashed the manacles against the wrist of the man on the bed—wrenched hard and snapped the other ring to the stout headpost of the bed.

The prone man came to life, emitting a frenzied scream.

HE MUST have screamed in hopes of startling Nace, for his eyes, open and dark, looked quite sane. Whatever his object was, it did him no good.

"Damn you!" he shrieked, and kicked at Nace. The gaunt detective dodged.

The fellow on the bed flounced about. He grasped the green skeleton leg and flung it at Nace. Nace dodged. The bones, hooked together cleverly with wire, clattered loudly against the wall and fell to the floor.

The man continued to convulse like an animal in a trap. In an instant, his free hand came up with a gun. He had been reposing upon it.

The weapon tangled in the bed clothing. Lunging, Nace captured the gun wrist. He twisted. The man on the bed screamed again. This time he had a reason, for Nace's bony hands were capable of opening horseshoes.

Nace had the gun when he backed away. He unloaded it as he backed to the desk. He struck the weapon, broken open, upon the desk. The blow was terrific. The steel bit deeply into the hardwood. Nace hit again. That smashed twisted barrel and cylinder upon the frame so they would not close together properly. He flung the useless revolver into a corner.

Moving swiftly, Nace went to the door.

There was a girl in the hall, blinded by the tear gas. It was obviously she who had fled into the basement after trying unsuccessfully to snare his feet in the clothesline loop.

She was trying to get out through the front door.

There was some tear gas in the hall, seepage from the basement.

Shutting his eyes, Nace ran to the girl, captured her arm and jerked her back into the room where the orange light glowed.

She struck madly at him. Her fists landed twice before he ducked away. He shut the hall door.

The girl was worth the look he gave her. She was dark-haired, dark-eyed, with a trace of suntan. She had an excellent figure.

"Rosa Andricksen?" Nace asked sharply.

She said nothing, but rubbed briskly at her eyes, accelerating the tear flow in hopes of soon clearing her vision. She wore a gray sport dress, very trim.

Nace waited five minutes, seven, ten. The man on the bed squirmed, fought the handcuffs. But there was scant chance of his getting away. He said nothing, except to vent hisses of rage.

Once Nace asked him, "Are you Reel?"

The man only snarled.

The girl began to be able to see.

"I am Lee Nace!" Nace told her.

She did not answer. Turning slowly, she eyed the man on the bed. Her movements were graceful.

Then she sprang headlong at Nace.

CHAPTER IV

Sinister People

HER STRUGGLE WAS silent, ferocious. She took Nace a little by surprise and he was on the floor before he recovered himself. She was strong. He had fought lots of men who were easier to handle.

Too, he did not like to paste her one on the jaw. That handicapped him. She clawed at him, tore the pocket of his coat. His pipe and tobacco and other articles spilled across the floor.

"Cut it out, sister!" he roared. "I'm Nace! If you're Rosa Andricksen, I'm the guy you sent for!"

The effect of this was surprising. She stopped struggling, held her head up to bring her ear close to his lips.

"What did you say?" she asked in a very pleasant voice. "I'm a little hard of hearing!" It was the voice that had phoned Nace!

"A little!" Nace snorted, then, very loudly, "I am Lee Nace! Sometimes people are kind enough to call me a private detective."

"Oh!" The girl disentangled herself. "I thought you were one of Reel's men!" She pointed at the man on the bed. "That's Reel!"

She seemed contrite, although there was a queerly set, vacant look about her face. Moving over, she picked up his pipe, tobacco and matches. She thrust the articles in his trouser pocket, as if he were a little boy.

"What's behind this mess?" Nace yelled.

"I don't know," the girl replied in the queerly soft voice the hard-of-hearing sometimes use.

Nace gave her a hard eye. "Now don't start slipping me fast balls, sister!"

There was something he did not trust about her manner.

"What?" she asked in her gentle voice.

"Tell me the truth!" he shrieked. "Was it you who called me?"

"Yes!" she breathed gently. "It was I."

"Why did you do it?"

"What?"

The adder glowed purple on his forehead as he bellowed, "Why did you call me?"

"Oh! This man," she pointed at the fellow handcuffed to the bed, "came to my apartment tonight and seized me. He took me to that bungalow. I got to the phone and tried to call you. I didn't think I had gotten you."

"What did he take you to the bungalow for?" Nace roared.

"I don't know," she whispered.

"Did you know Jimmy Offitt?" The bellowing was making Nace hoarse.

Her answer surprised him.

"No," she said gently.

Nace scowled. There was something wrong here. It did not hook up. He eyed her wrists, her ankles. Purple marks showed where she had been tied recently.

That gave him an idea. He swept into the hallway, got the clothesline wire with which she had tried to snare him, and came back.

Although she squealed and struggled, he tied her wrists and ankles. He did not bind so tightly as to cause pain, but when he was done, he was sure she would not get away.

He left her sitting on the floor, glaring at him, and went out to investigate the rest of the house.

THE PLACE was big, like a castle. Nace put a fresh stem in his pipe, thumbed in tobacco, and lit up. He left tobacco smoke in each room, mingling with the Oriental incense odor.

There seemed to be no servants. In two of the rooms, he found cobras picketed. He found the snakes because he was looking for them. Had he been prowling, burglar-like, he probably would have been bitten.

One upstairs bedroom was fitted with Chinese ornaments—a dragon tapestry, idols, and such.

In one corner was a trunk, plentifully plastered with steamer labels. The trunk seemed to have gone over most of Europe. Some of the customs stamps bore dates. They ranged over a period of the past three years.

Nace opened the trunk. It seemed to hold curios—timetables, hotel advertisements, bottles of perfume, bits of lace. The things most travelers pick up. But the Oriental nature of the things indicated this was the room of the Chinaman, Hoo Li.

On a dressing table was a picture of a plump Chinese. In the drawer of the table was a passport with the same picture. It was Hoo Li.

With the passport was the printed sailing list of an Atlantic liner that had docked in New York some three weeks ago. Nace ran through the list. As he came to names that interested him, he underlined them. When he was done, he had seven names.

M. J. REEL
HOO LI LUNG
BARON VON AUSTER
MOE MEVINSKY
JOHN HEAVY
JIMMY OFFITT
ROSA ANDRICKSEN

Nace swore, fingered his notched left ear.

"The whole outfit came into the States on a liner three weeks ago," he grunted. "And the black-haired queen told me she didn't know a thing about this! The hell she doesn't!"

He barged for the stairs. Somewhere outdoors, an automobile engine started. Nace took the stairs, six at a jump.

The girl sat in the hallway. She was still wired hand and foot. But the door behind her was closed.

Nace tried the door. It was locked. There was no key in it.

The automobile engine was receding rapidly down the driveway. Nace plunged through the front door. Tires screamed as the car skidded into the street. Nace caught a glimpse of the machine as it scudded under a street lamp. No one but Reel was in the vehicle.

Nace knew his chances of catching the car were nil. He did not try. He swung around the side of the house, fanning the ground with his flashlight, lest there be more anchored cobras.

A window in the coffin of a house was open. It gave into the orange-lighted room. Reel had departed by this route.

Entering, Nace inspected the handcuffs. They had been unlocked off Reel's wrist.

Dark-faced, Nace glowered at the source of the orange light. The base of this was a weird green skull. He went over, seized the light and smashed it on the floor.

The green skull was only plaster. It flew all over the room, a myriad of pieces.

He went to the door, hard-heeled, made sure no key was in this side of the lock. He kicked the lock out. That eased his anger somewhat. But the scarlet serpent was still hot on his forehead when he towered over pretty, dark-eyed Rosa Andricksen.

His voice a low, tearing whisper, he said, "Are you going to give me the handcuff key and the key to that door, or do I have to hunt for them?"

His voice had been pitched very low. Had she been the least bit deaf, she could not have heard him.

"I'll give them up!" she said, proving there was nothing wrong with her hearing. She had, it was plain, faked the deafness so as to enable Reel to overhear Nace's words.

NACE THREW the keys away. His hair was down over his eyes, and his jaw was knobby. His stubby pipe was sunk deep in his jaws.

"You jumped me that last time to get the key to the handcuffs from my pockets," he said grimly. "I'll hand it to you, sister! You're the slickest dip I ever ran into,"

She smiled impishly up at him. "You don't seem to like me!"

He scowled. "That means you won't talk?"

"I did talk," she replied. "I told you that Reel came to my apartment tonight, got me, and took me to that bungalow, and I called you. Then Reel brought me here. I got away—I was tied in the basement. I set that wire loop on the floor of this hall. I was after Reel. But you came along."

Nace grinned wryly. "You've got one thing I like."

She blinked. "What's that?"

"Nerve!"

He went into the room where the orange light had burned. He had not yet taken the time to search it thoroughly. Under the window where Reel had escaped stood a large window-seat chest.

Nace opened the chest lid.

Cr-a-c-k! went his pipe stem.

He swore a deep thumping oath in his chest. Then he called, "Have you seen Hoo Li tonight?"

"I know no one by the name of Hoo Li!" she replied.

He went back and untied her. "In that case, I'll show him to you!"

He led her in and showed her what was in the window box. He knew by the way that she gulped and began to tremble that she had not known what was there. No actress was *that* good!

Hoo Li lay in the box. He was knotted grotesquely—that is, his body was. For he was quite dead. Upon the moon features were five grisly purple splotches, a tiny puncture in the center of each. It was as though a sinister, poisoned claw of bones had grasped.

Nace indicated the green skeleton leg which had been upon Reel's chest, and which Reel had flung at him.

"That must have killed the Chinaman," he said dryly. "Reel took it off the body when he wanted to play dead. He played dead to fool me, of course. He wanted to stick around and see what that rumpus in the hall was, and he figured playing dead was a good way to do it." Nace frowned at the girl. "That's what happened, wasn't it?"

She shuddered. "I guess so. I was really a prisoner, and got away! That much is the truth."

Nace went down into the basement. He found wires that obviously had been used to bind the girl. He came back.

"I believe you," he said. "Now, what else do you know?"

"Nothing."

"You came back from Europe with all this crowd three weeks ago. What were you doing in Europe? And what is this green skull thing they want?"

She shivered. "I wish now that I had not called on you for help."

"Why did you?"

"I was afraid Reel was going to kill me." She shivered again. "He would have, too."

"You made a deal with him a minute ago?"

"No." She sounded earnest. "I merely let him go. He would have killed me even then. That's why I came into the hall and locked the door."

NACE FROWNED shrewdly down at her. "I see it! You're after the green skull, too. You let Reel loose in hopes he would get it, so you would have a chance of seizing it from him."

The girl blinked at him—tears were in her eyes. "You *are* clever!"

"And you and Jimmy Offitt were working together!" Nace suggested.

She suddenly burst into tears. Her shoulders shook convulsively. No acting about this! He held her close with an arm about her shoulders and let her sob.

"Jimmy Offitt was my brother!" she said at last. "My name is Rosa Offitt."

"Go on," Nace urged.

She shook her head. "No! I will not tell you any more! And I wish you would go clear away! Forget all this! Report the bodies, if you want to. Tell the police what you know. But go away!"

Nace grinned wolfishly.

He took his Panama from inside his vest, yanked it low and glowered from under the brim.

"Nix, kid!" he snorted.

He led her outdoors, and headed for the Plaza.

"Where are you going?" she wanted to know.

He told her.

"So that's where Baron von Auster, Moe and Heavy are hanging out!" she gasped. She seemed genuinely surprised at the news.

There was no excitement around the Plaza—no one lurking near. Nace made very sure of that. Then he took the girl in and rode the elevator to the sixth floor.

The corridor was quiet, except that, from down below somewhere, a radio was making soft mutter.

Nace had brought his canvas bag. He got out his listening apparatus and planted it against the door where he had eaves-dropped earlier in the night.

He heard no sound. Gently, he tried the knob. The door was unlocked; it swung open. Lights were on in the apartment. Without crossing the threshold, Nace stared inside.

"So Heavy is the latest guy to take the three-strike!" he murmured grimly.

HEAVY WAS a pile on the floor. He looked like the victim of some horrible joke, a prank concocted by a twisted mind—a brain with a twirk of utter fiendishness in its makeup.

Nace was tough. But the sight on the floor was too much. It got him. He swung forward with long strides and knocked a hideous green skull away from Heavy's features.

Some sinister jokester had arranged the skull in a position of biting hungrily. Brownly poisoned pegs, substituted for front teeth had brought death to Heavy. A knot on his skull, however, denoted he had first been knocked out by a blow from behind.

Pivoting from the macabre sight on the floor, Nace got the girl. She had not tried to flee, but possibly that was because he had been keeping an eye on her.

Nace went from room to room of the apartment. He found no one. The stereotyped nature of the fittings told him the place had been rented furnished.

He tried the inner doorknob for fingerprints, using white powder from his carry-all. The knob had been wiped clean.

His attention next went to the green skull. He picked it up between two books he found in a case, and placed it on a table, under a lamp.

An article called the green skull was behind the mess, it seemed. He wondered if this was the skull. He found nothing to bolster that belief.

He frowned at the girl while stemming his pipe. "This wouldn't be the green skull everybody is after, would it?"

She hesitated—not thinking up a false answer, but debating whether she should tell him the truth or not.

"No," she said at last. "That—is not it!"

"What does the green skull look like?"

"I do not think I'll answer that."

"Now, look here—"

She held up both hands. "Oh, don't start yelling at me! I'm trying to think it over—trying to decide whether to tell you the whole story or not."

Nace squinted his eye that had been darkened in the fight on the baseball diamond that afternoon. Then he turned his attention back to the green skull.

The color, use of a few chemicals from an analysis kit in his bag showed, was due to nothing more mysterious than malachite green aniline. The skull had apparently been soaked in the concoction, a form of green dye.

The skull itself was undoubtedly genuine. It was impossible to tell with certainty how long the owner had been dead.

"Do you know where this came from?" he asked the girl.

She took time to debate her answer.

"Hoo Li, the Chinaman, was a devotee of an Oriental cult known as the *Hara Sabz Haddi*, the cult of the green bones," she said finally. "Instead of the usual form of image, a green skeleton is used by the *Hara Sabz Haddi*. Hoo Li carried one around with him. I don't know where he got it—the Orient probably."

Nace took another squint at the green skull. "It has got the characteristics of an Oriental skull, all right."

"It must be part of Hoo Li's religious rigamarole," the girl said slowly. "He was a fanatical follower of his cult. He tried to convert all of them to his heathen religion at one time or another. I think Reel was half won over. He had green skulls on the brain. Take that reading lamp, the one with the orange bulb, for instance."

"You know a lot about them!" Nace said.

"I ought to!" she retorted.

"You were one of the gang, eh?"

"No!" She sounded emphatic, "But my brother and I have followed them and watched them for weeks, both in Europe and America."

"So that is why you all came into the States on the same liner?"

"Yes!"

NACE FELT of his notched ear, felt of his bruised eye, and scraped blond hair down over his forehead. He felt an urge to grab the woman and shake her. She got under his sunburned hide. She was, he realized, about as clever as they came. She was playing a game—and she was going ahead with it, even though he did have her a prisoner.

She seemed worried.

"Did you find out anything while trailing Baron von Auster, Moe and—" she indicated the body on the floor, "—this man?"

Nace had not told her the details of his evening's procedure. Coming here, he had merely advised her that he expected to find the three men.

"Wouldn't you like to know?" he snorted, trying to exasperate her.

She shrugged. "I don't blame you for feeling huffy! In your place, I wouldn't answer, either."

Nace, contrarily, decided to feed her a little information. It might serve as a bait to attract a statement that would help to clear up the muddle.

"Baron von Auster and the other two were getting ready to go after Reel in hopes of getting the green skull," he said.

The words got results far beyond his fondest hopes. The young woman's hands clenched.

"What?" she choked. "They were—didn't—didn't Baron von Auster and his two have the green skull?"

"Apparently not," Nace said dryly.

"I—thought they had it!" she gulped. "I turned—turned Reel loose so that he could get it from them!"

"What made you think they had the thing?"

She hesitated. "Why, because, when Reel took me to the bungalow tonight, some one had already been there—and murdered my brother!"

"And searched the house?"

"No-o-o!" She drew the word out, as if agonized. "The bungalow had not been ransacked. Reel started to do that. But when I got to the phone, he became scared and fled, taking me."

Nace's adder sear flushed redly. This was a mixup. Baron von Auster's men had spoken as though they had not slain Jimmy Offitt. And now the girl was as much as saying Reel had not done it, either.

"Do you think Reel murdered your brother?" he asked bluntly.

She sobbed a little. "No. He did not act like it. He was very surprised when we—found the body!"

Nace went over and shoved his face close to hers. "If none of the others have that green skull thing, hadn't we better go after it ourselves?"

She said nothing.

He guided her for the door, saying, "We're going to that bungalow! The thing must be there!"

CHAPTER V

The Green Prize

THEY HAD A wide boulevard across town. Nace wheeled his roadster into the center, horn hooting steadily, and made fifty and sixty most of the way. There was not much traffic. Half a dozen cops ran gesturing into the street after he had passed. Some of them got his license number.

"It'll rain summonses in the morning, I'll bet!" he growled.

He parked his machine two blocks from the bungalow, after approaching with horn silenced. The girl got out willingly—a bit too willingly.

"You'd better decide to play ball with me!" Nace suggested.

She maintained silence.

"All right, sister," he told her. "When I settle this thing, it'll be in my own way. And I don't want to hear you squawking."

She began, "You're not getting paid anything—"

"Like fun I'm not!" he snorted. "I've already collected two thousand smackers—off Baron von Auster!"

She jerked back from him. "He paid you, and you double-crossed—"

"Nix! I took the jack away from him!"

"Oh!" She seemed to consider. "I'll pay you that much more to go away!"

He laughed softly, ironically, said: "I don't work that way!"

They wended, via backyards, to the vicinity of the bungalow. Stars overhead and a silver half of a moon cast pale light. In the shadow of a rose bush in somebody's lawn, Nace surveyed the street.

On the corner lot, the boys still played with their baseball. There were only four of them now, and their game had turned onto a makeshift version of two-old-cat.

Nace, surprised that the lads were still out, eyed his watch. It was only ten o'clock—he had thought the time to be much later.

Two cars were parked in the thoroughfare.

Baron von Auster's new, inexpensive sedan stood near the corner, under a tree that cut off the brilliance of the corner street lamp.

Nearer was a roadster, a black machine. Reel's car—the one in which he had fled his black coffin of a mansion.

Both vehicles were empty.

Nace glanced upward, saw a cloud approaching the moon, and waited until it flung darkness into the street, then eased himself across. The keys were not in the roadster ignition lock. He opened his pocketknife and wedged it in front of a rear tire so that, should the car roll, there would be a puncture.

He lifted the hood of the little sedan and tore out the ignition wires. It would take at least twenty minutes of work to get the machine going.

The girl watched these preparations in silence.

She said nothing, offered no resistance, as Nace guided her toward the bungalow.

Shrubs, small hedges, furred the lawn and offered concealment. Haunting these shadows, Nace skirted the bungalow with his companion.

Soon the rear door slammed softly.

Staring, Nace heard, rather than saw, a figure glide into the low bushes. It lingered a moment, then returned.

The closing rear door choked off the light. Nace was not quite able to identify the man, due to the creepers that draped portions of the rear porch.

He eased to the bush the skulker from the house had visited. Exploring, his hands encountered a fat, small traveling bag. The container was stuffed to capacity.

Nace opened it, found what felt like a bundle of candles. He lifted these out, brought them close to his eyes to discern what they were.

His grip tightened when he saw the labels. Dynamite!

WITH HIS fingers, Nace searched further. A box holding what felt not unlike blank .22 cartridges reposed in the bottom of the briefcase. Detonator caps!

A fuse, a cap crimped to the end, extended from one of the dynamite sticks through a knife slit in the handbag side.

Nace carried his find to the roadster. The explosive and the caps, he placed in the rear compartment of the car.

And there, in the rear compartment, he made an ugly discovery.

It was the body of Moe.

The round, greasy little form was still warm. A hideous claw of green bones clung to Moe's throat, the pointed fingertips hanging like embedded thorns.

Moe had been struck a blow upon the head to produce unconsciousness before the grisly thing of green was applied to bring death. This wound had flowed some scarlet, staining the floorboards of the compartment.

Nace considered, then moved to the new sedan. On the front floorboards, he found scarlet stains.

Moe had been killed in Baron von Auster's machine and transferred to the rear of Reel's vehicle, it would seem.

Nace grasped the girl's trembling arm. "Listen—I want a straight answer to this question! Did Reel get a telephone call just before I arrived? I mean—did you hear the phone ring while you were getting loose in the basement?"

She was slow answering, then said: "The phone rang. But I

did not hear what was said. That was not more than five minutes before you came to the black house."

"That explains it!" Nace breathed fiercely. "Baron von Auster gave Reel a call and they combined forces! They're both in that bungalow now—hunting the green skull!"

Nace now continued his preparations with the dynamite.

He made a bundle of a screwdriver, a can of tube patch, a couple of wrenches, which he found in the rear of the roadster with Moe's body. He substituted this for the dynamite. He inserted the fuse in the slit in the bag, leaving the cap in place because he did not care to risk getting a hand blown off in removing it.

He carried the body of Moe to a patch of shrubs and concealed it there in the murk.

Carrying the bag, which now contained the harmless bundle he had exchanged for the dynamite, and guiding the girl by an arm, he went toward the bungalow.

He replaced the valise beside the bush where he had first found it. Then he glided close to the rear porch.

Voices murmured in the bungalow, apparently in the living room. Nace tried the porch door, and it opened silently.

They entered. Nace kept his grip on the girl. But she moved with a stealth equal to his own. They advanced until the voice murmur became distinguishable words.

"That is too bad," growled Baron von Auster. "It is possible the green skull is not concealed here after all!"

"That is conceivable," admitted another voice. "We can only search. And since we have combined forces, our chances of finding it are considerably greater!"

The girl brought her lips close to Nace's ear, breathed, "Reel!"

Nace nodded. He had guessed the two in the front room were Reel and the baron.

"Joining hands was a wise move for both of us!" Baron von Auster agreed. "It is regrettable that each of us thought the other was using that green skeleton to murder!"

"Yeah," muttered Reel. "Which one do you think is really the killer—the girl, or that detective, Nace?"

"I do not know. One or the other, it is obvious!"

Nace scowled blackly. It seemed those two had put their heads together and decided he or the girl was the green-skeleton killer. He looked down sidewise at the dark-eyed girl. He could see her face faintly in the dim glow from the front room. Her features were pale, set.

She glanced up at him, shook her head, shrugged, breathed, "I did not do it!"

The door into the front room was about half-open. Nace took a chance and looked through the crack.

The two men were systematically taking the room apart and slicing paper off the walls and digging beneath with knife points. Each had a pistol thrust in his belt, where it could be gotten at handily.

A spike-snouted, silenced automatic lay on a table. This was one of the unusual guns Moe and Heavy had carried earlier in the night.

Nace considered briefly. Then he flung himself into the room. He scooped up the gun on the table before the two men could move.

"Catch a couple of high balls!" he rapped.

The two might not be baseball fans, but they understood the lingo. Reel's hands went up. But Baron von Auster only glared.

"*Nein!*" he sneered. "The gun is empty! We drew the cartridges before we placed it there!"

Leering, Nace squeezed the automatic trigger.

Chung! It was loaded, all right. The bullet streaked so close to Baron von Auster's head that he ducked wildly. His hands went up.

ADVANCING GINGERLY, Nace disarmed the pair. Because

there was no place else, he stuffed their guns in the belt of his trousers.

The girl stood back, dark eyes thoughtful, and watched.

Nace frowned at her. "I have a hunch you know where that green skull jigger is hidden! You and your brother got it from these two. Don't you think it is about time you were digging it up?"

She surprised him by nodding agreeably. "I'll get it!"

She stepped to the radio. It took most of her strength to twist the heavy cabinet out from the wall.

"The thing should be hidden in a spare tube in the radio," she explained.

She reached into the instrument with both hands. Her left hand brought out a vacuum tube. The silvered glass of the bulb concealed what was inside.

Her right hand whipped out a small automatic which had been hidden in the cabinet. She pointed the weapon at Nace.

"I'd hate to shoot you!" she said grimly.

He blinked. He had not expected anything this desperate. He had his silenced gun trained in her direction. But he greatly disliked the idea of firing upon a woman.

"What are you going to do now?" he asked angrily.

"Get out of here!" she retorted. She hefted the silvered vacuum tube. "I'm going to dispose of this to the agent who is here from Europe to purchase it. Then I shall hunt you up, after waiting a sufficient time to permit the agent to get out of this country, and tell you the whole story."

"Yeah?" Nace was not sure whether to believe her or not.

She backed for the door.

Then disaster came. She had her back to Baron von Auster and Reel, all her attention riveted on Nace.

Baron von Auster sprang. He seized the girl, using her for a shield from Nace's bullets. With a free hand, he trapped her automatic. Twisting, he got it.

The thing happened in flash seconds. Nace suddenly found himself looking into the snout of the little automatic.

"You will drop your weapon, *mein Herr!*"

Nace did not debate long. He might have plinked Baron von Auster through the skull—except that the gun in his hand was unfamiliar and felt unnatural. He did not trust himself to miss the young woman.

He dropped his gun.

CHAPTER VI

The Green Skull

LAUGHING A BIT hysterically, Reel came over and relieved Nace of his weapons.

Nace gave the girl the blackest look he could manage, "You fixed things up nicely!"

She shivered. "Thanks!"

"That was no compliment!" he snorted.

"I mean—thanks for not shooting and maybe hitting me! That took nerve."

He grinned in spite of himself and the undoubted danger. This young woman not only had nerve, but it was evident she had walked the paths of danger before.

"Ruhig!" gritted Baron von Auster. "Quiet! Now we will inspect the contents of that radio tube!"

Together, he and Reel worked on the tube. They gave it a twist. The glass bulb came free of the base—it had merely been glued in place. The bottom of the bulb was open; the filament, plate and grid elements had been removed. The silvered coating of the tube still concealed what was inside.

Reel shook the bulb. An object wrapped in tissue was jarred out. He tore off the tissue. The green skull was disclosed.

The thing was not what Nace had expected. It was flat, not unlike a silver dollar, except that it was enameled green. On the face was a raised design of a skull.

"This is it, *mein Herr!*" chortled the baron.

Nace watched intently. He saw Reel place the plate between his palms and give a twisting motion, as though loosening the crystal of a watch. The plate screwed apart!

It was composed of several flat, thin discs. The surface of these discs had a strangely dull look.

Reel scrutinized the surface of the discs.

"It will take a powerful microscope to read the inscribed data," he declared.

He went into the kitchen. There was a sound of glass breaking. When Reel came back, he had the bottom of a milk bottle in hand.

"This will magnify sufficiently to show whether the disc is genuine."

He held the bulging glass over the discs. "Yes, it is the real thing! All the information is here! Location of frontier fortifications, size and number of guns—"

Nace's jaw sagged. He saw it all now. This disc—or the several discs—held writing engraved with a special mechanism which reduced the letters to such smallness that they were invisible to the naked eye!

The idea was not new—Nace knew of a novelty shop in New York where one could purchase ordinary pins upon the heads of which was engraved entire poems.

The discs held military information! The location of secret fortifications in some European country! Reel was an espionage agent. Baron von Auster, Moe, Heavy, Hoo Li—all had been working with him.

As for the girl and her brother—Nace eyed the young woman.

"You are in the employ of the government of the country from which this military information came, aren't you?" he asked dryly.

She hesitated.

Baron von Auster and Reel scowled at her.

"You might as well tell him!" Rell sneered. "We know the thing he has just said is the truth!"

"Yes," she told Nace. "That is right. That is why I was working alone—not telling you anything. I was afraid you would destroy the green skull—or give it to your own government."

Nace lowered his uplifted hands enough to thoughtfully touch his notched ear. She had judged him accurately. He had no sympathy for espionage systems. Trouble-makers! He would most certainly turn that green skull over to the American Intelligence—he would yet, if he could get his hands on it.

He eyed Reel, asked suddenly, "Did you know the body of Moe is in your roadster?"

Reel did not know it. His start of surprise showed that. He gulped, "What?"

Nace sighed. Reel's actions had given him his final clue. He knew who the murderer was—it couldn't be anyone else.

"You had better watch your friend, Baron von Auster," he said dryly. "His system seems to be to kill everyone, so that he may collect for the sale of this green skull, and keep the money all for himself!"

REEL AND Baron von Auster exchanged looks. They were not friendly looks.

Nace continued grimly, "Baron von Auster stole Hoo Li's green skeleton, poisoned the thing, and started killing everybody. He did in Jimmy Offitt, probably when Offitt wouldn't tell him where the green skull was hidden.

"He killed Hoo Li to get him out of the way, just as he killed his two men, Moe and Heavy. And just as he intends to murder you, no doubt!"

Reel had started trembling a little.

Nace, guessing partly, filling in what he did not know with what he thought had occurred, went on, "Baron von Auster killed Moe in his own car, and transferred the body to your roadster, Reel. Why do you think he did that, if not to frame the blame on you, should the chance come?"

Red glared at Baron von Auster.

The latter shrugged. *"Nein!"* he told Reel. "You are wrong! Come! Let us go in the kitchen and discuss this privately! I can explain everything, *Ja!"*

They tore wires off the radio and bound Nace and the girl, wrist and ankle. Then they stepped into the kitchen.

One of them kicked the door shut. Voices murmured for a moment.

Then there was a loud gasp, a blow, a stifled cry! Another blow! A form collapsed noisily to the floor. After that, silence!

Nace gave the girl a stiff-lipped grin, said, "It looks like one of them hit into a double-play!"

The back door slammed. But a moment later, it opened again. Sounds indicated the unconscious body was being moved by the survivor. But it was not moved far.

A series of moans, a gasp or two, followed. Then Baron von Auster's voice shrilled out.

"Himmel!" he wailed. *"Mein Herr* Reel! You are not going to kill me with that dynamite? Please?"

A sharp slapping sound stopped the cry. It might have been a palm against flesh. There was more shifting about in the kitchen. Five minutes it lasted. An age!

Came a scraping rasp—a match being ignited. Then a fizzing. That would be the fuse burning.

Baron von Auster screamed shrilly. "He is blowing me up with the dynamite—"

A blow ended that cry.

The kitchen door slammed. Feet pounded away in rapid flight.

NACE, ROLLING with difficulty because of his wired ankles and wrists, reached the girl. She was seeking to work toward the door. Lacking Nace's agility, she was not making much headway. Her face was white; fear stared from her eyes.

"Cool off!" Nace told her, low-voiced. "There's no dynamite in there! I took it out, hid it in Reel's roadster, and substituted screwdrivers and stuff! You saw me do it!"

"He may have found the—exchange!" she gulped.

"I don't think so! Here—I'll get your hands loose. Then you free me!"

Nace worked furiously at the girl's tyings. He tore his fingernails, scratched her wrists. The bindings finally gave.

"Now get mine!" he directed.

She obeyed—to his relief. A moment later, they were both free and on their feet.

A report thumped in the kitchen. The percussion cap exploding! The sound resembled a small firecracker. The fact that the dynamite was not in the bag had not been discovered.

Nace and the girl ran into the kitchen.

A man lay face-down beside the handbag. The valise itself was partially torn open from the blast of the percussion cap. Nace turned the man over. He wore the Baron von Auster's summer evening dress.

It was not Baron von Auster—but Reel. He was lifeless, skull crushed in, evidently from a blow by the baron's gun.

The girl gasped, "But I thought—"

"Baron von Auster is pulling a fast one!" Nace grunted. "He thought the explosion would tear the body up so it couldn't be identified. See, he even changed clothes with Reel! The baron figured he'd have no trouble getting away if everybody thought he was dead! The pick-up order would go out for Reel."

Nace charged out the rear door.

Flame jumped at him from the shrubbery. Lead took part of the glass from the kitchen door. Baron von Auster had evidently waited to see how his scheme worked.

Threshing leaves denoted that he was in flight.

Nace let him go, then followed at his leisure. The girl bobbed along at his side.

"He's getting away with the green skull!" she groaned. "That means my country—it will lose valuable information! In case of war, it will mean the death of thousands of men!"

Nace snorted. He was not going to get steamed up over wars in Europe.

The chase arched around to the street. Baron von Auster began shooting again. Lead squealed, slashed savagely at leaves. Powder smell filled the street. The *chung, chung, chung* reports of the silenced automatic were vicious.

Nace made himself and the girl as thin as possible behind a tree.

The baron ran on and tried to get away in his little sedan. But Nace had plucked out the ignition wires.

Back to the roadster belonging to Reel, Baron von Auster ran. He sprang in. The keys were evidently in his possession. He must have had the foresight to take them against just such a contingency as this.

The machine lunged ahead.

The jackknife Nace had planted pierced the tire. Air began escaping to the tune of a shrill, erratic hiss.

Leaning against the tree behind which he had taken shelter, Nace watched. The roadster fled under a street lamp.

The flat tire was making the rear end bounce up and down.

The girl half sobbed. "He's getting away—the murderer of my brother—"

Nace dropped an arm on her shoulders. "Wait, kid! He's going to get his, unless I'm mistaken."

A moment later, Baron von Auster got his. The ground jarred. A roaring explosion slammed against Nace's eardrums. Windows broke all over the neighborhood, amid much brittle jangling.

Rosa Offitt held to Nace with both hands, trembling.

He crooked an arm around her shoulders. "The jarring set the dynamite. You wait here, and I'll see how it came out."

He ran forward. The roadster was spread over much of the street. The body of Baron von Auster was not greatly mutilated, although the man was undeniably dead.

In a coat pocket, Nace found the troublesome plaque—the green skull.

He went back and showed the girl the grisly trinket.

"Now I pay you off for not playing ball with me!" he said dryly,

"You mean—you won't give it to me?"

"That's exactly what I do mean. This thing goes to the American Intelligence, if they want it."

Her reaction surprised him somewhat. She sighed. "That's all right, I suppose. You know—we have no fear of the Americans attacking us."

Nace squinted down at the girl. He was, he made a mental note, going to take a future interest in her. She was a swell number.

She shrank against him, as if for comfort, shivering. "What about Baron von Auster—?"

"That guy," Nace told her grimly, "fanned out!"

The Diving Dead

The man in black looked like a crow in mourning. He said he was an undertaker— and had a coffin ready for Detective Lee Nace. The police sergeant looked like trouble—went out of his way to make things tough for Lee Nace. The redheaded girl looked like a million. She brought haunting memories to Nace. The corpse in the cabin looked like a horrible nightmare. It plunged Lee Nace into an amazing race with a grim and terrible death.

CHAPTER I

Coffin Bait

IT WAS THE morning of Friday, the thirteenth. Nace accidentally broke the rear-view mirror on his roadster while driving downtown. A black cat angled his path when he was leaving the parking lot. Near his office, a ladder slanted over the sidewalk and Nace forgot to go around it.

Crass superstition? Sure it was. Nace paid no attention to any of it. Maybe it was his hard luck that he didn't, for the pay-off was not long in coming.

In front of his office building, Nace met Police Sergeant Gooch. As far as Nace was concerned, Gooch was another black cat.

"Hello—tall, blond, handsome!" Gooch smirked around a cigar.

Nace gave him a bony-faced leer.

"You're going for your morning shave, I suppose?"

Gooch's teeth mashed his cigar angrily. He had a prolific blue beard, and was touchy about it. He shaved three times a day it was rumored.

"The same old cop-loving Lee Nace," he said wryly.

"Sure! I love cops." Nace pumped a breezy fist against Gooch's fat middle. "I'll prove it. C'mon up to the office. I'll give you a cigar. I keep a special brand for you public servants."

Gooch smiled dreamily, picked the Havana from between his teeth, and held it so Nace could see the maker's name on the band.

Nace's neck slowly became purple as he looked at the band. On his forehead, a small scar reddened out like a design done with red ink and a pen. A long time ago, a Chinaman had hit

Nace above the eyes with the hilt of a knife that bore a carved serpent. The scar, a likeness of a coiled adder, was ordinarily unnoticeable, but came out vividly when Nace was angry.

"You got that stogie out of my office!" he rumbled savagely.

Gooch's round face was placid. "I hope you don't mind—"

"Mind!" Nace shoved his angular face against Gooch's cherubic one. "If you think I'm gonna have flatfeet busting into my place, you're crazy! I'll prefer charges! I'll have you clapped in your own holdover! I'll—"

"Now, now, honey, don't have a hemorrhage!" Gooch

*Lee Nace saw the man
go for his gun.*

fished a folded paper out of his tight blue suit, presented it.
"Look, dear!"

The document was a search warrant for Nace's office.

Nace cradled back slowly on his heels. The serpent still
coiled redly on his forehead. His eyes were smoky, far-off.

"What the hell, Gooch? What the hell? Is this one of your little ideas, or—"

"Wouldn't you like to know?" Gooch blew smoke airily, then started off.

Nace planted in front of him. "You'd better tell me—"

"Tell you—nothing! It's police business! We don't roll around gabbing—"

Nace jerked the cigar out of Gooch's teeth, threw it in the gutter. Simultaneously, his other hand dove under Gooch's coat and came out with four more cheroots of the same brand.

Gooch grasped at his pocket, but was too late to save the Havanas. He made a slit-eyed, wrathful face, lower lip protruding beyond his upper. He gave a difficult, thick laugh.

He walked away, putting the search warrant in his pocket.

THE ELEVATOR boy stared, fascinated, at the cherry serpent on Nace's forehead as they rode upward. Nace found his office door locked, and knew Gooch must have used a master key.

Nace ducked a little, from habit, as he went in. He was tall enough so that the top of a door occasionally brushed off his hat.

He roamed, gaunt and angry, around the outer office, opening a tall green metal box of a clothes locker and probing desk drawers and other places. Tramping into the inside room, he wandered down a long workbench, delving into cabinets. Nothing was greatly disarranged, but evidence showed that Gooch had made a thorough search.

Frowning, Nace lunged back into the outer office and slammed down at his desk. He dug out his pipe and a silk pouch of rough cut. He rasped a match alight on the under side of the desk, applied it to his pipe and sat scowling. The serpent scar gradually went away from his forehead.

"Damned if it don't beat me!" he muttered. "Gooch gets funny ideas of a joke! Maybe that was one of 'em!"

As if that dismissed the affair, he took the morning paper

out of his pocket, cracked it open, and settled back to read.

He was over as far as the sport page when a strange-looking man came in. The fellow walked slowly, kept his head down. He wore a black suit, black derby, a black string tie, black cotton gloves on his hands. He was the picture of a crow in mourning.

"Good morning, sir!" he said solemnly. "I am in search of a Mr. Lee Nace."

Nace put his paper down. "That's me."

"I believe you must have made a mistake about the address you gave us," the newcomer murmured. He took off his black derby as if he had just thought of it. "There was, I am sorry to say, no such address."

"What kind of an address?"

"Why—where we were to take the coffin."

Nace placed his pipe atop his paper. He grinned widely, then scowled sourly, as if practicing making faces. On his forehead, the serpentine scar coiled redly.

"What the hell?" he said savagely. "Is this somebody's lousy idea of more humor? Did Gooch send you?"

The man in the crow garments looked even more mournful.

"Perhaps I should have explained," he murmured. "What I mean is the coffin bearing your brother's body. It's in a hearse downstairs."

Nace picked up his pipe, laid it down. He gave the man a hard eye. "You wouldn't kid me, buddy?"

The man seemed injured. "Perhaps there has been a mistake—"

"You're blasted right there's been a mistake!" Nace snorted. "I don't know anything about a coffin or a dead man. Anyway, I haven't got a brother!"

The other fumbled his derby. The hat was sized down by a stuffing of newspapers in the sweat band. "Are you Lee Nace, the private detective?"

"Sure."

"When you telephoned me, you said—"

"I didn't telephone you!" Nace got up from behind the desk and came around and stood close to the man. "I still think this is a joke, buddy! Maybe you're in it, and maybe you're not. Be a good guy and spill the works!"

The man absently adjusted the newspapers in his derby. "I am from Lake City. My name is Stanley, and I own the Quiet Service Funeral Parlor. Yesterday, a Mr. Nace telephoned me—"

"I'm betting his name wasn't Nace!"

"He used that name. He said he wanted the body of his brother taken to New York. He told me to come to a home in Lake City for the—er, remains, and I did that. Then I drove all day and all night—"

"Was there anybody at the house where you got the body?" Nace inserted.

"Oh, yes! Two of them. One was a big, redheaded girl. The other was a man, a big man. He had a purple nose. The body was there in a coffin. Like I said, I drove all night—"

"The two at the house have names?"

"They forgot to tell me—"

Nace picked up his newspaper, popped it into a wastebasket. "Go on with the yarn."

"I got in New York this morning—"

"If I know my geography, Lake City is on the Lake Erie shore, just across the Ohio state line. That right?"

"That is correct. Lake City is a beautiful little town of—"

"You made a damn quick trip for a hearse!"

The man put his black derby on. His mien was not so mournful now. "I opened her up a little. She's fixed up with a siren. We use her for an ambulance sometimes. Anyway, I tried to find the New York address them people give me, and there wasn't no such thing. So I got your office address out of the phone book and came here."

Nace set teeth in his pipe stem, fanned a match over the bowl. He did not mention the fact that his phone was unlisted. His name and number were not in the directory.

"Well," he said. "It looks like the next move is yours."

The man adjusted his derby. The headgear was sizes too big, but the folded paper in the sweatband made it fit snugly. "They told me in Lake City that you would pay me for the trip."

Nace snorted. "Do I have to tell you the answer to that one?"

The visitor recovered his mournful look. "If this is a joke, mister, it's on me, not you."

"Sure." Nace puffed his pipe bowl hot. "I think I'll take a look at your passenger from Lake City."

"Of course!" said the black clad man.

He walked ahead of Nace into the tiled hall, and thumbed for an elevator. Nace began slapping his pockets with great vigor.

"Wait a minute!" he grunted. "Forgot something!"

He swung back into his office. But he did not put anything into his pockets. Instead, he made sure the hall door had set its spring lock, so his visitor could not follow him. Then he snapped open a desk drawer and took out a steel skullcap, lined with sponge rubber. This bore a blond mop which exactly matched Nace's hair.

He put it on, adjusting it by a mirror on the inside of the clothes locker door. The thing made his head look a little bigger, but only a close observer would notice that.

He rejoined the man in the raven garb. They rode the cage down to the lobby. Nace, with a habitual duck as he stepped out of the elevator, headed for the street.

"Wait!" said his guide. "I parked the hearse around behind."

"Sure. I guess it would collect a crowd out in front," Nace said. But he began to get a cold feeling around his spine.

They circled back of the elevators, and went down a long

passage with shoe soles clicking on cold concrete.

They came out in a pit of a courtyard, concrete floored. A slit between two buildings gave access to the street. There was a circle of big iron doors, loading platforms, dirty windows. The air smelled of rubbish, gasoline and disinfectant.

THE HEARSE was black and long. The windows were backed by light tan curtains, fully drawn.

Nace's guide took off his black derby and climbed in, after flinging open the double doors at the rear. Tan curtains whizzed on the slide as he brushed against them. He reached back and closed them, although they had let in light.

"Come and look," he invited.

Nace clambered in and forward, seeming not to notice that the somber man maneuvered to a position behind him. The fellow opened the forward half of the coffin.

Nace did not look surprised when he saw no body in the pearl-colored interior.

Instead, he sank a little, bending both knees. He had a good idea of what was coming. He wanted to take it on the top of his head.

The blackjack made a whistle, a *thunk!* Its leather burst and shot sprayed the hearse interior.

Nace fell, ears belling, colored lights crawling around in his eyeballs. The man had either never used a blackjack before, or he had meant to kill. Only the steel skullcap had saved Nace.

The man spurred Nace with a foot. "You're supposed to be quite a guy in the big town. But take the word of an elm-peeler from the sticks, you ain't so hot!"

He went back, closed the rear doors. Nace opened an eye and studied as much of the coffin lid as he could see from his position on the floor. It bore no lock, much to his relief.

The man came back, humming cheerfully, and flipped open the other coffin lid. He got hold of Nace's shoulders and lifted. Nace let himself be dumped into the coffin and lay there, feet sticking out. The man pushed at Nace's feet.

"Yah!" he snorted. "You *would* be too long to fit!"

He scrambled out the back. Nace heard the rattle of the lock on the rear door, but did not worry greatly. He could kick a window out if necessary.

Starter gears gnashed iron teeth. The engine came awake with a hoot. It moaned a few times as the man pedaled the accelerator.

Then several things happened in slap-bang order. Shoes scuffed on concrete as a man rushed from some hiding place. The wild footsteps reached the hearse. Blows whacked. A gasp made a sound as if paper had torn.

The hearse seemed to spring backward. Evidently the driver had slumped against the shift lever, knocking it into reverse. Nace's head hit the coffin and so hard that the shock trickled to his toes.

The vehicle came to a stop with the engine killed.

"You would give your pal Tammany a run-around, would you?" growled the newcomer, harsh-voiced.

Nace got up and sat on the coffin edge.

CHAPTER 11

The Pop-Eyed Dead

LEANING FORWARD, NACE picked the curtains apart a crack. He got a good view of the new arrival.

The fellow was a little, dapper hawk. He was around five feet, weighing maybe a hundred and twenty. He was twitching scuffed skin off the fist with which he had just struck blows. He flexed the fist, snapped crimson drops off, then blew on it.

Seizing the dark-clad man, he hauled the fellow from behind the wheel, exhibiting amazing strength for one so small.

The man in black was so dazed that he could not stand erect.

Leaning down, the little man slapped. The blows had the crack of a pistol shot.

"I should smear you, Jeck!" he gritted.

The sitting man put both hands over his cheek, wailed, "Listen, Tammany—!"

"Listen—hell! I've listened to you too much already!"

"I couldn't find you, Tammany!" Jeck put up black-gloved hands, as if to shield off more blows. "They started to take Jud Ogel's body to Nace. And I couldn't find you. I tried everywhere, and I couldn't get you. What was I to do? The body-moving gag looked like a stall to get the stuff out of town."

"Was it?"

"That's the funny part! I grabbed the hearse near Hudsonville, in Jersey. There wasn't nothin' in it! Not even Jud Ogel's body!"

Little Tammany snapped more red from his fist. "Well, when I found everybody concerned had left for New York, I set sail myself. Understand me, I'm not saying I believe a word of your talk. But we'll play like I do. Who's this bird, Lee Nace?"

"A private dick. I called a newspaper and got some dope on him. He has a rep."

"Bad or otherwise?"

"Search me! He's something the police don't like. But that don't mean anything. The private shamus that they would like don't live."

Tammany swelled his knot of a chest. "Let's wake him up and talk to him. I saw you put him in the back."

"He'll take a lot of awakening, I guess." Jeck shoved up on his feet and stood, legs weaving at the knees.

"I hope you didn't kill him! He seems to be the key to this whole mess!"

Nace angled silently to the rear door. The serpentine scar was bright on his forehead. So they thought he was the key! And he had no idea what it was all about!

Nace wore elongated, ornate cuff buttons. He removed the one from his left sleeve. He worked at the two halves with his fingernails. Hidden lids came open. Two tiny darts were disclosed.

The lock at the rear rattled, then the doors whisked back. Tammany was first to show himself. Nace flipped a dart. It flew too swiftly to be seen, but materialized like a tiny thorn, clinging to Tammany's neck.

The blank look on the stricken man's face alarmed Jeck. He sprang forward, only to get Nace's second dart in the cheek.

For perhaps a count of ten, both men stood still, faces becoming blanker. Tammany was the first to pile down slackly on the concrete. Jeck followed him, seeming to turn into a pile of black cloth.

Nace hopped out and dumped both men into the hearse.

It was early, but someone might look out of the neighboring windows and see what was happening.

Locating a set of the web straps used in lowering caskets in graves, Nace employed them to bind both men securely. He tore padding out of the caskets and made two gags.

The men would sleep for two hours or so. The drug on the darts produced an unconsciousness that lasted about that long.

Nace searched them, finding money, cigarettes, and cards that showed them to be Thomas Tammany and Leo Jeck, members of the Lake City country club. There was nothing really important.

Nace's height made him seem awkward as he got out of the hearse. He went around and looked at the name done in small silver letters on the front door. The Quiet Service Funeral Parlor, of Lake City. He eyed the license number, fixing it in his memory. The gasoline tank was nearly full. The gas was a colored variety—dark amber.

NACE ENTERED his office building, banging his heels along the concrete corridor. The adder was gone from his forehead. He stoked his pipe on the way up in the elevator.

From his office, he put in a long distance call to Lake City. He held the wire, listening to clicks and animated feminine cries as the connection was built up.

"Hello—Quiet Service Funeral Parlor?" he said at length. "I want to find out something about a hearse of yours." He gave the license number.

"We only got one hearse!" a wheezy voice came back at him. "We rented it out to a feller yesterday."

"Who was he?"

"Said his name was Smith, from a little town over in Pennsylvania, where he has a funeral home."

"What did he look like?"

"Say—has something happened to our hearse?"

"It's safe here in New York, but we're hunting the bird who

was driving it. Describe him!"

"He was a big man. The main thing I remember about him was his nose. It was purple looking."

"Thanks, buddy!" Nace hung up. Black-clothed Jeck, when he had first appeared, had declared a redheaded girl and a purple-nosed man had consigned him the body in Lake City. Jeck's story had been a lie, of course, but the part about the man with the purple nose was significant.

Nace got up and walked slowly around the chair. He went to the window and stood looking down. His pipe bubbled and hissed and smoke made a fog against the pane.

Detective Sergeant Gooch sat in a squad car across the street. Beside him in the machine was Honest John MacGill. Honest John was three-hundred pounds of plugging, straight copper. Men like him backboned the police department.

The tense manner of both policemen showed they were watching Nace's office building.

Nace caught their gaze. Sergeant Gooch waved a cigar he was smoking, then took off his hat and poked a finger inside to show he had been carrying some of Nace's weeds there. Scowling, Nace pulled down the window shade. There was no particular hate in his scowl. Gooch and Honest John were all right. But they did love to ride a private operative.

Nace, thinking of the search warrant, swung over to the telephone. He had a friend down at headquarters that might be able to tell him what was behind the warrant. Sergeant Gooch would never part with the information, it was sure.

He picked up the phone.

A CONTRALTO voice behind him said, "I think you have galloped around long enough!"

Nace spun. She was tall, with red hair and eyes a contrast in blue. Her form was moulded exquisitely upon large bones. The bluing was worn off the double-action Colt which she held.

Nace sucked angrily at his pipe. She had been concealed in

the inner room. Nace growled around his pipe stem, "What kind of a game—"

"You might as well save that!" She gestured her gun at the window. "Why did you pull down the shade just then?"

Nace gave her surly silence for an answer.

"It won't take long to find out!" She whipped to the window with a feline grace, and ran the shade up. "Ah—my friends, the policemen! Well, they aren't doing any good down there!" She worked at the fastening to get the window open. She was, he could see, going to call Gooch.

Nace pulled his pipe out of his teeth and pegged it at her gun hand. He had practiced long hours at throwing things. His aim left nothing to be desired. The pipe tapped her knuckles.

Pain tightened her finger on the trigger. The gun coughed. Plaster geysered off the wall. Nace took a gangling leap, grabbed her arm, shook it. The gun went skidding across the room.

Holding her tight in his arms, Nace ran to the inner office. He had no idea what it was all about, but the thing smacked of a frame-up.

His eyes roved the inner office with practiced speed. There was no sign of evidence planted to connect him with some crime.

He had the redhead's arm pinned, but she began to kick at his shins and scream loudly.

Nace carried her back, picked up his pipe, then, still holding her, went to the window and looked down. Sergeant Gooch and Honest John MacGill were not in the squad car. They must have run into the building, drawn by the shot.

The girl had changed her screaming to words.

"Big Zeke!" she shrilled. "Help me!"

Came a banging at the hall door. The spring lock had secured the panel automatically when Nace entered. With a crash and jangle, frosted glass cascaded out of the door. A man shoved head and shoulders inside.

The man was almost as tall as Nace, fully twice as heavy. His hands were rust-colored, huge, shaggy with tobacco-hued hair. His nose was big, and a network of veins that seemed to lie on the surface gave it a purple color.

He beaded Nace with a blue revolver that was a twin to the girl's weapon. Nace spun the girl away, flung himself backward. A bullet dug plaster on a line with the space he had vacated. More bullets came. They pursued Nace, always a yard or so behind, as he pitched into the inner office.

He slammed the door, twisted the key. His face and hands were pale, but the adder scar was a scarlet stamp on his forehead. Lead began clouting splintery holes in the door.

Nace jerked a coil of linen rope from behind the cold radiator. The rope was there for just such an emergency as this. One end was already secured to the radiator. He jerked up the window and flung out the rope. This window was on the side of the building. It was six stories down to a rooftop.

Something over a dozen feet to the right climbed the spidery metalwork of a fire escape.

Nace went down the rope hand over hand. Although the rope reached to the roof of the building far below, Nace did not descend the whole distance. He stopped perhaps thirty feet down and began to swing himself. The hard brick bruised his shoulders, knees, elbows, and scuffed his fists. But he was soon able to grasp the fire escape and swing onto the steps.

He bounded upward, trying to blend speed and silence. He reached the top and jumped over a high coping onto a tarred roof.

From the window below, Sergeant Gooch's voice roared, "He slid down the rope to that roof below!"

That was exactly what Nace had hoped Gooch would think.

NACE RAN to a roof hatch and descended to the top elevator landing. Luck was with him, for he found a cage waiting. He rode it down to the lobby level and swung out through the passage to the cement-floored courtyard.

He opened the hearse doors. Jeck and Tammany still slumbered inside. Nace picked up the black derby Jeck had worn and dug the newspapers out of the sweatband. He unfolded them, found they were the first two sheets from a small weekly.

It was the *Lake City Chronicle,* dated three weeks back. It proved nothing except that Jeck habitually wore this somber garb.

Nace closed the hearse doors, locked them, then traveled at a long-legged walk out of the courtyard.

He went to the parking lot where his weather-beaten roadster stood. Unlocking the rumble seat, he took out a rather bulky canvas bag that was closed with a zipper fastener. He put it in the front seat, then got in and nudged the starter with his toe.

He wheeled the roadster out of the lot, thence westward toward the George Washington Bridge. This was the most direct route to Hudsonville, the Jersey town where Jeck claimed he had seized the hearse.

He turned down the windshield and the breeze soon cooled the adder off his forehead. He discovered he had bitten his pipe stem sometime during the excitement, cracking it badly.

He replaced it from a case of spare stems that he drew from the zipper bag. The bag held a conglomeration of articles, ranging from intricate electrical mechanisms to an efficient assortment of skeleton keys.

This zipper bag was Nace's sack of magic. It held about everything he needed in his perilous profession. It was largely judicious use of the contrivances contained in the bag which had lifted Nace to a position of prominence.

A newspaperman had once dubbed Nace the "Blond Adder." The name had been unusual enough to stick. Nace knew the value of publicity in drumming up business, so he made it a point to always give the newspaper reporters a good story. Hence he was frequently on the front pages.

That Nace had spent several months in England as a paid

consultant to Scotland Yard showed he was good in his line.

THE GEORGE WASHINGTON BRIDGE rolled a greasy cement ribbon under the roadster. Nace took the main pike toward Hudsonville.

The little Jersey town was a long shot on Nace's part, but he had to take hold of the mystery somewhere. Having not the slightest idea what it was all about, he had selected Hudsonville.

Houses alternately thinned out and became plentiful as he passed through villages. The roadster hit rough pavement and he held the canvas bag on his knees so it would not jar about.

A roadside sign told him he had three more miles to go.

A hulk of a filling station, a brood of tourist cabins behind it, appeared on the left.

The roadster shot past. Then it squatted a little and rubber wailed as Nace applied the brakes. He backed down the pike and into the filling station.

He had noticed that two of the pump measuring jars were filled with amber gasoline. Gas of that color had been in the hearse tank.

No one came from the station. Nace honked his horn. The blare went unanswered. Nace got out and went into the station, but found no one. He called loudly. Somewhere in the distance, a rooster crowed; there was no other sound.

He swung back toward his roadster, holding a match over his pipe bowl and pulling in smoke. Instead of getting into the car, he spun on his heel and came back.

He started a rapid search of the cabins. They numbered ten. The first seven were empty. This was slack season for the tourist trade.

Red rivulets had crawled from under the door of the eighth cabin and were thickening and drying in the morning sun. Nace took his pipe out of his teeth. He had an expensive habit of biting the stems off when sudden developments came. He nudged the door inward with a foot.

A stocky, curly haired man lay on the floor. He wore the stained white coveralls of a filling-station attendant. Four bullets had tunneled through his chest.

A form swathed in a sheet was on the bed. Nace did not investigate this ominous figure immediately, but studied the man who had been shot.

A cheap automatic was half concealed by the body. Nace turned the corpse over, and saw a shiny deputy sheriff badge pinned to the grimy coveralls. The cheap automatic had discharged one bullet into the wall, and had jammed in extracting the empty shell.

The man, obviously a combination of filling station attendant and deputy sheriff, had come investigating something suspicious, and a jammed gun had been the death of him.

Nace flung out a long arm and peeled the sheet off the bed. This disclosed the figure of a corpse in underwear.

CHAPTER III

Sergeant Gooch's Tip

A GHASTLY, POP-EYED look about the corpse instantly riveted Nace's attention. The eyes were half out of their sockets; the tongue stuck out, stiff and pale, farther than Nace had ever seen a tongue protrude. The whole cadaver had a strangely bloated aspect.

Nace grimaced, eased off his steel-lined wig and ran long, bony fingers through his natural hair. He got his zipper bag from the car, and took out a magnifying glass, together with various test tubes and chemicals.

The stuff he was using actually comprised a compact analysis kit. Unlike most private detectives, Nace had not served an apprenticeship with the police. He had spent those years at famous universities, studying medicine, chemistry, electricity and similar subjects. Few knew it, but he was a licensed doctor; he had been admitted to the bar as a practicing lawyer, and he had written a textbook on electrochemistry.

Twenty minutes later, he left the vicinity of the filling station and its flock of tourist cabins. The curly haired deputy sheriff-station attendant had been dead only a few hours.

The death hour for the pop-eyed corpse had been at least two days ago. The cause of the fellow's death was one of the blackest mysteries Nace had ever encountered. To all appearances, the man had literally swelled to the bursting point from some strange inner pressure. The direct cause of death was suffocation, after ruptured cell walls had filled his lungs with blood.

The hearse driver, it was Nace's theory, had driven into the tourist camp and rented a cabin in which to leave the body. Nace thought of Jeck. The man might have been the attendant's murderer. Jeck's conversation with Tammany had shown that he had overhauled the hearse with the expectation of finding something of value in it. He might have been searching when the deputy sheriff intervened.

Nace nursed the roadster around a curve at fifty-five. "Jeck and Tammany are on the prowl for something they want bad," he summarized. Then he thought of the redheaded girl and the purple-nosed man. "Those two are not exactly soft, either."

Back in town, Nace did not return his roadster to the parking lot. Sergeant Gooch and Honest John MacGill knew his custom of keeping it there. He slid the machine into the curb some two blocks distant.

Carrying his bag, he strode to the corner. He did not round into the street on which his office faced. Instead, he leaned against the corner just out of sight. He produced a small pocket mirror and ostensibly combed his blond mop. The mirror gave him a view of the street.

A squad car full of plainclothes men was at rest in front of Nace's office.

Nace went around and peeked into the areaway where the hearse stood.

Honest John MacGill was ensconced comfortably on the front seat of the hearse.

From his zipper bag, Nace drew an iron egg of a smoke bomb. He dropped it, spewing a black worm, on the cement. He let the worm grow into a huge, writhing monster that gorged the crack of an entryway.

"Help! Fire, fire, help!" Nace piped in a shrilly altered voice. He waited, concealed in the dark vapor cloud.

Into the smoke lumbered Honest John MacGill. Puffing, sneezing, he yelled, "What the hell kind of a fire is this? Where's it at?"

Leaving Honest John lost in the smoke, Nace ran past the hearse and into the basement of the office building. A freight elevator carried him to his office level. There was no attendant in the freight elevator. He ran it himself.

It deposited him around an angle in the corridor. The spot could not be seen from his office door.

Nace produced a key and let himself through a door that bore no lettering. A leather chair built for comfort, a smoking stand on which stood a rack bearing half a dozen pipes exactly alike, a powerful reading lamp and numerous cases filled with books and magazines comprised the fittings. This was Nace's study. Not even the building attendants knew it was here. He even cleaned the place himself.

The smoking stand had a large cylindrical base. Nace lifted the top off this. Two square glass panels were revealed. In one could be seen Nace's outer office. In the other was portrayed the inner room, his laboratory.

It was not a television machine, but a complex arrangement of mirrors and perfectly straight tubes.

Sergeant Gooch was visible, seated at the office desk, a box of Nace's cigars open before him. His mouth was pulled down at the ends, putting wrinkles in his blue-bearded jowls.

Policemen and detectives were parked around the office and others were in the inner room.

Sergeant Gooch's lips moved and he waved both hands.

Nace hastily slapped two small switches beside the glass view-panels. On the walls of the room where he crouched were two innocent-looking oil paintings. At the touch of the switches, these became diaphragms of loud speakers, which reproduced what was being said in Nace's office and laboratory. They operated from sensitive microphones and a vacuum tube amplifier. The mikes were well hidden in Nace's office.

"Broadcast it again to the squad cars!" Sergeant Gooch was bellowing. "Maybe some of them didn't get it the first time. Describe the redheaded dame and that purple-nosed lunk who was with her. And while you're doing it, describe Nace again, too."

Nobody made a move to comply with the command. Sergeant Gooch liked to yell. His men could tell from the exact tone of his voice when he was giving an order he really wanted carried out. He was not using that tone now.

"The call is going out every half hour!" somebody told him.

Sergeant Gooch threw one of Nace's cigars, with no more than an inch smoked, into the cuspidor, and took a fresh one. He fired it with Nace's desk lighter, handling the lighter roughly, as if he hoped it would break.

"Hell! I'd give a brass monkey to know what this is all about!" Gooch made a face in the cigar smoke. "If the red-headed dame and her shadow with the violet schnozzle hadn't pulled their freight, I might know something!"

SOMEBODY SNICKERED. Gooch looked pained. "Aw, d'you have to rub it in?"

"I can't help thinkin' how you and Honest John was actin' when we got here! Ha, ha, ha! Ironed to the radiator with your own handcuffs! We could hear you yell and rattle the cuffs two blocks away!"

Nace grinned wolfishly at the two glass squares into which he was staring. It would appear that the Titian and her damson-nosed companion had turned upon Gooch and Honest John when they came in.

Nace was more than mildly surprised. The girl had been in the act of summoning the police when he seized her.

Sergeant Gooch got up with the box of Nace's cigars and passed the cheroots around. "It was kinda strange how that happened. The dame seemed glad enough to see us. The big guy kinda stood around and moped. Then he threw down on us with the revolver. The fire-top didn't seem to approve of that. She looked at the big guy like she was ready to knock his block off. But she helped dress us up with our own jewelry. And they went out together."

Sergeant Gooch came back to the desk with the cigar box. He took a fresh weed for himself. "They got clean away. We charged around huntin'. And were we surprised when we found them two guys sleepin' in the hearse!"

"The hospital should be letting us know what ailed them two slumbering beauties!" vouchsafed an officer.

"Yeah." Sergeant Gooch rasped fingers over his chin shag. "You know, the sleep them fellers was havin' had all the earmarks of Lee Nace's work. Some damn funny things happen to people who mix themselves up with Nace."

At this point, Honest John MacGill arrived. He was swabbing at his eyes with his sleeve—they were watering from the effects of the smoke.

Sergeant Gooch pointed his cigar at Honest John. "A fine lot of help the department gives me! Look at 'im! I set 'im in the hearse and he breaks out in tears, probably from thinkin' of funerals—"

"Aw, can it!" Honest John growled. "When I find the dang joker who threw that smoke bomb in the alley and then hollered fire—"

Gooch got up, squawking, "What's this about a smoke bomb?"

"That's what I said!" Honest John leered about truculently. "If I thought one of you monkeys—"

"It wasn't anybody from the department!" Sergeant Gooch told him grimly. "Smoke bomb! Ha! That's something else that smacks of Nace!"

"Damn the luck!" Honest John howled. "I'll bet that's who it was!"

Sergeant Gooch teetered on his heels. "Sure it was Nace! He used that smoke bomb so he could get into the building, I'll bet!" Gooch went to the window, leaned out and gestured at the plainclothes men in the squad car below.

Nace could not see his moving arms in the picture that was reflected by the arrangement of mirrors and straight tubes, but he guessed that Gooch was signaling some of the officers to the rear. He drew back inside.

A detective asked, "What put you on the trail of this mess, anyway?"

"A telephone call!"

SERGEANT GOOCH gestured everybody toward the door. "Somebody called me about daylight and said Nace had murdered a man and was hiding the body in his office. Well, bless your Uncle Gooch, that sounded fishy! But it was a chance to worry Nace a little, and there is nobody I enjoy worryin' more! I got a warrant and come up here and turned his place upside down!"

"What'd you find?"

"Hell—what I expected! Nothin'! C'mon, you guys! We'll frisk this building!"

Sergeant Gooch was opening the door when the telephone rang. He came back, picked up the instrument.

"Yeah, this is the pride of the cops… He did!… They did? Both of 'em?… Ow-w-w! What is this town comin' to!"

Gooch ground the receiver savagely upon its hook.

"What's happened?" somebody asked him.

"Happened! Happened!" Gooch flung his cigar out of the window with great carelessness for the heads of pedestrians below. "Them two guys we found asleep in the hearse! They jumped off stretchers while they was bein' carried into the hospital, and ran and got clean away! Can you beat that?"

From the door came a faint scraping noise. A detective sprang over and looked into the hall, after frowning at the mail box.

"It's the mail!" he said over his shoulder. Then, in a louder voice directed at the mailman, "Hey, Uncle Sam, what'd you drop for Nace?"

The mail carrier's reply was not audible to Nace.

The detective now began to work at the mail box, which

was a stout steel case affixed to the door. He tugged, swore, smacked the metal with the heel of his hand, tugged again. "I can't get the dang thing open! The mailman says he dropped in four letters!"

Sergeant Gooch ambled toward the laboratory, bristled jaw out, saying, "I'll see if I can find a hammer or a screwdriver or something!"

His long face knobby with angry muscle welts, Nace got up and jumped to a telephone on a bookcase. Instead of a bell, this instrument was fitted with a light that brightened when a call came in. Nace dialed the number of his office.

The phone was near enough the smoking stand base so that he could look into the glass panels and see what happened.

Sergeant Gooch, a hammer and screwdriver in one hand, answered the call.

Nace made his voice hard, angry. "This is Nace! What's the idea of you and your shadows cluttering up my place?"

With one hand, Gooch made frantic silent gestures at Honest John, directing him to trace the call. Honest John dived out through the door. Sergeant Gooch began stalling to hold Nace on the wire, telling Nace what a pal he was, thanking him for the cigars, and finally:

"I'm sorry about that search warrant business, Nace, old boy, old boy. The thing was all a big mistake—"

"You're a liar!" Nace advised him. "You have never in your life admitted you could make a mistake!"

Honest John had worked swiftly. He put his head in the door, whispered loudly, "The phone is in an office on the top floor of this building!"

NACE HUNG up. There was a phone upstairs all right. The instrument he was using was tapped into that line, but the instant he hung up, jack switches automatically cut it off so the tap could not be traced.

Gooch and his men bolted out of Nace's office.

Nace gave them time to get well on their way upstairs, then ran to his office, got four letters out of the mailbox, and whisked back to concealment. He shuffled the letters.

Three advertisements, he discarded at once.

The last letter was postmarked from Lake City, Ohio, the day before. It was somewhat bulky. He opened it. There was a letter.

> Dear Cousin Nace:
> I have your note requesting that our relations be strictly of a business nature. That such would be the case was, of course, my understanding before I appealed to you.
> The retainer which you request for your services seems rather large, but I am enclosing it. Please consider yourself hired.
> I am also bringing the body to you in New York, as per your request, although I am still doubtful about this being the best procedure. You may expect us shortly after you receive this letter.
> Julia Nace

Clipped to the letter were two five hundred dollar bills and three one hundred dollar bills.

Nace frowned. The adder scar was a faint pink shadow of itself upon his forehead.

"Julia Nace," he said slowly. Then he placed her. She was one of his relatives he had never seen. They were connected with some kind of a shipping business on the Great Lakes.

Nace felt absently of his steel-armored wig. The brother, Jerome, had died a few weeks ago, he remembered now.

He thought of the redhead, wondering if she was Julia Nace, grinned, said, "As a relative, she would be easy to take!"

Julia Nace, it appeared from the note, had been writing letters and receiving answers, under the impression she was in communication with the branch of the family tree that had gained fame as a detective.

Today was Nace's first contact with the affair, by letters or otherwise. Somebody had been playing the girl for a sucker.

NACE CLICKED the switches which shut off the two loudspeakers disguised as paintings. He replaced the pedestal of the smoking stand. He opened the door into the hallway. No cops were in sight.

Nace whipped silently to the freight elevator, entered, nursed the door shut, and sent the cage downward. He stopped the cage on the second floor, making as little noise as possible.

This was not the first time Nace had found occasion to leave his office building without being observed. He crossed to a large metal cabinet that stood against the end of the corridor. He opened the door, wedged through many soiled garments, found a secret catch and got the rear open.

A moment later, he stepped out of an exactly similar cabinet in the next building. This building was very long, extending the remainder of the block. Nace walked down passages, descended stairs, and mingled with the crowd at a furniture auction being held in a room opening off the lobby.

He bought a cheap but bulky wicker chair and walked out carrying it on his shoulder in such a manner that it concealed both his height and features from Gooch's detectives. Nace walked a block, rounded a corner, and threw his chair into the first empty truck he saw.

He had been doing some thinking. Jeck and Tammany must have awakened in the ambulance en route to the hospital. They would, of course, have no idea what had happened to them during the last two hours.

Their first move would be to try to get a line on what had occurred. The logical place for them to seek information would be in the vicinity of Nace's office.

Nace turned into an alley, with the idea of entering a rear door of a store and going forward to watch the street before his office.

He no more than stepped into the alley before guns began clapping thunderously. Lead squawled, chopped brick around him, ricocheted. A slug did something hot, painful, jarring, to the back of his neck.

Nace slapped flat on the alley bricks. That was the old stand-by trick of a man under fire. Sometimes it made those shooting at him think they had scored a fatal hit.

It worked. Down the alley, a taxi motor boomed. The cab went out of the alley like a racing whippet out of a starting box.

Nace shoved up from where he had dropped. He burned alternately hot and cold. He did not shoot at the receding hack—for the very good reason that he did not carry a gun. Muscles and wits, Nace maintained, were more to be depended upon than firearms. A man putting all trust in a gun was likely to be at a loss if disarmed.

He glimpsed the license number of the hack. Who rode the cab, he could not tell. Nor had he been able to see who had shot at him, so swiftly had the thing happened.

He turned away, feeling the back of his neck. His wound was only a scratch, but had the bullet come an inch closer, it would have parted his spine.

He worked away from the vicinity, keeping out of sight of policemen. He turned his coat collar up and stuffed his handkerchief under it to hide his hurt.

TWO HOURS later, he was sitting in a speakeasy, a small bandage taped over his neck, when a newsboy came in with the latest editions. Nace bought a paper. A front-page item caught his eye almost immediately.

A taxi driver had been found in his machine beside a Long Island road. The license number was that of the cab carrying the gunsters who had fired upon Nace. The driver was dead when discovered—skull crushed in.

The spot where the taxi had been found was a quarter of a mile from a commercial airport.

Nace got his hat, paid his bill, and tramped out of the speak. He secured his roadster from the spot where he had parked it, and headed for Long Island. He snapped on the radio under the dash and shortened down the wavelength to pick up police broadcasts.

For a time, the instrument mumbled nothing but routine business.

"All cars attention! A pickup order for Lee Nace, the private detective." Nace smiled without alarm. But his face froze at the next words from the radio. "This man Nace is wanted by the New Jersey authorities on a murder charge. Witnesses saw him departing from a tourist camp where the bodies of two murdered men were found."

The radio launched into more routine.

Nace took a side road to avoid the spot where the taxi and the murdered driver had been found. He pulled up at the edge of the airport tarmac.

"I want," he told the field manager of one of the city's largest aerial taxi services, "to hire a plane to take me to Lake City, Ohio."

The manager grinned. "What is this, a gold rush?"

"Why?"

"You're the third. About an hour ago, two other planes left for Lake City. They got off about fifteen minutes apart."

Nace recited monotonously, "One carried a redheaded girl and a purple-beaked guy. A man dressed in black and a little, hawk-faced fellow hired the other ship. Which pair went up first?"

"The girl and the fellow with the sunrise face."

"Give me the fastest ship you have!" Nace said grimly.

CHAPTER IV

Peril House

THE AFTERNOON WAS well along when Nace's hired plane sloped down out of low-hanging cotton-tuft clouds and wheeled a slow circle over Lake City.

Between four and five thousand would catch the population of the place. A three-story structure was the tallest building in town. This was the schoolhouse. Some of the streets were unpaved. Plumes of dust trailed such vehicles as were using the near-by country roads.

The sun-irradiated blue smear of Lake Erie began at the edge of town and stretched away until it was lost in a gray haze. Near town were docks, moored launches and cruisers, and small boats drawn up on a pale beach.

Perhaps a mile down the shore, there was an empty dock, warehouses, and a great rambling old house situated on a vast but seedy-looking lawn.

Nace had been unable to secure a fast ship, and knew he had not passed the two taxi planes from New York. The ships were not to be seen. Nace hoped they had arrived, landed their passengers and departed. They could have beaten him here by a couple of hours.

His own ship let him out in the stubble of an oatfield. He had brought his zipper-fastened canvas bag. Carrying it, he hoofed into town.

He found a car with a taxi sign on the windshield. The driver told him Julia Nace's place was about a mile away on the lakefront. It was, Nace discovered, the establishment with the empty wharf, warehouses and old rambling house.

The hackman also said three or four planes had circled the town within the last two hours. This was fair evidence that his quarry was ahead of him. He could not account for the fourth plane. It might have been a barnstormer.

He rode the taxi halfway out, dismissed the machine, and hoofed it the rest of the way. Nearing the place, he vaulted one of the fences that paralleled the road and eased through brush and small trees. He was taking no chances.

From a distance of a hundred yards, he surveyed the sprawling house. As he watched, a farmer in a wagon passed along the road. A small terrier trailed the wagon. The dog bounded across the rambling lawn to the front door of the ramshackle house.

The actions of the dog then became strange. It reared upon its rear legs, as if to look in the open door. Then the animal spun and fled at full speed, tail tucked under.

Nace let the wagon get out of sight. Then he sprinted for the door of the house

He did not know what he was expecting. Whatever it was, he was disappointed. When he veered inside, he saw only a composite of worn hall carpet, ancient stairs with a worn runner, and brightly figured wallpaper.

There was mail on the hall table—circulars from a marine engineering concern, a boat builder, a nursery, and a telephone bill. All were addressed to Miss Julia Nace.

Nace opened a door, found himself in an old Colonial living room. There was a picture of Nace's grandfather, Silas Murray Nace, over the fireplace mantel. The venerable old gentleman was garbed in the uniform of a buck private of the Confederate army.

Grandfather Nace was tall, blond, angular of feature.

Nace cocked a critical eye at the picture, remarked, "The block the chip came off of."

He did not waste more time admiring his ancestor. He began a search of the house. He found the kitchen well stocked with food. Adjacent, he found a windowless, rather large room that had evidently once been a pantry. But it now bore a bed, a dressing table, a hooked rug. Feminine garments were draped on hangers.

Two Winchester repeating rifles rested on nails driven into the walls. There was also a box of a rural telephone on the wall. Nace lifted the receiver and listened. A dead silence told of cut wires.

Stepping back, Nace absently tamped tobacco into his pipe.

HE THOUGHT of the way the dog had acted. Opening his zipper bag, he got out a bullet-proof vest. Peeling coat and shirt, he put the protector on underneath.

The big pantry was a poor place for sleeping. There were no windows. But the door was strong. It struck Nace as a likely bower for someone in fear of attack.

Suddenly, in the direction of the front room, a woman began screaming. Her shrieks had the ripping quality of a soul torn out. They were full of rasp and choke, rather than being loud, and there were no words, but only the enstrangled cries.

Nace moved, but not toward the front room. Instead, he pitched through the kitchen door, banked right around the house, and stretched himself to reach the front door. Lifting on his toes, he floated to a comparatively silent stop in the doorway.

The redhead lay on the floor, well down the hall. Her long, finely moulded form was slightly atwist, with knees drawn up and both arms under her. Her head was canted on one side, so that her face was toward him.

Her eyes were open so widely that they seemed to protrude.

Nace ventured a doubtful step across the threshold.

Something seemed to squeal behind him. The squeal was so sharp, sudden, as to be something of a snapping report. It was a bullet, and it hit Nace in the back, directly over the heart.

He sprang convulsively upward and forward, came down with a noisy crash, and rolled completely over twice, bony limbs rattling on the floor.

Noise of the rifle shot swished across the clearing, hit the house, and an echo glanced back, a single crack like a stick breaking.

The redheaded girl got up from the floor, both her hands gripping a sawed-off shotgun on which she had been lying. She ran past Nace to the door. She stocked the shotgun to her shoulder and looked out.

The uncertain waving of the muzzle showed that she could see no target. A rifle bullet came through the door with a piping squeak. It hit the wall, scooped a fistful of plaster upon Nace's prone form.

The girl backpedaled from the door. Nace got up, trying to reach his back with both hands. The bullet-proof vest had saved him, but the slug had carried an energy of many hundreds of foot pounds. He stumbled into the room that held the picture of Grandfather Nace, fell prone on the floor and lay there, writhing a little agony.

The girl went to the window, picked the curtain back, and looked out. She stood there perhaps a minute, then turned. Her face was very white under her red hair.

"I can't see a sign of him!" she said, hot excitement in her contralto voice.

Nace pulled up on hands and knees and went to the window. His back was a mass of dull pain. He watched the brush at the edge of the lawn for three or four minutes, but could discern no trace of the rifleman.

He got to his feet and stood with his back pressed tightly to a wall. This seemed to ease the pain a little.

"Whoever fired the shots was trying to kill both of us!" said the girl.

Nace wiped a cold sweat of pain from his forehead with a jerky gesture that dislodged his steel skullcap of a wig. His eyes held a bleak suspicion.

"Suppose I choose to think the shots were part of that act you were putting on?" he grated.

Her hands tightened angrily on her blunderbuss. "The second shot was aimed at me! Couldn't you see that?"

"I saw that it missed you! If the sniper out there was your pal, he might have planted the second shot to draw suspicion from you."

The girl shrugged, rested her shotgun in the crook of an arm. "I was putting on an act, all right. But the shooting was not part of it. I was upstairs and saw you come prowling around. So I came down here and screamed and laid down on my gun. I thought I'd get a chance to hold you up when you came in. I wanted to get my hands on you."

"Why?"

"I've got some questions I want to ask you!"

NACE STUMBLED to one window after another, peering through them, until he had surveyed all sides of the house. He could discover no one. He came back to the girl, saying, "Shoot your questions!"

She snapped angrily, "You doublecrossed me!"

"There's where you're all wet!"

"I wrote you letters telling you all about this trouble!"

"If you did, somebody's been lifting 'em! I only got one! It enclosed a retainer fee!"

The girl cocked and uncocked her gun absently. "I mailed that last letter myself, from the post office. The others, I simply put in the rural box out in front."

"You can see what happened!" Nace told her. "Now, give me the lowdown on this!"

The girl went into the pantry bedroom off the kitchen, came back carrying both Winchesters. She did not offer the rifles to Nace, but stood them against the wall, where he could easily reach them.

"You've heard of Mel Caroni?" she asked.

"Sure! Who hasn't?" Nace snorted. "He was Chicago's gang big shot. But he's in Atlanta now—income tax. They say he's broke."

"You bet he's broke!" the girl said grimly. "He converted everything he had into cash and jewels, and tried to skip the country. A coastguard cutter sank his boat out on the lake, not fifteen miles from here."

Nace raised his eyebrows and lowered his mouth ends to register understanding. "And Caroni's hoard sank with the boat?"

She nodded. "Caroni hired us to recover the stuff. You know, we own the Lake City Salvage Company."

The girl took four shotgun shells from a pocket of her sports skirt and toyed with them. "The night after we located the wreck, there was an explosion which killed my father and two of the crew, and sank our salvage boat. My brother and the rest of the crew escaped."

"Where do Tammany and Jeck hook in?"

"They're two of Mel Caroni's gangsters," she explained. "After the explosion, we refused to have anything more to do with the salvage job. They seem to think we got Caroni's treasure. They've been hanging around."

NACE FLEXED his arms, bent his back a little, grimacing. He went to a window and started to lift the shade.

A bullet planked through pane and shade and thumped loudly into the wall.

Nace dodged back involuntarily, then bent forward again, plucked up the shade and stared out. He saw no one.

Broken glass emptied from between shade and window sill as if the fragments were coming out of a sack. Fully two minutes, Nace stood and stared.

"What about your brother?" he asked over his shoulder.

The redhead dropped shotgun and shells and splayed both

hands over her face. "It was ghastly! Awful! We found him down by the lake shore! His eyes and tongue—they protruded! He was all swollen! I don't think the Lake City doctors knew what had killed him. But they claimed he had been bitten by a snake!"

"What kind of a snake?"

"Water moccasin! Usually, you don't find them this far north! But the shore here is infested with them."

Nace did not take his eyes from the outdoors. He could discern no sign of the sniper.

"And Jud Ogel?" he prompted.

"We found him day before yesterday!" The girl picked up shotgun and shells. "Jud Ogel was in exactly the same condition as my brother. I immediately wrote you! Yesterday morning, I got word to bring the body to New York, where experienced chemists could be put to work to find the cause of death."

"A stall!" Nace said. "You had Zeke rent a hearse and start the body for New York, huh?"

"That's right!"

"Zeke gave a fake name when he hired the hearse!"

"Did he? I guess he didn't want to connect me with the affair."

"And Zeke's story is that somebody stole the hearse?"

"Two masked men! One of them called the other by your name."

Nace moved to another window and continued his staring outdoors. "Now maybe you can explain why Zeke tried to shoot me!"

"Zeke said he just kind of went crazy from thinking you were connected with the murders of my brother and Jud Ogel. He wasn't responsible."

"Who is Zeke?"

"One of the divers working for my father's—my company.

Jud Ogel was a diver, too!"

Nace tried a third window. "Where is Zeke now?"

"I don't know. He came out here while I remained in Lake City to buy groceries. When I got here, there was no sign of him."

Nace was perspiring. "Who do you think is the villain in this bit?"

"Tammany and Jeck!" she said promptly.

CHAPTER V

Corpse Under the Carpet

NACE MOVED OVER to the door, making faces as his back pained him. He looked out, shivered.

"You cover me with the shotgun," he suggested. "I'm going out."

"That'll take nerve!" The girl eyed him, shrugged, took up a position with her shotgun. "I guess you've got it."

Nace left the door at a headlong run, and lined for the nearest brush. The serpent was a blaze on his forehead. Each instant, he expected to be shot at. He was in a cold sweat when he plunged into the bushes. No shots had come.

He worked toward the lake, stopping often to listen. Trees grew thicker and larger. The ground sloped down sharply. Through the leafage, he caught the blue shimmer of Lake Erie.

Came a soft flutter in the ground plants. Nace sighted a slimy, writhing reptile. One of the moccasins! The venomous thing plopped into the lake. He heard two more of them as he worked toward the wharf. The place was alive with them.

Then he heard the girl cry out from the house. It was a single wail, full of blood-curdling horror. And it was very muffled.

Nace sprinted for the rambling old house, heedless of noise.

Someone shot at him with a rifle. He could not tell how far the bullet missed him—perhaps a yard. He sighted the steel snout of the rifle, waving about in the bushes. The sniper was beyond the house, a bit to the right of it. None of the fellow's person was visible.

Nace angled over and got the house between himself and the gunner. No more bullets came.

He dived into the kitchen, crossed it, hit the hallway.

"Julia!" he yelled.

"Down here!" Her voice was in the basement.

Nace found the basement door open off the hall. He rattled his feet down rickety stairs.

The redheaded girl stood in one corner of the musty cellar, beside a pile of old carpets. She had pulled a carpet off an object. She looked at the thing that she had uncovered, and shrieked again, hysterically, in spite of herself.

Nace went over and stared. Then shoved the girl away, saying, "Quit looking at it, dammit!"

THE BODY of Tom Tammany had been under the carpet. The man's eyes and tongue protruded. All over, he was swollen and purple.

Nace ran for the cellar stairs, gritting, "This thing is getting damn bad!"

He gained the hallway, veered into the sitting-room, and got one of the Winchesters. Ordinarily, he did not use a firearm. But this was going to be an exception.

The redhead came up from the cellar, choking, "While you were out, I thought I would search the house for Zeke—"

Replying nothing, Nace began a careful scouting, first from one window, then another. The girl got the other Winchester and also began peering from windows.

Five minutes later, the girl cried from the front door, "Look who's coming!"

Detective Sergeant Gooch came stamping from the direction of the road. He held a blue service revolver in each hand. Before him, he herded Jeck and Zeke.

Coming near, Sergeant Gooch stepped to one side, so that he could cover Nace and the girl, as well as Jeck and Zeke.

"Drop that artillery!" he snapped.

"Be yourself!" Nace growled. "You're out of your bailiwick!"

Gooch cocked both his revolvers. "Bailiwick, hell! Something's happened to Honest John, and I ain't fooling! Drop 'em!"

Nace told the girl, "This crazy cop has shot more people than he's got fingers and toes! We'd better do as he says!"

"Where's Honest John?" Gooch demanded savagely. "He left me to go on a lone-handed scout, and he ain't come back!"

"How should I know?" Nace asked. "I didn't even know you two were in this neck of the woods!"

"Somebody reported your car at the New York airport," Gooch explained grudgingly. "We learned you and the rest of the gang had chartered planes for Lake City. So we followed. Officially, we're investigating the murder of that taxi driver. We beat you here. Our police plane was fast!"

Nace gestured at Jeck and Zeke. "Where did you tie into these two?"

Gooch glared at Jeck. "I caught this monkey running down the road with a rifle. A minute later, the other guy came out of the brush of his own accord."

Big Zeke wrinkled his purple nose and spoke up in a harsh rumble. "I was followin' Jeck. I been followin' him for the last hour!"

Nace snapped at Jeck, "So it was you who shot at me!"

"No, it wasn't!" Jeck disclaimed.

"That's right! It wasn't him! I been watchin' him!" Zeke made the statement vehemently.

The girl roved bewildered eyes. "Then who was it?"

Nace scowled blackly at Sergeant Gooch. "It strikes me as damn funny—you two guys showing up here. Are you sure you're not doing anything but upholding the law?"

Blood sheeted under Gooch's blue beard stubble. "For a little bit, I'd knock you into the middle of next week!"

"Any time you feel lucky, old son!"

Nace leered. "Was it a man or a woman who telephoned you that wild story about a body being in my office?"

"Man."

"Okay." Nace took out his pipe and yellow silk pouch. He dunked the pipe in the pouch, making the act a small gesture at Jeck. "I don't suppose you know anything about who killed that filling station attendant, shot at me in that New York alley, or murdered the taxi driver?"

Except for the black gloves, Jeck still wore his crowlike garments. "Listen, wise guy, all I did was grab that hearse because I thought Caroni's treasure was in it. There wasn't nothing in it, not even a body—"

"He's a liar!" Zeke yelled.

"There wasn't nothin' in the hearse!" Jeck repeated sullenly. "I went to get you, Nace. I thought you might know where the swag was, and I could make you cough up! After you put me and Tammany to sleep and damned if I know yet how you done it—we woke up on stretchers. We was scared, and got right out of town. We didn't shoot nobody."

Nace ran plumes of smoke from his nostrils. "Why were you prowling around out here?"

"I was lookin' for Tammany. We separated just after we got to Lake City. Tammany disappeared."

Sergeant Gooch waved his guns as if they were pennants, and shouted, "Pipe down! Pipe down! We can go into this later! What we're gonna do now is find Honest John!"

Nace, raising his voice angrily, shouted, "Let's find out where we're going first! Somebody around here has got his hands on that Caroni treasure! He knows he's got to keep it secret, because Caroni's gangsters would take it away from him. So he's been killing everybody who finds out he has it. I think I know how he's been pulling the murders so as to leave his victims looking like they were about to explode, but I've got to get some proof."

Sergeant Gooch roared, "If you know anything about them

killings, you've got to tell me "

"In a horse's neck!" Nace told him. "Let's go hunt Honest John!"

They trooped out of the house.

"I think Honest John went toward the warehouse and wharf!" offered Sergeant Gooch.

AS THEY made for the warehouse, Nace observed each of the others in turn. They were all glancing about nervously as if expecting more shots.

The redheaded girl came close to Nace, shivering, "Do you suppose the person behind this is someone we haven't even seen?"

"I'm not going to risk a laugh by saying what I think!" Nace told her.

The warehouse was big, heavily timbered. It extended out over the water. The wharf itself was only a continuation of the warehouse floor.

The massive door was unlocked. Nace shoved it in. There was a passage the length of the structure, with stall-like storerooms on each side.

Just inside the door, they found Honest John's hat, shoes, trousers and coat. The latter two garments were almost as large as small tents.

Nace scrutinized one of the stalls. It held parts of marine engines. He tried the next storeroom. It held great piles of well-greased chain hawsers. This was all equipment for salvaging operations.

In the third cubicle were stored coil of one-, two- and three-inch manilla rope. Some of the coils were new, still in burlap coverings.

Honest John MacGill sat on one of the rope coils, clad only in his underwear. He was dead and swollen and his eyes and tongue almost hung out of his head.

"Stick right here, every one of you!" Sergeant Gooch rapped

"Nace—you watch 'em!"

He ran down the passage, popping his head into stalls, searching.

Black clad Jeck spun, tried to pull a gun from a shoulder holster. Nace took four quick jumps and swung a bony mallet of a fist. Jeck folded down and flopped end over end, like a crow shot on the wing.

He squirmed, dazed, but not unconscious. "I ain't had nothin' to do with this!" he whimpered.

Nace kicked the gun into a corner, blew on his fist. The adder on his forehead was a pale salmon. "You picked a swell way to show it!"

Sergeant Gooch came back. His face was like dough, stuck full of short blue pins. He was almost crying with baffled rage.

"There ain't nobody else here," he said thickly.

Nace turned on the redheaded girl. "Were your brother and Jud Ogel in their underwear when you found them dead?"

"Yes, they were!" she replied, then turned swiftly and walked out.

"Hey, you! Come back here!" Gooch ripped.

Nace gave the police officer a scathing eye. "I hope you don't expect her to stay here and look at that body!" He followed the girl outdoors.

IN A moment, Gooch followed, covering Jeck and Zeke with his revolvers.

"We'll go to the house!" Gooch snapped. "I'm gonna ask some questions! I'm gonna get to the bottom of this, I am!"

They moved to the house. Nace, hanging back, let the others enter first.

"The telephone is out of order," he said shortly. "I'm going after the local coroner and sheriff."

Sergeant Gooch sniffed, half from anger, half from grief. "Now listen, Nace! We won't get anywhere by ringin' these hick cops—"

"The old copper spirit!" Nace answered. "Nobody can do anything quite as well as a New York flatfoot!"

He heeled around and strode across the lawn to the road, thence along the pike in the direction of Lake City.

Once out of sight of the house, however, he slipped silently into the brush. Working through it, he reached the lake shore, then turned left. He used only enough caution so that those in the house did not hear him. He ducked into the warehouse.

CHAPTER VI

murder By Suction

I n ONE OF the stall-like storerooms nearest the wharf end, he found an assortment of diving suits. These ranged from light metal head rigs—nothing but a helmet and short shoulder mantle to ponderous, all-metal suits for deep-water work.

The fact that Honest John was in his underwear indicated that he had been planning to use a diving suit. The detective would naturally have removed his outer clothing so that he would not be soaked in case the diving garb leaked.

But none of the diving suits had been used within the last hour or so—not one was wet. Bending low, Nace scrutinized the place, catching the light from various angles.

There was a faint deposit of dust on the floor. It was scuffed with many tracks—tracks of men in bare feet, and prints of men in shoes. And in two spots, lack of dust marked where two diving suits had recently lain.

After these discoveries, Nace took great care not to mutilate the tracks in the dust.

He lifted one all-metal suit, complete with helmet, and carried it out into the passage, thence toward the dock. He lowered it, reentered the warehouse. In an end stall in the structure, he found a powerful air pump, already set up. No doubt it was there for the purpose of testing diving suits. There was plenty of air hose.

The compressor was operated from an electric motor. It made some little noise when he switched it on. It might be heard at the house. He found an electric lantern, waterproofed for diving use.

He began donning the diving suit. This proved to be something of a task. The rig had not been tailored for a man of Nace's unnatural height. It was of ample girth, however, permitting him to assume a crouching position.

Nace was basing his procedure on a well-grounded suspicion. Honest John had been in a diving suit, or about to get in one, which meant he had been preparing to enter the water for some purpose. That purpose could hardly have been anything except the securing of the Caroni treasure.

Honest John must have discovered the possessor of the treasure making a dive to see that the hoard was safe, and had been murdered for his pains. No doubt Tammany had been slain for the same reason. The killer, knowing the wet suits would betray the loot hiding place, had gotten rid of them, probably dumping them off the dock.

The Caroni swag, unless Nace's guess was far wide, was concealed somewhere around the dock, under water.

Nace adjusted the air valves on the suit. The air pump was fitted with automatic controls. It would need no attendant for the short dive that he expected to make.

He closed the thick glass window of his helmet, clumped to a ladder, and laboriously let himself into the water.

The sun was low. The wharf shadow lay over the water where he was descending. This made the depths gloomy. With foresight, he had switched on the electric lantern before starting down. It diffused a pale luminance.

The water was much deeper than he expected. He settled on the mud bottom, began to play his light. Almost at once, he picked up footprints in the mud. They had been made recently—fine mud was suspended in the water in and around each print. Nace followed them.

The trail angled in toward the wharf piling. Nace tugged the air hose carefully behind him. He saw one of the moccasins, swimming under water. Farther in among the piling, he discerned another. The writhing, repulsive things made him shudder.

A few feet within the forest of piles he found what he had expected.

Several rubberized bags were stacked close together. He grasped one of them with the claw-like pincer which served as hands on the metal diving suit.

Treading slowly, feeling his way back through the fog of mud he had stirred up, he returned to the stair-ladder. He climbed laboriously, the sack clinging to one claw. Reaching the wharf finally, he dropped the bag and began to work upon it with his iron claws.

The rubber-coated fabric was tough. He wrenched at it, tore it.

Pieces of jewelry, many neat bundles of currency, cascaded out. It was beyond a doubt, Caroni's treasure. The rest would be easy to get. It could await capture of the murderer.

Nace suddenly sensed a faint jarring against the wharf planks. He tried to spin. He knew the jarring was from the slam of feet as men leaped toward him.

Before he got around, a stout manilla rope looped over his shoulders. It snugged. Nace, as clumsy as a pile of scrap iron in the ponderous metal suit, was jerked off his feet. He slammed down with a great rattling and banging.

It was then that he saw his assailants numbered two. Jeck and Zeke! They piled fiercely upon him.

Nace rolled, seeking to get slack in the rope, so he could free his arms. The armored diving suit was a protection against the blow of any fist or club. Jeck and Zeke apparently did not have guns. At least, they were not flourishing any.

Nace lifted a great metal blob of a weighted shoe and crashed it down on Jeck's foot. The foot flattened out as if it were a meatball that had been stepped on. Jeck screeched, fell, and almost succeeded in tying himself in a knot around his injured foot.

Zeke jumped upon Nace's steel back, like a gigantic, rusty bullfrog upon a small turtle. He was a bigger man than Nace, possibly stronger. That, coupled with the unwieldiness of the diving suit, kept Nace from arising. He was, in fact, held helpless.

Zeke got hold of the rope and succeeded in securing the awkward metal arms of the diving suit.

"Quit yer whinin'!" he snarled at Jeck. "C'mon and hold this bird in his tin nest! I got somethin' to try!"

Jeck wailed, "That girl! She got away from us at the house—"

"Never mind her! She ran toward town for help, and it's more'n a half mile to the nearest house! We got time!"

Zeke left Nace, ran along the wharf, and disappeared in the warehouse. Jeck got up on one foot, hopped over, and sat on Nace. When Nace yelled, Jeck unscrewed the glass window and opened it so he could hear the words.

"You would have done better to keep out of this!" Nace told him. "I was sure you didn't pull those murders!"

Jeck showed surprise through his pain. "How'd you know that?"

"It was all Zeke, right from the first. There was nobody in the hearse when you grabbed it. That made it pretty certain that Zeke had already ditched the body, killing the filling station attendant while he was doing it. Then he tried to kill me in my office. That showed he was scared of me.

"He telephoned the police that lie about the body, so as to get me in trouble so I couldn't help the girl. Probably he intended to plant Jud Ogel's body in my office. I have no proof of that, of course. Neither can I prove that he shot at me and murdered the taxi driver, but he wasn't with the girl, and he could have done it.

"When he came back here, the first thing he did was to look and see if his treasure was safe. Honest John and Tom Tammany saw him doing that, and he killed them both. Then he tried to potshoot me and the girl. He probably threw the rifle he had used into the lake. And he claimed he had been following you so as to draw suspicion from himself. You'd better be wise, Jeck, and let me go!"

BEFORE NACE'S argument could get results, Zeke reappeared. He carried a great, writhing, poisonous water moccasin, gripping it just back of the head.

Leaning over Nace, Zeke gritted, "I'm gonna put this thing in the suit with you! That's what I done with the girl's nosey brother, when he caught me lookin' at my swag. Then I'm gonna close your suit up tight and reverse the air pumps. They'll suck all the air from your suit. Your eyes and tongue will stick out. You'll look like hell when they find you! Like Jud Ogel looked!"

"I figured that's the way you did it!" Nace told him hatefully.

"How come you figured that out?"

"That purple beak of yours showed you were a diver. Most old-time divers have schnozzles like that. It's the pressure that does things to the fine blood vessels under the skin. You being a diver, it was natural you'd think of a stunt like this taking pressure out of a diving suit to do your murdering."

Zeke shoved the moccasin's head close to the helmet opening. It was so near that Nace shrank back to avoid its darting tongue.

"You ain't gonna do much more fine deductin'!" Zeke grated.

Redheaded Julia Nace came racing out of the warehouse. She held a revolver—one of Sergeant Gooch's police specials. She ran in a semicircle.

While Zeke still gawked at her, the revolver cracked flame.

Before Nace's face, the head of the moccasin disappeared as if by magic. The bullet had shattered it.

Zeke straightened, yelling. He flung the only weapon at hand—the snake. It gyrated, contorting in the air, toward the girl. She ducked from the hideous thing in spite of herself.

Zeke rushed her. She shot at him. Missed! She fired again,

and the bullet tore flesh from his shoulder. Then his fist caught her on the jaw and she dropped as if poled. She hit the wharf hard and did not move a muscle.

Whirling, Zeke ran back. Halfway to Nace, an idea seemed to hit him. He sprang upon Jeck, gibbering, striking with his fists.

Jeck went down, knocked unconscious. Zeke rolled Jeck on his face. Then he backed away, took a running jump and came down with both feet in the middle of Jeck's back. There was a sickening pop as Jeck's spine broke. He must have died instantly.

Zeke screamed madly, "By hell, there ain't nobody gonna get a split of that swag! I bombed the salvage boat so I'd be the one to get it in the first place! I've had to kill men since to keep it! I'll kill a few more! That woman, too!"

He leaned down, grasped the window of Nace's suit, preparing to close it. He could not resist one last boast.

"I'll reverse the pump and it'll suck the air out of your suit! That'll fix you! I altered that pump especially for these sucking jobs!"

Then he jumped, howled, and clapped both hands to his eyes. He weaved back wildly, pawing at his face. He came blindly to the edge of the wharf and plunged over.

There was a loud splash. A silence! Then more splashes. Zeke began screaming. His voice was horrible.

"I can't swim! Help! I can't—"

An ominous *guggle-guggle-guggle* ended that. There was no more noise. Zeke had drowned.

Nace lay in silent agony. He opened a tear gas bomb that he had the foresight to carry inside the diving suit.

THIRTY MINUTES later, he was rubbing his eyes and confronting the redheaded girl and Sergeant Gooch. The redhead had regained consciousness, unhurt except for an aching jaw.

They had found Sergeant Gooch bound securely in the house.

Gooch was growling, "Them two came to an understanding, then they grabbed me—"

"They wouldn't have come to an understanding if you hadn't left them alone while you tried to third degree me!" the redhead snapped.

Gooch flushed under his blue beard stubble. "I thought—"

"I doubt it!" said the girl. "I haven't seen you show any signs of being able to think!"

Nace eyed her steadily. "Say, are you going ahead with this salvage business that your father ran?"

She hesitated. "No. Why?"

Nace grinned widely. "For years, I've been looking for a woman assistant. You've got everything it takes. How'd you like the job?"

"I think I'd go for that in a big way!" she said promptly.

"Fine! We'll show these New York cops some things!"

Sergeant Gooch emitted a forlorn groan.

The Tank of Terror

Grim and horrible were those warnings
of the Big Boss. They were found in
automobiles, office buildings and in homes.
They were the mutilated corpses of men
boiled in oil. And they told the Oklahoma
police not to be too inquisitive. Into this
hotbed of horror came Lee Nace to buck
a triple-decked deal of the Big Boss—a
reward-hungry newspaperman—and the
two-gun Robin Hood of the oil company.

CHAPTER I

Hot Oil

SHE WAS TALL, blonde, streamlined. The roadster was long, cream-colored, and also streamlined.

She was making motions at powdering her nose, using a pancake compact with a mirror fully four inches across. She held it braced against the steering wheel.

Utter concentration rode her long, beautiful face. The big, flat powder puff dabbed the compact with strangely erratic frequency. It slapped only the mirror—never the powder cake.

Oklahoma sunlight, white and hot, sprayed blonde and roadster. To the right, it cooked evergreen stucco buildings of the Tulsa Municipal Airport. To the left, it toasted flat classroom and barrack structures of a school of aeronautics.

In spasms, the sun leaped from the blonde's compact mirror. Her powder puff, whipping systematically, was dividing the beam into dots and dashes.

On hands and knees beside the airport waiting room, Lee Nace crawled. He was very long, bony, blue-eyed. He was gathering together the wind-scattered sheets of a letter.

Standing and staring at Nace were six or seven people who had been his fellow passengers on the recently arrived New York plane.

They were fascinated by the scar on Nace's forehead. It was a perfect likeness of a small coiled snake—an adder. A Chinaman had once hit Nace in the forehead with a knife hilt which bore a serpent carving, and he was destined to forever carry the scar.

The man was too quick.

Ordinarily the scar was unnoticeable. But it flushed out redly when he was angry or worried. He was worried now.

Inside the ornate, modernistic waiting room, a male voice was shouting: "Telegram! Wire for Private Detective Lee Nace! Telegram!"

Nace continued picking up the sheets of his letter. He pretended to read each. When he had spilled the sheets, he had taken pains to make it seem an accident.

Slyly, over the paper, he read the heliograph message being flashed by the blonde's compact mirror.

"A reception committee!" she sun-flashed. "Three of them, man with the telegram is one. The other two are wearing coveralls—to hide bullet proof vests."

Nace captured two more sheets of his letter, pretended to read, but kept his eyes on the mirror.

"The one with the telegram is 'Robin Hood' Lloyd," the girl continued. "He's Oklahoma's bad boy."

She ended her transmission.

Nace arose and barged in under a striped canopy which could be telescoped out to meet arriving planes. He entered the flashy waiting room.

"TELEGRAM FOR Lee Nace!" droned Robin Hood Lloyd.

The Robin Hood was a lean, young-old wolf. His chin bore scars, irregular, wavy lines—marks of an ancient beating with knucks.

The men sat side by side on a modernistic divan. They were chunky. Their faces might have been meaty blocks covered with a good grade of brown saddle leather.

Both wore khaki overalls. Both had newspapers spread open in their laps.

Headlines on the papers read:

OIL SCANDAL GROWING!

There was a picture of a man with a flowing white beard. He looked like Santa Claus. Under that was another black-faced type line.

EDITOR APP LEADS STOLEN
OIL INVESTIGATION

Nace sidled, long-legged, for the seated pair. These men did not know him, or they would not be using the telegram ruse to spot him.

He was still moving when his long arms shot out. His hands, long-fingered, bony, swung hard against the right ear of one man and the left ear of the other. Their heads, driven together, made a hollow *bonk!*

Each man gave one convulsive quiver as he became unconscious. Then they lay back on the modernistic divan, mouths agape, eyes pinched. The newspapers slid off their laps, revealing frontier six-shooters.

ROBIN HOOD LLOYD stood and stared, a yellow telegram envelope dangling from his right hand. Suddenly he dropped the envelope and began to shake his right hand madly.

A small revolver, dislodged from an armpit, dropped out of the sleeve and hung swinging on a string.

Before Robin Hood could seize his hideout weapon, Nace's fist lashed. It hit the handiest spot—the undershot jaw which gave the Robin Hood his wolf look.

Oklahoma's bad boy flippered his hands convulsively. He was not entirely knocked out, and feeling himself going down, wheeled in an effort to land on all fours. He failed and hit the floor all spread out.

The sound as he came down was a metallic clank, as of a pile of scrap iron on the tile floor, rather than a man.

Nace had read about this Oklahoma cut-up in the New York papers. The fellow went around armored like a knight of old—not only with a bullet proof vest, but with steel leg and arm shields.

The Robin Hood rolled on his back, made a tent over his face with his hands, and moaned loudly.

"The wild and wooly west!" Nace said through his teeth. "I'll show you how we handle 'em back where the lights shine bright!"

He rushed—bent low, long arms hanging down.

He never did know exactly what happened next. One of the men on the modernistic divan unlimbered with a gun. Or maybe it was both of them. A bullet slammed against Nace's right side. It spun him just enough so that the second slug got him in the stomach. The Robin Hood managed to draw back both feet and kick him in the head.

Nace's eyes became two gory bonfires of pain. His insides felt as if they were torn out. He started to cave.

It soaked through his dazed brain that he would die if he did. He hauled up, swayed around, and ran blindly for the white blur he knew was the sunlit door.

When he got outside, he knew it only because he seemed to be in a white-hot snow storm. He pawed his kicked face, beat his body where the bullets had hit.

He wore a bulletproof jacket which had saved his life, but the slugs had mauled him horribly.

Flaying his tortured brain, he managed to remember where they had stacked the baggage from the plane. He veered for the luggage heap. His canvas zipper bag was there. He wanted it. It was his war sack, his bag of tricks, his life preserver. He was too drunk with pain to realize he could not get to the bag before the trio in the waiting room could come after him.

Nace never carried a gun. He subscribed to a theory that toting a firearm tended to make a man helpless, if ever he was caught without it.

FINALLY HE snapped out of the daze. He swiveled around drunkenly on a heel.

His hand, clawing inside his coat, fished out a little metal tear-gas firing cylinder. He exploded it in the waiting room door.

On the opposite side of the building, the roadster engine was moaning anxiously. The blonde waited, tense at the wheel.

The Robin Hood and his two followers floundered out into the sunlight. Blinded by the tear gas, they were holding hands to keep track of each other. They acted like three small boys trying not to get lost.

"Come on, guys!" rapped the blonde. "Blow!"

The blinded Robin Hood tried to climb into the roadster hood, under the impression that he was getting in the back seat. He hauled out a single-action gun, jabbed it above his head and fanned out its five slugs. Then he found the car door and piled in. "O. K. That'll hold 'em! Blow!"

The roadster seemed to snug its oilpan belly to the ground, then jump. Scooting away, it left a rain of gravel.

"Did you get the dirty so-and-so?" the blonde demanded.

"Hell, no!" The Robin Hood held his jaw with a clench so tight that tendons on his hands whitened like chalk rods.

"Damn! Did he hand one on my kisser!"

"My heroes!" The girl's voice was dry. But her eyes were brightly glad.

As if it were clawing cats, the wind tore her blond hair about. It was so very blonde, that hair, that it was plainly dyed.

Nace staggered around the airport waiting-room, covering as much ground to right and left as he did ahead.

The field operation office was in the same building with the waiting room, but there were doors, probably closed, through which the tear gas had not penetrated.

Like a dude out of a bandbox, a man popped out from an office window. He wore striped trousers and a gray lap-over tea vest. The pearl grip of a derringer protruded, charm-like, from his watch pocket. He pulled his tiny gun, leveled it. The thing made a sound like a giant firecracker and kicked his fist back in his face.

He looked foolish when the slug dug a geyser of dirt not a hundred feet from where it stood.

Nace leaned, white-faced, against a wall, said, "Better get a bow and arrow!"

The dapper man looked around and grinned. "When I do hit 'em, though, I make a big hole! Say, Skipper, you look like hell!"

The pain had faded the adder scar off Nace's forehead. It was coming back slowly.

"And I was the cookie who was gonna show how it's done in the east!" he said dryly. "I done swell! Yes, I did!"

The nattily dressed man reloaded his derringer with a cartridge as thick as his little finger. "Y'know who that was?"

"Mr. Lloyd, I believe."

"You said it, Skipper! Oklahoma's contribution to the wild and woolly west—the Robin Hood himself. The lad who can walk down Main Street in Tulsa, from the Louvre to Brown-Dunkin's, and not a cop can see him—because they're afraid to. 'Officers again escape Robin Hood,' is the streamer an

Oklahoma City rag runs every time he had a gun fight with the law."

Nace grimaced. "You talk like a newspaper man! What sheet?"

The dressy man skidded the derringer back into his watch pocket. "The *Telegram!* Halt Jaxon's the name. Oil editor!"

"Know Ebenezer App?"

"I ought to! He pays me!"

"Let's go hunt him up!" Nace suggested.

Dapper Halt Jaxon made a whistling mouth. "You must be Lee Nace, the private shamus the governor hired to come from New York to come here and work with the boss!"

"The same!"

Nace walked behind the waiting room and came back with his canvas zipper bag. "Do we go?"

"We do!"

Jaxon led the way to a roadster. It was a speedster, low and yellow, remindful of an overgrown canary.

CHAPTER 11

The Hot-Oil Ring

THE CANARY CAR tweeted a horn when it pulled out of the airport parking. It tweeted a different one wen it turned into Sheridan Drive, heading toward town. Not once during the trip in did it sound the same horn twice.

"I was sent out here to meet you!" Halt Jaxon offered a cork-tipped fag from a silver case.

"I need something stronger!" Nace produced a stubby pipe and a silk pouch. "Whew-w-w! What a reception! Is that the usual thing out here?"

"If you're going up against the Robin Hood, it is! I guess you're out here on this hot-oil trouble."

"What hot-oil trouble?"

"For cryin' out load! Don't you read the newspapers?"

"Where'd you get the idea your troubles mean anything to Broadway rags?"

"Oh! So it's like that! Well, for the last year or so, most of the Oklahoma oil fields have been shut down. They passed laws—"

"Proration!"

"Go to the head of the class! The governor had to stick the militia in some fields to close 'em. They're just discovering that, while the fields were shut down, somebody stole a lot of oil!"

"What do you call a lot?"

"We ain't pikers! Thirty or forty millions!"

"Barrels?"

"Dollars!"

Nace felt tenderly of his shoe-bruised face. "You wouldn't kid me?"

"I might, but I ain't. I tell you, they're just getting into the damn mess! The governor has investigators all over the state. Wherever they dig, they turn up a dead cat.

"Down at Bowlegs, they found a farm of 55,000-barrel crude tanks plumb empty. In the Oklahoma City field, a lot of leases are running salt water where they should be making oil. The oil has been pulled out by mysterious persons unknown— lifted, heisted, stolen!"

"Can't they put a finger on anybody?"

"Sure—small fry! But some great big bright brain is behind the whole thing! They can't learn who! I'm telling you, Skipper, it's the most colossal robbery in history."

Nace wiped crimson off his fingers. "What'm I supposed to do? Make news for App's paper?"

"App owns a lot of production up in the Osage which ain't production any more. He'd like to know who pinched the oil! And any news fit into print, we print."

The canary car swung past MacIntyre airport. Off to the left, derricks in the Oil Exposition grounds stuck up, a horny, cactus-like cluster.

"THE HELL of it is the way they get drowned in hot oil!" Halt Jaxon said.

Nace stuffed his pipe, then looked at the stem. It was cracked. He took a small metal case from his zipper bag, extracted a fresh stem from the assortment it held. He chewed an average of a stem a day out of the pipe. The total often reached three or four when the going got tough.

"What's this—drowned in oil?"

"Several state investigators have been found that way. Also oil men and roustabouts. They're simply drowned—and pretty badly scalded."

The tower of the Exchange National swelled up ahead. Immaculate Jaxon tooled his canary roadster toward it, trying out different horns on the traffic.

"They all got too close to the master mind!" Nace mixed his question with a mouthful of smoke. "That it?"

"It's a guess! Yours is as good as anybody's!"

"The bodies found in any particular oil tank?"

"Never in any tank!" Jaxon touched a button; a horn gave a cow-like moo. "They find the bodies in the damnedest places. One was leaning against a lamp-post as stiff as a board. Some of them have been in hotels, houses—all over."

"That's a hell of a note!" Nace drew on his pipe.

The roadster paused for the traffic light on Main, then made a turn.

"App left this message in the office mailbox!" Jaxon fished a finger daintily in the pocket of the tea vest, as if afraid of soiling it. He produced a strip of coarse white copy paper.

Nace took it, read:

Jaxon:
Lee Nace, a private detective, will arrive on the three o'clock plane. Meet him and bring him to the hotel Crown Block, room 1820.

The note, typewritten, bore only a typed signature—"App."

Nace stiffened his brake leg instinctively as the gaudy roadster shaved another car. "Don't they have any traffic laws down here!"

A moment later he said, "I hope App don't think there's anything secret about this! I'm sunk if he does!"

"Yeah, that's right!" Jaxon agreed. Then he added, "Unless you sent some agents ahead?"

"Who do you think I am? The army?"

Jaxon grinned. "Well, I didn't know! The A. P. has carried stories about you! You're supposed to be good. I thought maybe you had help. You'll need it!"

Nace nodded toward an up-and-down sign which said, "Telegram," and asked, "That's the plant, huh?"

"The sweat shop itself!" Jaxon maneuvered his roadster around a corner.

The wind was from the south, bringing a smell of distilling crude from West Tulsa refineries.

Jaxon asked unexpectantly, "What about the blonde in the Robin Hood's car?"

Nace looked interested. "Well, what about her?"

Jaxon laughed. "I see you didn't get a close look! What a form she had! Oh, man!"

THE CROWN BLOCK HOTEL was not quite the largest in the southwest, but it was generally conceded to be the most sumptuous.

When an oil man hits it rich, his first act was to take a suite in the Crown Block. It did not matter whether he made his strike in Seminole, Borger, Oil Hill, or East Texas. He took a suite in the Crown Block. It was sort of a ritual—a man's way of telling the cockeyed world he was on top.

Jaxon swerved his roadster in to the curb. They got out, Nace with his canvas zipper bag. There was a flurry, then hard looks, when bellboys tried unsuccessfully to capture Nace's bag.

They walked a gauntlet of doormen in Czaristic uniforms, and waded in a sea of rich, thick carpet. A silent elevator wafted them up, and they single-filed down the corridor, more rich carpets sponging underfoot.

The door of 1820 was massive, shiny, of mahogany, with a ponderous wrought-bronze lock.

Nace's eyes roved with habitual alertness. Suddenly he grunted, lifted one foot off the carpet and hopped to the wall, propped against it, he began untying his shoe.

"Must've picked up a rock at the airport!"

His hand, apparently resting against the wall as a brace,

made a slight rubbing motion.

There was a small, irregularly shaped chalk mark on the wall. This was almost unnoticeable to the casual eye.

When Nace took his hand away, the mark was gone.

Nace tore a bit of inner sole from his shoe, put it back on. Then he opened his canvas bag. He took several expensive looking cigars from a case and pocketed them.

The adder scar, seeming to come from nowhere, was once more coiling redly on his forehead.

"Let's go!" His voice was dry, with a bit of a rattle.

Jaxon rippled knuckles on the door. A voice invited them in. Opening the door, Jaxon stepped back politely to let Nace in first.

Three men appeared suddenly, shoulder to shoulder, inside the room. The Robin Hood and his two followers!

Frontier six-guns bulked big in their fists.

The blonde, without uncoiling herself from a chair in which she sat, said, "Come right in, boys! Cut yourself a piece of cake!"

Nace ambled into the room, hands held far out from his sides. He was so very tall that he instinctively ducked a little as he entered.

Halt Jaxon rolled his eyes, made faces. "So the note was a come-on!"

"Can the guff! Come on in here!" The Robin Hood made a meaningful gesture with his thumb and a gun hammer.

Gun snouts followed Nace and Jaxon, crowding them to the wall. The blonde uncoiled from her chair, closed the door, and stood with her back pressing the panel.

Her blonde hair was done in a flat patty on the back of her neck. She slid slender fingers under this, and brought out a tiny derringer, similar to Jaxon's, but of smaller calibre.

The Robin Hood eyed the small gun with wolfish concentration. "Where'd you get that, sister?"

"From Monkey Ward!"

"Don't get sassy!"

NACE PUT in, "Where's the western chivalry I've been hearing about?"

The Robin Hood switched the tall private detective from head to foot with eyes which were unafraid and predatory. He growled, "You behave and keep that mouth shut, and maybe nobody'll get hurt."

He came over and slapped Nace's arm pits, lifted coat tails. Frowning, he searched more intensively. "I'm a son-of-a-gun! You ain't heeled!"

He fell to examining Nace's bullet-proof vest. The thing seemed to fascinate him. He thumbed open his own vest and compared it with Nace's.

"Where'd you get that?" he asked. "I might buy one like it!"

"Made it myself," Nace advised. "Let's get down to business."

"Sure! Sure!" The Robin Hood turned to his two companions. "I want to talk to Nace alone. Take this over-dressed hombre away. Haul him off to that cabin north of Shell Creek. Hold him until you hear from me."

Jaxon was standing beside a floor lamp. As the two men approached him, he elbowed the lamp violently.

The fixture slammed one man in the face. The fellow ducked back, startled. Jaxon flung upon the other, grasping the gun wrist with both pudgy hands.

The Robin Hood made a growling noise. He slapped his coat violently—two big sixes appeared as if by magic. He hesitated, growled again, then jabbed the guns back out of sight.

He leaped for Jaxon.

The blonde, running toward Jaxon, got in the Robin Hood's way and also in the way of the man the floor lamp had hit. She grabbed Jaxon by the throat and began choking.

Freeing one hand, Jaxon slapped her with the back of his

fist. The blow reeled her away. She collided with a chair and went over, tangled with rungs and armrests.

"Beat it!" the Robin Hood rasped at her. "We'll handle this!"

The blonde, still mixed with the chair, fumbled at her nape for the gun under her hair.

Nace, leaping to her, harvested the gun with a single clutch. He pocketed it. Going on, he came up behind the Robin Hood. Both his hands went under the tail of the man's coat. They grabbed a belt, pulled. There was a snap. Nace's hands reappeared with the Robin Hood's gun belt and both big revolver holsters.

The man the lamp had hit drew a gun. Nace flung the captured belt, whip fashion. Both six shooters flew out, but the holsters popped loudly on the man's face. The fellow squawled, lost his weapon. Nace round-housed a fist to his middle. The man closed like a book.

The Robin Hood was whirling. Nace let knuckles fly at the scarred wolf jaw. They landed squarely.

Arms fanning spasmodically, the Robin Hood reeled toward the window. Unable to help himself, he popped head and shoulders through the sash. He all but fell to his death, eighteen floors below.

The Oklahoma badman wore cowboy boots. Clutching their narrow toes, Nace hauled their owner back in.

Jaxon and his opponent swore, swapped blows, on the floor.

The blonde untangled from the chair, ran to a table on which her purse lay and scooped it up. She unclipped it, spaded a hand inside, then shoved purse and hand at Nace and Jaxon.

"Hold it!" she snapped.

Nace promptly jutted his hands above his head. Jaxon tore free of his dazed foe, lurched up and dived at the girl.

Nace tripped him. Jaxon tumbled end over end like a soft ball.

One of the Robin Hood's men crawled for his fallen gun. Nace, his hand still raised, jumped sideways, and mashed his fellow against the wall.

Ducking, Nace scooped up the gun. Continuing the same movement, he fell behind the bed.

The Robin Hood and his two followers staggered out of the room. The girl followed, banging the door shut.

JAXON BOUNCED up from the floor, screaming. "You tripped me! There's ten thousand reward for that guy—and you trip me—"

"I kept you from getting a lead pill!" Nace snapped. Rapidly, he gathered the guns scattered around the room.

When they ran into the hall, an elevator door was sliding shut.

"Gimme one of them guns!" Jaxon yelled.

"To hell with you—hothead!"

Jaxon made faces, ran back into the room.

Nace bore a staccato thumb on the elevator button. Time crawled. A minute! And still no cage came!

"Here they go!" Jaxon squawled from within the room. Nace ran to his side. Jaxon was hanging out of a window. On the sidewalk far below, the Robin Hood, his two men, and the blonde, were legging it for a corner.

Jaxon tore at one of the guns in Nace's hands. Nace held on tightly, would not give it up. The runners below disappeared.

Cursing, his round face purple, Jaxon squealed, "A fine cluck you are! I could have potted the Robin Hood from the window. Damn your hide! Ten thousand reward—"

Nace waved a fist under his nose. "Shut up, or I'll feed you a mess of knuckles!"

Jaxon squared off belligerently. "Any damn time you feel lucky—"

"Just a newspaper fathead!" The adder scar above Nace's eyes was red as ink. "You dope! You balled things up!"

"I did like hell!"

"The Robin Hood had something on his mind. He wanted to talk, and I wanted to hear him. But did you give us a chance? Yes, you did—not!"

Jaxon hardened his fists. "I don't give a damn about that! You wouldn't come across with the gun! That costs me ten thousand! It burns me up!"

He swung a fist at Nace's face. Nace rolled back from the blow; his right arm came up; his hard knuckles smacked against Jaxon's biceps. It was an agonizing blow.

Jaxon yodeled from the pain in his muscles. Nace collared him, hauled him to the door, and gave him the boot.

He slammed the door after the stumbling, enraged oil editor.

Nothing happened for a few seconds; then elevator doors clanged in the hall. Nace looked out. Jaxon was gone.

Going to his canvas zipper bag, Nace carefully replaced the cigars which he had taken out before entering the room. Two were broken. He disposed of these in the bath.

Carrying his bag, he descended in a tardy elevator and left the hotel. He took a cab to the new Union Station, changed to another, and went to a small hotel on Boston.

There was a derrick firm on one side of the hotel, a well-shooter supply house on the other. Walking up two flights, Nace found a room number. He knocked on the door. Silence answered.

Car horns honked in the street below. Over on Main, news-boys were yelling the *Telegram*.

Nace knocked again, a peculiar signal—two taps, then two more, widely separated.

The blonde opened the door.

CHAPTER III

Drowned in Oil

NACE WENT In, closed the door. He lowered his bag, then opened it. From it he took a sensitive microphone, fitted with vacuum cups. He stuck this to the door. Wires led from the microphone to an amplifier in the bag, thence to headphones.

The device was a highly sensitive sound pick-up. It would amplify any noise from the corridor a thousand fold. Should anyone approach, the instrument would make the noise like that of an elephant stampeding.

"Any chance that they suspect you are my agent?" he asked the girl.

"Don't make me laugh!" The blonde patted her hair. "With this layout I don't even know myself. Gosh, Nace! What if this platinum dye won't wash off?"

"I guess I could stand that!" As he took out the pipe, and plugged it, Nace eyed her.

Her first name was Julia. Her last name was the same as his own—Nace. She was a cousin, very distant. She had not been an operative in his agency for long and she was already good, and getting better.

She had what it took.

"You didn't lose any time getting lined up!" he said, making the words both a compliment and a question.

She laughed. "It was easy! Half the people in town know the Robin Hood by sight. But you can save our blarney! I haven't learned anything!"

Nace fired his pipe, then clamped one receiver of the sound pick-up to an ear.

"What do they want with me?" he queried.

"A talky-talk!"

"What about?"

"Search me. The Robin Hood is all hot and bothered about nothing. When he learned you were coming to town, he said he'd go out and meet you. I didn't know until later that he only wanted to talk."

"Everybody in town knew I was coming, huh?"

"The Robin Hood has his ways of learning things! He must have a spy on the *Telegram*."

"Is he mixed up in this hot oil?"

"Sure! But there's a catch to that, Nace! I don't know how he stands—whether he's in the ring, or out of it."

Nace eyed a fly-specked telephone. "Do you think you're safe, kid?"

"Believe it or not, this Robin Hood is the McCoy. He packs two guns and he's killed his men. He'll fight anybody. But he doesn't shoot in the back, doesn't shoot unarmed men, and respects women."

"Chivalrous, huh?"

"That's straight, Nace! Not one of the gang has made a pass at me; I haven't heard any dirty stories, and they make their eyes behave. Different from our eastern mobs, eh?"

Nace took off the listener receiver. He went to the telephone, picked up a directory, and thumbed through it.

"Who did you tell 'em you were?"

"Just a little girl who got turned out of the California pen a few weeks ago! For fifty dollars a New York printer faked me a newspaper clipping with my picture and everything."

Nace found his number. He placed a finger in the dial nobs. When the selector had made his connection he requested,

"Ebenezer App, please!"

Probably twenty seconds later, he began, "This is Nace. I just got into town... Oh, Jaxon told you, did he... It was a fake note that led us to the hotel."

A metallic gobble of words poured from the receiver. Nace listened to them for some time, asked, "Who was it?" twice, and hung up.

"App says he found out who's behind the hot-oil ring," he told the blonde. "He said he accused the fellow and made him admit it—and for me to come over and make the pinch."

"Who is it?"

"App said he'd spill that when I got there. He flatly refused to name the fellow over the phone."

TULSA WAS a town of a hundred and fifty thousand. Unlike large cities of the east, alleys ran behind the business houses.

Leaving the hotel with his zipper bag, Nace stepped from the rear door into an alley. He swung rapidly for the corner. Newsboys on the street were shouting, "Oil scandal grows! Last oil drowning victim still unidentified." Every paper bore App's Santa Claus picture. "Mr. App pushes investigation."

Nace ignored them, striding toward the Telegram Building. His eyes roved alertly. He saw men in field boots, Osages in bright blankets, pasty-faced clerks with puckers between their eyes that meant eye-strain.

The Telegram was a tall narrow building of brick. Extremely pretty girls ran the elevators.

Nace thought of Julia as he rode up. Ordinarily she was a red-head. The combination of her looks and her brains was hard to find. She had been under his instructions for a month now. Numerous methods of signaling had been part of the trailing. Sun flashing with the compact mirror was one.

The tiny chalk marks, which he had stopped in the corridor of the Crown Block Hotel to erase, was another. They had warned him of the ambush in the room.

Nace swore. He had gone into that room deliberately. The reckless Jaxon had defeated his chances on learning something—perhaps something valuable.

Nace found a door bearing the name, "Ebenezer App, Publisher."

He went in and found himself in a reception room—green carpeted, tan walled, fitted with leather chairs and a reception desk.

A girl with stringy brown hair lay across one of the chairs. She wore square-toed shoes and a brown frock with a starched white collar. She had a very long nose.

Blood was drip-dripping from her nose to the carpet.

Nace opened a door marked, "Mr. App—Private."

The office beyond reeked of emptiness. The furniture was expensive and in good taste.

App's picture hung on the wall. The Shavian beard bristled. His cheeks were ruddy. His eyes were fenced with little wrinkles. With the addition of a big white mustache, he would have made a perfect Santa Claus.

Coming back, Nace examined the girl with the long nose. When he moved her, her mouth fell open and let a little crimson come out. But she had only been struck on the jaw with a fist or a blackjack.

The fifth paper cup of ice water from the cooler revived her.

Jaxon came in when she was rolling her eyes and gurgling. He had combed his hair, put on a fresh shirt. Once more he looked as if he were right out of a bandbox.

He demanded, "What the hell's going on here, Nace!"

At this, the girl leaped up. She dropped her cup, pointed both hands at Nace, screamed "He's the man who hit me!"

Jaxon sneered, "I wouldn't put it past him."

Nace laughed at Jaxon, fists up and hard. The oil editor spun and fled from the office like a frightened peacock.

Nace turned back to the girl but did not approach her lest

he frighten her. "You're mistaken, you know! What happened?"

"A man came in! He said Mr. Nace was waiting outside!" The girl's voice was scared. "He went in to see Mr. App. And then someone must have hit me. I didn't see who it was."

That was all she knew. When he had finished his questioning, Nace ambled out into the hall. Jaxon stood there, undecided. He walked off hastily at sight of Nace.

Nace went down to the city room. There was a big picture of App's Santa Claus countenance on the wall. Nace asked for a late edition, got it, was stared at, and left the building. He hopped a cab at the corner, said, "The morgue the city uses."

UNLIMBERED ON the cushions, Nace studied the newspaper, centering his attention on the unidentified man, who had been drowned in oil. The fellow had been found near Reservoir Hill two days ago.

There was little else of interest—except that no one seemed to know who he was. The body was being held at the morgue.

On the front of the morgue, a sign said, "Funeral Home."

It was a plain building. Fifteen years ago, when Tulsa was a village it must have been a private mansion. The doors had been enlarged to permit of coffins being carried through.

Nace found a bright-eyed little man in charge. They went into a room where there were long marble slabs and much noise—laughter, shouts.

The funeral home, it seemed, also conducted an ambulance service. The ambulance drivers and an assistant undertaker were rolling craps on a marble slab. They had turned a stiff body on the slab and were using it as a backstop for the dice. They reminded Nace of small boys trying to show how callous they were.

In the rear of the room, the undertaker uncovered a cadaver.

The dead man was tall, lean. His skin, where the oil had not been wiped off, was strangely white. Fingernails, hair, eyebrows—all were gone.

Nace studied the long, sharp features. Somehow, they struck him as vaguely familiar.

"Hot oil got this one!" he said. "And I don't mean stolen oil, either!"

"The oil must have been scalding hot!" the undertaker agreed. "That's what made his hair and fingertips slip."

"Have the others been like this?"

"You mean scalded? Sure!"

Once more Nace squinted at the features of the dead man. He could not get rid of the idea he had seen the fellow before.

"O. K.," he told the undertaker.

He went back, and stopped in front of the crap shooters bouncing dice against the body. He scowled at them.

"Cut it out!"

The dicers glared at him. "Who the hell're you?"

"Cut it out!" Nace said, and beetled his brows.

The trio scowled, changed feet. The strange crimson scar on Nace's forehead seemed to disquiet them. Then they gathered up their dice and went out, trying to maintain a dignity.

Disgust rode heavy on Nace's long, bony face.

The undertaker began, "What was the idea—"

"When you're dead, do you want three guys bouncing dice off your ribs—"

From the direction the three dice rollers had taken, came gasps, low cries of surprise.

"Stand still, you monkeys!" gritted an ugly voice.

Nace came to life like an electrical machine switched on. He dived for the door, whipping out his tear-gas firing cylinder. Reaching the door he got a glimpse of a man—a man he had never seen before. The fellow had a bulky, shapeless body, a long neck, and a chicken-like head.

He carried an automatic shotgun, the barrel sawed off at the magazine.

Nace shoved out the tear-gas cylinder and let it bang.

Squawking, the man with the shotgun clutched at his eyes with one hand. With his other hand he slapped the automatic shotgun against his hip. He pulled the trigger three times.

The gun was ear-splitting. Across the morgue room other explosions crashed like echoes. Holes the size of washtubs opened magically in the wall. Plaster, lath, and bits of brick rained. Marble slabs upset on their stands.

Nace jumped clear of the door. Now he retreated further, dragging the undertaker.

THE SHOTGUN was firing explosive slugs. They were capable of tearing a man to pieces.

Nace ran to a window. It was frosted glass. He boosted it up and dropped outdoors.

He waded through flower beds, leaping high, and circled the house.

The shot-gunner came out of a side door. He was blinded by the tear gas, feeling his way. He carried his automatic weapon in one hand.

Nace chopped knuckles at the gunner's elbow. Pain reaction caused the man to release his gun. Nace sprang upon him.

They rolled briefly on the ground, grunting, swapping blows. Then Nace stood erect, his foe unconscious and cradled in his arms. Stooping again, he picked up the shotgun.

The fight, the shots and explosions, had excited the neighborhood. Heads were hanging out of windows. A few pedestrians, positioned close to trees, stood and stared.

Glancing about, Nace saw a small flivver touring which had been parked there since he entered the funeral home. He ran to it.

On the front floorboards, covered by a gunny sack, lay a dozen extra explosive shotgun slugs.

Nace propped his burden in a seat of the little car. He tossed the automatic shotgun in the rear. Then he went to the touring. He ramped the starter. The engine began to chatter, shimmy the fenders, and shake the steering wheel in his hand. He meshed gears and drove away. A bit later, he was guiding the flivver down a tree-canopied avenue of residences.

From time to time, Nace reached over and slapped his slumbering companion. The man was slow to awaken. Opening his zipper bag, as he drove, Nace dug out liquid ammonia in little cloth-covered glass phials. He broke one of these under the man's nose. The fellow eventually sneezed, grimaced, and began to paw about aimlessly.

"Who sent you and your artillery after me?" Nace demanded.

The man made mumbling animal noises. He was still a little beyond speech.

Nace looked back. A small coupe seemed to be following him. He could not make out the driver. Nor could he be entirely certain that the car was on his trail.

He reached over to sting his companion into wakefulness with another slap.

A cream-colored roadster lunged out of a side street. Angling over expertly, it sideswiped Nace's flivver. The little car, knocked out of control, jumped at a tree.

By springing suddenly erect, Nace kept his face from hitting the windshield as the car struck. His chest met the glass. It caved; he slid across the hood. His shoulder jarred the tree, and he tumbled to the ground, only slightly dazed.

Skidding all four wheels the cream-colored roadster had stopped as soon as it side-swiped the flivver.

The flivver was up on the curb, leaving plenty of room underneath. Into this space Nace crawled.

Glimpsing the feet of a man who had dropped out of the roadster, Nace wriggled for them. The feet were encased in cowboy boots. Hooking both hands about the boots, Nace pulled. There was a single profane bark and the owner of the boots sat down heavily.

It was Robin Hood Lloyd.

In going, Nace tried to haul him under the flivver. The Robin Hood drew a heavy frontier six. But he made no effort to shoot.

"Damn you!" he snarled. "Why don't you carry a rod!" He tried to bat Nace in the face with his gun.

Nace dodged back and pulled harder. The Robin Hood came sliding under the flivver.

The fight which followed, Nace was always to remember. The Robin Hood battled with fists and his revolver. He kicked, gouged, bit. Anything went. Nace returned all he received. They bruised themselves against the flivver chassis and against the concrete curb.

THEN THE chicken-headed man entered the fray. He crouched down and looked under the car. He had secured his automatic shotgun, from where Nace had placed it in the flivver seat. Deliberately, he aimed at Nace.

Glimpsing the man, Robin Hood Lloyd threw up his six. Its boom seemed violent enough to blow the flivver off their backs.

The shot-gunner sagged, leaking scarlet from a blue-rimmed pit which had suddenly appeared directly between his eyes.

Nace and the Robin Hood separated as if by mutual agreement. They crawled out on different sides of the roadster and stood erect.

"Before I'm through with this, I'm gonna beat hell out of you!" the Robin Hood snarled. "But not now! I hear old Ebenezer App has been kidnaped! Anything to it?"

Nace hesitated briefly. "Yeah. And just before it happened, App found out who is heading the hot-oil ring!"

"Thanks!" Backing swiftly, the Robin Hood climbed into his roadster. The engine was running and the car got under way quickly. It volleyed off in the direction of town.

A few seconds later Nace saw a coupe pass the corner on a side street, a block distant. The tree shadows made it impossible to tell who occupied the machine. But it was the same coupe which had tailed Nace.

Nace ran around the flivver. One glance told him the man with the shotgun was dead. Getting his zipper carryall from the car, Nace set out across the back yards. He ran the first few blocks, then slowed down to a walk as he heard the business district. Excitement was noticeable in the Telegram Building when he entered. In the glass enclosed circulation room off the lobby, groups of clerks stood under a Santa Claus picture of App and talked. The pretty elevator operators were flushed and perturbed.

In the city room, Jaxon was talking to four policemen. The dressy oil editor glared at Nace. "There's the bum now!"

The policemen came over, jaws out, eyes wintry. One jingled handcuffs suggestively.

Nace got in first word. "I'm a private detective—"

"We know all about you, brother!" frowned one cop. "We don't like your kind! And we don't like the way you're getting around this man's town!"

The adder leered redly at them from Nace's forehead. "So what?"

"So it's the can for you."

Nace put his zipper bag on a reporter's desk, opened it, and extracted a yellow fold of paper.

"What's that?" questioned the officer.

"Telegraphic commission from the governor—appointing me a special investigator in this hot-oil business."

The policeman scowled. "Let's see that!"

TEN MINUTES later, Nace was alone in the newspaper morgue. The policemen had gone their disgruntled way. They didn't like it, but Nace had a special permission from the governor.

Jaxon, after making ugly grimaces to express his personal opinion of Nace, had gone off somewhere—probably to the oil editor's sanctum.

The morgue was a dingy room, a fly-specked Santy picture of App on the wall. There were great steel filing cabinets. These held drawers, and the drawers were gorged with envelopes. There were pictures, mats, clippings, cuts.

The cabinet bore alphabetic file letters. Nace was looking under the "L" guide.

He found a quart of white mule, a pair of dice and two packs of cards, which some reporter must have hidden.

There were four envelopes on Robin Hood Lloyd, all fat. They traced his life from the cradle, his associates, his family, his boyhood chums—all were named.

The file was a potential fortune. It contained material enough to write a book on Oklahoma's bad boy who was probably destined to take a place alongside Jesse James.

Nace read the clippings, replaced them, then left the morgue. As he was passing the city room, a copy boy ran out.

"Somebody on the 'phone wantin' you, Mr. Nace!" he said.

"I'll take it in the booth," Nace told him, and entered a little glass enclosure, and picked up an instrument.

Julia's voice came to him.

CHAPTER IV

The Oil-Boiled Trail

"WHAT'S EATING YOU?" Nace asked quietly.
Julia said, "I followed them!"

"So it was you in the coupe!" Nace chuckled.

"Sure! I didn't have anything else to do so I trailed you to the newspaper, then to the morgue, then away. That is, after we left the newspaper, I followed the Robin Hood, who was following the guy who was shagging you. That's why I didn't warn you—"

"Don't get me dizzy!" Nace chuckled. "Where are you now?"

"In a bungalow at the foot of Reservoir Hill. I tagged the Robin Hood to a house at the top of the hill."

"Describe the house!"

"I'll do better than that! Here's the number." She gave him a street and numerals. "There's several houses on the hill and this is one of the biggest."

"O. K.," said Nace. "What do you make of this jamboree?"

"Search me, boss! I'm fairly certain the Robin Hood is somebody big in the oil ring. But just now he's sure going around like a chicken with its head cut off!"

"You know there's a body in the morgue now."

"Yes?"

"I just identified the corpse by pictures and clippings at the *Telegram*. It's the Robin Hood's kid brother."

"Hm-m-m!" Julia made a thoughtful humming sound.

"That may explain a lot, boss!"

"I wouldn't be surprised."

Julia said hastily, "Are you coming out here?"

"What's the address of this place you're telephoning from?" Nace demanded.

Again she gave him a street and a number. "I'm going to hang around on the front porch!" she advised. "The lady who owns it is an old dear. So she'll let me stay."

Nace drew on his pipe and ran a smoke plume into the upper part of the booth. His forehead, wrinkling, bunched the crimson snake scar. He thought for a minute.

"Hold the wire," he said.

"What?"

"I've got to see a man about a dog!"

He planted the instrument on the booth shelf, but did not hang up the receiver. Whipping out of the booth, he dived into a hallway and went up a flight of stairs four at a time.

He knew the newspaper phone P. B. X. operator was in an office on the same floor with the morgue. He had noticed the phone room door.

Rising on tiptoe, he gave a good imitation of floating as he went down the corridor. Nearing the frosted glass panel of the P. B. X. room, he ducked low, so his shadow would not show. He gave the knob a gentle try. It gave; the door swiveled in.

The phone girl looked around, gave him a forced, uneasy smile. Her lids shuttered up when she saw Nace's peculiar scar. The sight seemed to frighten her.

"Wh-what do you want?"

"A look at your board!" Nace told her.

The girl's jaw dropped. Her swivel chair squeaked as she spun. She reached both hands for the web of connecting cords on the P. B. X. board.

"None of that!" Lunging, Nace brushed her hands back.

The girl leaped up, mouth agape to scream. Nace plastered a

hand over her mouth and forced her back in the chair.

Slotted brass holders under each jack on the phone board bore designation cards. Nace examined these; he followed cords with his fingers. His inspection lasted at least a minute.

He frowned at the P. B. X. operator. The serpent on his forehead seemed to coil and uncoil, as the winkles came and went.

"You've got my connection cut in on an outside line," he pointed out grimly. "What's the idea?"

The girl shrank down into her chair. "You're crazy."

NACE SHOVED his telegram from the governor under her nose. She seemed reluctant to look at it.

"Read that!" he said harshly.

The girl read. She began to shudder. Her hands opened and shut like the paws of a stretching cat.

"Do you know that a murder accomplice can draw a life sentence?" Nace asked fiercely.

The girl spread her hands over her face and began to sob.

"Cough up," he commanded. "You're in a tough spot, kid."

The girl blubbered, "I didn't know it was anything very wrong. If I had I w-wouldn't have done it for fifty dollars a week."

"Who hired you?"

"A man I met at the dance."

"His name?"

"Chick Oliver."

Nace thought of the chicken-headed man who had taken the Robin Hood bullet between the eyes. "Was he a little, squatty guy with a long neck and a head like a chicken?"

"T-t-that's him!" stuttered the frightened operator.

"He was killed about twenty minutes ago!" Nace said ominously, knowing it would do no harm to frighten her a bit more.

She began to rock from side to side and whimper.

"What conversations were you to connect outside?" he asked.

"Anything for Mr. App!" she moaned. "Then, a little while ago, I got a call asking for anything you received."

"What number did you connect the calls to?"

She gave him a phone number, then quavered, "I h-h-hope I h-h-haven't done any harm!"

"Oh no!" he jeered. "You haven't done anything but nearly get me killed and get App kidnapped and probably murdered."

The girl rolled over so she could mash her features against the arm of her chair.

Nace trailed downstairs, grim faced. He found the city editor—a youngish man with too much belly—and asked, "Got a back number directory?"

The directory was produced. Nace looked up the number the girl had given him.

"Clarence Oliver," was the name which followed the number. The address was out on Eleventh. A high number! That meant it was far out.

NACE WENT back to the P. B. X. girl's cubby. He had remembered his interrupted conversation with Julia.

The phone operator still sobbed in her chair.

Nace put on her headset and snapped levers. He called, "Hello!" several times but received no reply. Julia had left the wire.

"Did you touch these connections?" he asked the operator.

She shook her head, and tears fell off her chin.

"Keep your trap shut about this!" Nace advised her. "Maybe it'll come out all right."

He now called the house from which Julia had talked. A pleasant-voiced old lady—she sounded like an old lady—answered him.

"The blonde girl?" the old lady echoed, seeming surprised. "Oh, two men came for her a minute ago, and she left with them."

Nace turned somewhat pale, the scar on his forehead got

proportionally redder. His eyes acquired a frightened look.

"Thank you!" he told the old lady in a thick voice and hung up.

A TAXI carried Nace out Eleventh. The machine travelled between forty and fifty, with the horn open. Eleventh was a mixed street. Scattered along it were small stores, greenhouses, root beer stalls, pig stands. There was an ice cream factory and oil-field tool concerns. They passed the Tulsa U. stadium.

Clarence Oliver's house was a little brick, very neat. The walk was of red concrete. There was a garage to the side, and a tennis court behind.

Watching both windows, Nace ran up the walk. He tried the door. It was locked. He batted the glass out with his fist, turned the spring lock inside and walked in.

The room was loaded with cheap brown furniture, bridge lamps, card tables, a radio. The rug was flowery. All the stuff looked new.

A faint odor reeked in the air. Nace sniffed. He breathed one word, "Oil."

Nace crossed the room, almost running. The hallway beyond was square; four doors opening off it gave to bath, kitchen and two bedrooms. Nace tried the bath. Nothing there.

He knocked open the end door and found himself in a kitchen, ornate with a white enamel. The oil smell was stronger here, mingling with cooking odors.

A man-sized bundle reposed on the floor, near one wall. It was swathed in canvas. Nace found as he worked over it that underneath the canvas were layers of oilcloth.

Four Winchester rifles had been tied into the bundle to give it stiffness. No doubt the men who had carried it here had wanted it to look rigid, as if it were a piece of furniture.

It was the body of a man. His color was white, parboiled; his clothing was oil-soaked. Nace looked at the face. It was almost unidentifiable. There was a wad of white hair, which might have been a beard which had slipped. A Santa Claus beard.

"App had that kind of a beard!" Nace muttered.

THEN HE fell to straining his ears. He could hear footsteps out in front, coming up the walk. He went silently to a window.

There were three of them, all strangers. They approached suspiciously.

Nace eased backward quietly and sidled into a bedroom. While the three newcomers tramped on the front porch, Nace worked at his sleeves. He wore cuff links which were oversize, long, and narrow. Under his prying fingernails, tiny secret lids opened in the links. He took out small darts.

The darts were but little larger than pins. The tapering rear ends bore tiny metal vanes to make them travel straight when thrown.

The three men entered the house with the noisy abandon of fellows who felt themselves at home.

"Things don't look natural around here without Chick!" one remarked.

"I'd like to know exactly what happened to Chick!" muttered another. "Did Nace get him? Or did the Robin Hood?"

"We'll find out from the evening papers!" grunted a third man. "What we've got to do now is get rid of old App's body."

They filed past the bedroom door.

Nace threw a pair of his darts in one-two succession. He flung them hard. The men jumped, clapped hands to their arms, swore. Then both reeled crazily and crashed full length on the floor.

Eyes popping, the third man stared at the first two.

"What the hell?" he began. "What ails—"

Nace lunged at him, hands outstretched, fingers splayed. A moment later they were entangled, and rolling on the floor. The man got a gun out of his clothing. Grasping the hand which held the weapon, Nace beat it against the floor. Squealing, the fellow lost his gun.

The next instant, the fellow had produced a knife. The suddenness with which he did this smacked of the supernatural. He struck—the blade *zinged* across the front of Nace's bulletproof vest, opening his clothing.

Nace fell on the knife and hand with his chest. The other was strong, and Nace's weight was not sufficient to pin him down. The man jerked free, sprang up.

There was only one thing Nace could do. He picked open the secret lid in one of his cufflinks, shook out a dart, and flung it. The other ducked wildly. But Nace had calculated on that. The dart thorned into the fellow's face.

Almost at once, the man crashed down.

Nace scowled at the recumbent form. He had not wanted to use that third dart. He had hoped to question one of the men. But now all three would be unconscious at least two hours. The darts were daubed with a drug which produced a stupor lasting that long. Nothing, as far as Nace knew, could revive the men before the two-hour interval was up.

Nace began searching his victims. He turned up money, keys, soiled handkerchiefs. After the fashion of crooks, they were carrying nothing which would identify them.

A coat pocket disgorged an object which caused Nace to spring erect and swear thickly. He turned the thing in his hand. It had an ugly significance. It could have come into the possession of these men in only one fashion—with the capture of its owner.

It was the girl's flat pancake compact.

CHAPTER V

The Hilltop Prowl

NACE RAN TO the telephone. The number he requested was the one from which the blonde had called—the
house at the foot of Reservoir Hill. The wait which followed
was so long that he began to think he was not going to get his
party. But the pleasant-voiced, elderly lady finally answered.

Nace asked for a description of the two men with whom
Julia had departed. In return, he received an accurate word
picture of two of the trio who lay unconscious in the room in
which he stood.

"Thank you!" he said, and hung up.

He bent over the three, shook them angrily, knowing however that it was useless. That they had seized the girl, there
was not the slightest doubt. But it would be two hours before
anything could be done toward making them tell where they
had taken her.

Nace went to the tennis court in the back yard. With his
pocket knife he stripped off the thin, strong cords which sup-
ported the net. Carrying these back into the house, he bound
the three senseless men. He tied efficient gags between their
jaws, then plastered these over with adhesive tape which he
found in the bathroom.

There was a small basement under part of the house. It held
only a gas-burning furnace. He left his prisoners there.

His taxicab was still waiting where he had left it a short distance up the street. He got in, perched tensely on the edge of

the cushion, and directed, "Reservoir Hill! And make it snappy!"

Reservoir Hill was a knob at the north of the Tulsa City limit. A zig-zagging drive climbed its abrupt slope. The top offered a birdseye view of Tulsa, and mansions clustered there.

Behind the hill was the Osage—a hilly wilderness of scrub oak, spotted with oil derricks and compression pumping stations and a small refinery or two.

Nace dismissed his cab at the top of the hill and went on afoot. There was the faint sound of oil wells pumping in the distance. The tang of crude hung faintly in the air. Nowhere in Tulsa did it seem possible to escape the odor of oil.

The mansions on top were even more magnificent than they had appeared from below. In architectural style they ranged from Spanish, Irish and old English, to American Colonial. The fact that they were expensive, and the grounds well maintained, kept them from seeming garish.

There were no sidewalks along the wide, smooth, concrete parkways. Nace walked in the road, keeping to the left. Street names were painted, in black and yellow panels, on the raised curbs. His eyes searched these.

When he found the one he wanted, he walked on as if it were of no consequence.

He still carried his canvas zipper bag. Indeed, the valise seemed to be out of his hands only when he was in action. He lugged it along instinctively, much as another man wears his hat.

Sheltered by an ornamental hedge, he lowered the bag, opened it, and took out a small but powerful telescope. He wielded this until he located the house to which Julia had trailed the Robin Hood.

Somewhere near, a voice purred, "So now you've turned peeping Tom!"

NACE'S FIRST reaction was to jump for cover. He did that. Concealed on the other side of the hedge, he scuttled twenty feet, then stopped.

The voice made hateful laughter. "Scared of little old Jaxon, Skipper?"

Nace angled south a few yards, then worked through the hedge. He found Jaxon hunkered down behind a squatty fir tree.

Jaxon returned Nace's blank look with an unpleasant smile. "So now I'm in your hair again!"

Nace glared. "Hell, but you're funny."

"Oh yeah?" Jaxon seemed to consider the insult. "I reckon I don't rate an explanation of why you're here."

Nace wrinkled the serpentine scar on his forehead. "I'm not quite sure what you rate."

Jaxon leered. "If you're wondering how I got the tip-off on this place, Skipper, I'll tell you! It was the phone girl. She listened in when your platinum-haired dame called you. Mighty slick, your sending the blonde on ahead! I didn't give you the credit."

"Why are you out here?" Nace asked him levelly.

"Didn't I just tell you? For the Robin Hood and the ten thousand reward on his head."

"Blood money, eh?"

"Any money is good money, Skipper—"

Nace flung out a hand and shoved. Sputtering angrily, Jaxon upset. Getting atop Jaxon, Nace clutched and got the little derringer from the oil editor's watch pocket.

Sitting up, Jaxon lashed out with two angry fist blows. Nace dodged the fists, vanishing from their path in a way that seemed uncanny.

"Gimme that owl head!" Jaxon said.

Ignoring the request, Nace told him, "You can either go back to town, or you can behave yourself and go with me."

Jaxon considered this, straightening his double-breasted gray vest with angry jerks. In getting the derringer, Nace had torn the watch pocket. Jaxon fingered the frayed edges.

"You couldn't get rid of me!" the oil editor said finally.

"Okay!" Nace told him. "But you make one crack-brained move and I'll crown you!"

"I'll get that ten thousand before this is over," Jaxon said grimly.

Nace opened his zipper bag to return the telescope. While he had the bag open, he removed four of his cigars, and pocketed them.

"I thought you smoked a pipe!" Jaxon grunted.

"What do you care what I smoke?"

They set off along the street, side by side.

The house to which Julia had trailed the Robin Hood was situated on a street a block to the right. They headed for it, cutting across yards and haunting the shelter of shrubbery.

The house was probably the most unattractive on the hill, but at the same time one of the largest. It was gray brick, squarish of line, rambling—not unlike a cluster of big gray boxes jammed together.

The body of the house had a height of two stories. Atop this sat a square room, the sides almost entirely of glass. These windows were not curtained, and Nace kept a close watch on them.

No one stirred. The absence of curtains lent the mansion a deserted aspect.

Jaxon whispered shrilly, "The Robin Hood may not be in there! He may have left!"

"Shut up!" Nace advised.

They crept up to within three-score feet on the house. There, behind a low, vine-covered fence of steel pickets, they reconnoitered. Using the telescope, Nace not only surveyed the house but also the yard and dwellings around them and behind.

To the rear, Nace saw something which caused him to start violently. However, he made an elaborate pretense and continued his survey of the surroundings.

Then he tapped Jaxon on the shoulder. "You're going back!"

"What the—"

"Don't argue! Beat it!"

Jaxon made an angry face. "If you think I'm gonna be left out in the cold on that ten thousand—"

Nace showed him a granite-hard fist. "You're going to be left cold on the ground if you don't do what I tell you."

Jaxon considered this; then, mumbling disgustedly, he crawled away.

He had covered no more than two dozen yards when the Robin Hood and his two followers popped out of bushes and seized him.

JAXON PUT up a violent struggle. He kicked, wielded his fists and tried to use his teeth. He sought to cry out, but a hand over his mouth stopped that.

Nace made no effort to go to his assistance, but merely looked on, as if it were all some drama he had staged. A swipe from a six-gun barrel finally reduced Jaxon to a limp pile.

The Robin Hood approached. His two followers came behind, dragging the oil editor.

Nace and the Robin Hood exchanged sour looks.

"You do the damnedest things!" growled the Oklahoma bandit.

"That's a matter of opinion!" Nace told him.

Diving out a quick hand, the Robin Hood searched Nace. He found the derringer which the private detective had taken from Jaxon.

"Hell!" he snarled, and tried to give Nace back the weapon.

Nace scowled, knocked at his hand. The derringer flew off in the shrubbery somewhere.

The Robin Hood sat back with a pained expression on his wolfish features.

"If I ever catch you with a gun in your hand, I'm going to

kill you dead!" he promised.

Nace replied nothing. In the eastern newspapers he had read of this fellow—and wondered how one man could garner such a reputation. Now that he was in contact with the Robin Hood, the answer was clear. The man had a code of honor and adhered to it. He was a character from the old, two-gun west, transplanted to 1933.

The Robin Hood shoved his wolf jaw out. "We're going in! There ain't nobody in there, but we'll go anyway! I want to talk to you."

They entered the house through a rear door which was unlocked and gave into a kitchen. The furniture, Nace noted, was swathed in dust covers. The place showed few signs of recent occupancy.

Jaxon was deposited on a divan. One of the Robin Hood's men went into the kitchen, ran water into his hat, came back, and doused the fluid on the recumbent oil editor.

"That bird's a neckpain," Nace said, indicating Jaxon. "Let's get out talk before he wakes up!"

"An idea!" The Robin Hood jutted his wolf face at Nace. "I want to make a deal with you, feller!"

Nace shrugged. "If the deal is to give you the name of the man behind this hot-oil business, when I find out who it is—nothing doing!"

The Robin Hood's long jaw lowered almost to his necktie. "How'd you know that was it?"

"What else could it be?" Nace spread his hands. "The man dead in the morgue is your brother. You're out to pay somebody for getting him."

"I'll be damned!" grunted the Robin Hood.

"That's what you came to the airport to see me about," Nace continued. "And you arranged the hotel trap in case you couldn't get to me at the airport. You did fix that hotel business, didn't you—leaving the note in the newspaper office for Jaxon?"

"Yeah!" the Robin Hood admitted. "Say—you're pretty sharp!"

Nace eyed him intently. "If you're not afraid of incriminating yourself, you can tell me some things."

The Robin Hood laughed harshly. "Say, feller, I ain't afraid of admittin' anything! If the law ever puts the shuck on me they've already got plenty to hang me! A little bit more won't hurt!"

Nace grinned. "You know, I'd kinda hate to see 'em get you, at that."

"To hell with what you think!" the Robin Hood scowled. "I'll blow your damned head off if I ever catch you with a gun! What do you want to know?"

"Have you been mixed up with this hot-oil ring?"

"Sure, I've been doing most of the dirty work." The wolf face became fiercer. "And I got it in the neck! The big boss is trying to hog the proceeds! I don't know who he is. I never have known!"

Nace waved his arm. "What about this house?"

"This is where the boss always met us. That is, he'd come and talk to us from one room, while we stayed in another."

CHAPTER VI

The Smoke Trap

NACE SQUINTED AT the Oklahoma badman, absently fingering the cigars in his pocket.

"Well, don't you believe me?" the man scowled.

"What difference does it make?" It was just as well, Nace reflected, to feed the fellow a little sass and keep him guessing. The Robin Hood might have likable qualities, but that did not mean he was a pleasant customer.

Should he get the idea Nace was no longer useful, he would be as likely as not to shove a gun in the private detective's hand and demand that they shoot it out, wild-west style. He was that kind of a character.

"I'm going to look around!" Nace said, and started for a door.

"I've already done that!" The Robin Hood scowled blackly. "You stick here!"

Nace pivoted. "You know that blonde girl?"

"Sure! And don't you go making cracks about her, shamus! She's a straight little number!"

"Don't I know it!" Nace said earnestly. "You don't, by any chance, know where she is?"

The Robin Hood hesitated. "I ain't seen her since we split up, after leavin' the Crown Block!"

"I thought so!" Nace's voice suddenly sounded old, weary. "She has disappeared! The lice working for the big brain back of the hot-oil ring grabbed her!"

The Robin Hood swore softly. "How d'you know that?"

That, Nace reflected, was something else to keep the fellow guessing. No good could come of letting the Robin Hood know that Julia was Nace's assistant.

Saying nothing, Nace passed through a door. He was cursed at, ordered to come back. He ignored profanity and summons, and began to search.

None of the upstairs rooms yielded anything. The glass-walled box of a room which sat atop the house was entirely bare of furnishings. There was a dust on the floor, a thin film. It was smudged and tracked where men, in the hours or days past, had crouched to watch the surroundings.

He ended up in the basement. This was very large, divided into several rooms—washroom, gym, billiard room, and a larger enclosure which held a furnace.

The furnace was an oil burner, and there was a fuel tank, almost as large as half a railway tank car.

It was very warm in the furnace room. Nace put a hand on the furnace. It was hot. He opened the doors. The fires were out. There was no room for anyone to have been concealed in the furnace.

He went over and started to climb upon the fuel tank, with the idea of peering in the manhole at the top. Instead of doing that, he sprang back, ran to the stairs.

"Come down here!" he called. "I've got something for you!"

There was no answer from above.

"Come here!" Nace repeated sharply.

No reply.

Nace climbed the stairs with long jumps, ran into the room where he had left Robin Hood Lloyd and his companions.

Jaxon glared at Nace over the twin blue snouts of a derringer.

"I'm gonna collect that ten thousand yet!" the oil editor gritted.

THE ROBIN HOOD and his two fellows had their hands at shoulder level. Their faces held fierce hate, and also wariness. The derringer held only two bullets. But that was enough to kill two men.

Waving his weapon to cover everyone, Jaxon sidled over and disarmed his prisoners.

"Jaxon—you nut!" Nace started forward.

"Get back!" Jaxon snarled. "I'd like nothing better than to sink lead into you!"

In a loud, wolf-howl of a voice, the Robin Hood said, "He had the hideout up his pants leg!"

"That's your hard luck!" Nace grunted. "You searched 'im—not me!"

"Shut up and plop down on your faces!" Jaxon ordered.

The Robin Hood's claw-like hands opened and shut. He exhibited all the signs of a man about to make a break.

"Go ahead—if you want to croak!" Nace told him, and lay his full length on the floor. "This lunk ain't foolin'! That ten thousand has got him crazy!"

Reluctantly, as if their joints were afflicted with a stiffness, Oklahoma's master outlaw and his two satellites followed Nace's example in flattening to the floor. They let Jaxon bind them.

When the job was done, Jaxon stepped back. His face was flushed, his eyes gleeful.

"Now to call a flock of cops!" he gloated.

He went to the telephone, picked up the receiver and listened. Making one of his faces, he flung away from the instrument. "Line's dead! Wires must be cut!"

He seized upon Nace's bag, stripped back the zipper, and peered inside.

"Regular bag of magic!" He leered at Nace. "I'll just take this along. I don't want you gettin' away and turnin' your buddies loose!"

He walked outdoors. The rear door slammed.

Nace sat up. Twisting, he managed to reach his left trouser leg with both hands. He grasped it at the cuff, one hand on either side of the seam, and made a tearing gesture. The seam pulled apart.

Six inches of thin hacksaw blade came out.

Jaxon had used wire clothesline for the binding. The hacksaw blade quickly cut through the bonds on Nace's ankles. He ran to the Robin Hood.

"Hold the blade!" he commanded. "I'll saw my wrists free!"

Eagerly, the bandit complied. It required perhaps a minute for Nace to loosen his hands. Twice, he gashed himself. Then he sprang erect.

"Now untie me!" growled the Robin Hood.

Nace laughed harshly. "Who said anything about untying you?"

The bandit snarled like a wolf in a trap. "Damn you! If I ever catch you with a gun, it'll be your finish!"

Ignoring the ominous promise, Nace glided to a window and looked out. There was no Jaxon. But the man had time to depart.

"Have you been watching this house all afternoon?" Nace asked the Robin Hood.

"Go chase yourself!"

"Have you? This is important!"

"Yeah—all afternoon!" the bandit admitted grouchily. "Why?"

"The blonde followed you here, and then disappeared. That proves she's not here—she couldn't have been brought in without you noticing."

"How come you know so much about that blonde?" the Robin Hood pondered.

WITHOUT ENLIGHTENING the puzzled outlaw, Nace dropped from a window and dived into shrubbery. He angled northeast. Reservoir Hill sloped down there with less abruptness.

Since it was the shag end of the hill, giving only a view of oil wells, a tank farm or two, and numerous long tin oil-well tool supply houses, there were no mansions.

Weeds grew profusely, and to the size of small trees. A single narrow drive, the concrete somewhat cracked, angled down the slope.

Nace ran along the road, eyes downcast. He was taking a long chance—or maybe it was not such a long chance, considering certain deductions he had made.

He soon found what he had hoped for—a car standing in the weeds a few yards from the seldom-used road. It was a limousine, large, the body custom made.

Nace went to it and looked in. It was empty.

"Julia!" he called.

An echo came back at him from the side of Reservoir Hill, but there was no answer. Nace walked a circle around the car, close to it at first, then more distant.

He found crushed weeds, more weeds which had been broken down, then straightened. A trail! He followed it a few yards.

Julia was tied in a ring around a small scrub oak tree—hands and feet lashed together in a ball. She was gagged with a handkerchief and copious quantities of adhesive tape, also blindfolded.

Nace freed her, helped her erect.

"What was it?" he demanded.

She began to describe the two men he had left unconscious in the little brick house out on Eleventh.

"Not that pair!" he said impatiently. "Or did they leave you here?"

"No," she said. "It was someone else—one man! But I was blindfolded! I can't tell you a thing about him!"

"O. K. It's back to town with you!" Nace cocked an eye at the sun. It was some slight distance above the horizon. "Better still, fog out to the airport and grab the Kansas City plane. One leaves in about half an hour!"

"Nix!" she said.

He scowled at her. "Are you gonna be contrary?"

"No!" she explained carefully. "I'm just not going to leave!"

He shrugged, then led the way back up the Hill. Julia bobbed along at his side. The wind stirred her blonde hair, and in brushing it out of her eyes, she pulled a handful where she could look at it. She grimaced, "If this stuff don't wash off—I'll be a sight!"

She was limping, stiffened as she was by being tied around the scrub oak.

"How'd you find me?" she demanded.

"By using the old bean. They had you, and they couldn't have taken you to their hangout, because the Robin Hood was watching. So they had to leave you somewhere. I took a chance on it being nearby."

"Do you know who's behind this?"

"Sure!" Nace told her. "But don't ask me who. So far, he's been too slick for me to prove anything!"

THE ROBIN HOOD and his two companions glared at them when they entered the rambling, blockish brick mansion. Nace had not gagged the trio. Outlaws that they were, they certainly would not yell for help.

The Robin Hood stuttered, "Who—what—for cryin' out loud!" Then he rolled over on his face and groaned loudly. It had dawned on him that the blonde was Nace's agent. He snarled, "If I ever catch you with a gun—"

Nace looked at the girl. "You heeled?"

She laughed. "Sure! They never found my hideout, and I had no chance to use it!"

Reaching under the patty of blonde hair on her nape—it

still retained some of its shape—she produced her tiny gun.

"O. K. Watch these cookies!" Nace gestured at the base-ment. "I'm going down and have a look. There's a furnace down there, and a fuel-oil tank. The outfit is rigged so that the oil runs though the furnace and is heated, boiler fashion."

The girl shuddered. "You mean—"

"That this is the joint where the victims have been drowned in oil—or boiled in oil, whichever way you want it."

She shuddered again. "What gets me is whatever suggested such a means of murder!"

"Simple! Hot oil! Get it? Anybody gets too close to the hot oil, and he gets cooked in the stuff! Every time one of those bodies was found, no one had any trouble understanding what was back of it!"

Nace descended the stairs, entered the furnace room and clambered upon the tank. He was wondering if there might not be a body in it. Apparently there was not.

The tank was so hot he could not bear his touch upon it. He perspired, not entirely from the heat; he was thinking of the boiled body in the house on Eleventh.

Concealed in a recess behind the tank were wires for lower-ing bodies into the boiling oil, and great bolts of oil cloth to bind the cadavers in afterward, and to spread upon the floor so that there would be no stains.

The cache was in a metal box which fitted in a niche that was disclosed when bricks were lifted out.

There was quite an armament with the other stuff—three army rifles, a half dozen automatics, sawed-off shotguns, and a machine gun. The latter was no diminutive Tommy, firing pistol cartridges, but a full-size weapon chambering long .30-calibre rifle slugs. It was a regulation military gun, air-plane type.

Nace was looking at it when the next development came.

"Nace!" the blonde called from above. "Watch out!"

NACE SCRAMBLED madly off the tank, carrying the machine gun. He ran for the stairs.

There was scuffling above. Before he came in sight of the stairway, he heard feet clattering down it.

Driving a hand inside his coat, Nace brought out one of the cigars. He clamped it between his teeth. Raking a match on a partition, he lighted the weed. He was puffing strongly when he came within sight of the stairs.

Blonde Julia stood on the steps. She was struggling, kicking. But she was held quite helpless by the man who was behind her, using her as a shield.

The man wore a long raincoat. His trouser legs were pulled up, so that only his hairy shanks showed below the raincoat. His features were entirely masked by two bandanas, one tied so that it hung behind, and the other in front, perforated with eyeholes. His hands were cased in cotton gloves. One held an automatic.

He pointed the weapon at Nace.

"Drop it!" His voice was hoarse, unreal—a disguised tone.

Meekly, Nace dropped the machine gun. He drew on the cigar and ran a plume of smoke from his nostrils.

"C'mon up here!" he was directed. "And get them hands up!"

Nace followed the orders to the letter.

The Robin Hood and his two satellites still lay on the floor, wired tightly. They glared, cursed in low voices.

"This is the big shot!" snarled the Robin Hood. "The guy who murdered my kid brother!"

"You had no business sending your kid brother punking around to find out who I was!" the masked man growled. Then to Nace, he snapped, "You get over against the wall!"

Nace backed until his shoulders were clamped to the wall. The cigar protruded stiffly from his teeth.

The masked man advanced, menacing Nace with the automatic, shoving the girl ahead of him. He slammed her against the wall, snarled, "You stay there! Behave, and you may live a few minutes longer."

Then he reached out to search Nace.

Nace blew smoke in his face.

The man cursed, straightened, and brought up a hand to knock the cigar out of Nace's teeth.

There was a loud crack. Sparks, tobacco, geysered from the end of Nace's cigar.

The masked man jabbed both hands convulsively in the air. He slanted stiffly backward, as if his heels were hinged to the floor. In his forehead, on the right side, but where it had penetrated the brain, was a circular hole somewhat more than an eighth of an inch across.

He crashed his length on the floor, hitting so hard that his heels flew up, then banged back.

Nace took the remains of the cigar out of his teeth, pinched out flaming shreds of tobacco, and pocketed it. The firing barrel inside the cigar, chambered for a .22-long-rifle cartridge, was expensive. Another cigar could be built around it. The thing was fired by a hard pressure of the teeth.

Stooping, Nace started to strip off the mask. Then he hesitated, eyed the girl, and asked, "Want to bet that I can't name him?"

She shuddered. "Don't be dramatic!"

He shucked off the mask.

The cherubic, Santa Claus features of Ebenezer App, white beard and all, were disclosed.

THE ROBIN HOOD, rearing up from the floor, cried out, "For yellin' out loud! The last hombre on earth that I suspected!"

"Sly old duck—he was!" Nace said grimly. He looked at the Robin Hood. "He owes his downfall to you!"

The bandit glared. "You're nuts! I didn't even suspect—"

"Maybe not! But it was your finagling around with me when I first got here that started App worrying. He thought I smelled a rat, because I hadn't reported to him. He decided to fake his own death and clear out, I guess.

"Probably that body on Eleventh Street is one of his own men who was about his build. He dumped the fellow in oil, then took him out and bundled some white whiskers in with the body."

Julia walked to the door and outside. She didn't like to look at dead men. She called back, "But you said you suspected who it was?"

"Sure!" Nace grunted. "When App told me over the phone that he knew who was behind the hot-oil business, he wouldn't say who it was. That was queer. It occurred to me that the old goat just wanted me to hurry over and find out he was kidnapped!"

Swinging over, Nace began untying the Robin Hood and his two men.

"What're you going to do?" snarled the bandit.

"Let you go bye-bye! You did save my life, you know!"

The Robin Hood purpled. "By hell, I wish I'd let the guy slug you with his shotgun when he looked under the flivver! I like you less than any guy I ever saw!"

"Just a pal!" Nace jeered.

"If I ever catch you with a gun, I'm gonna kill you!" the Oklahoma outlaw yelled.

In the distance somewhere, a police siren was wailing. That would be Jaxon and his policemen.

Leaving the bandit and his two men to get to their feet and finish untying themselves, Nace went to the body of Ebenezer App. He searched briefly—found a twin to the automatic which the man carried and dropped when he died. Nace picked up both guns.

He examined the weapons. Both were clipped full of cartridges.

He tossed one to the Robin Hood.

The bandit caught it. He stared, surprised. "What the—"

Nace rapped angrily, "You've been shooting off that mouth about what you'd do if you ever caught me with a gun! Well—"

"You're askin' for it!" the outlaw ripped. He jutted the gun at Nace.

There was a terrific roar—two shots, almost one, but with a slight stutter which marked a shade in timing.

The Robin Hood squawled. He waved his gun hand madly over his head. It was mangled, and scattered scarlet drops over walls and ceiling.

His automatic skittered along the wall behind him.

Without a word, but with an expression of agonizing chagrin on his wolf face, the Robin Hood whirled and dived through a window. His two men followed him. Running rapidly, they were soon lost to sight.

Nace went to the door.

Blonde Julia gave him a disapproving frown.

"Dramatics!" she snapped. "Some day, that stuff is going to be your finish!"

Nace pretended he hadn't heard, and watched a police phaeton moan up the hill and careen into the drive. Dapper Jaxon sprang out, along with numerous policemen. The oil editor was like a peacock hen with a brood of blue chicks.

"Hot after his ten thousand!" Nace said dryly. "Speaking of dramatics—you're gonna hear 'em when he finds his bird had flown!"

The Flaming Mask

The Chicago World's Fair had a new and amazing attraction—a red-hot meteor. Buried in this molten mausoleum was a man's skull, and a square-cut diamond. The papers played it up as an unlucky planet dweller hurled earthward to doom. But Lee Nace, ace detective, doubted that star dwellers wore square-cut diamonds—and he went out to take a look for himself. It was then that he came face to face with—the flaming mask.

CHAPTER I

The Hell Heat

THE ALLEGED METEOR fell slightly after midnight. The morning papers carried a story about it. The item was interesting. But it was not half as arresting as the astounding and horrible discovery which was made a bit later.

Agency Detective Lee Nace read the papers that morning. There was also a short double paragraph about himself. It was on the front page, and said Nace, renowned sleuth whom Scotland Yard had once kept in England for a time as consultant, had stopped off in town to see the Century of Progress. The meteor item was on an inside page.

Nace clipped the bit about himself, filed it in a brief case. That kind of publicity was good for his business.

The alleged meteor was taken to the Century of Progress grounds for exhibition. That afternoon, a scientist put it under a powerful X-ray. What he saw caused the scientist's eyes to pop. He called wildly to his associates.

A portion of a human skull was embedded in the upper part of the supposed meteor. Inside the skull were what appeared to be brains, thoroughly cooked.

In the lower portion of the meteor was a diamond. The gem was cut with large facets, a setting from a ring, perhaps.

The skull was that of a man.

Nace went out to look. No one invited him. Nobody paid him. He was simply interested in unusual murders. This looked like one.

Of course, the newspaper scribes wondered—in front page print—if the meteor was not a fallen star, and the skull that of an unlucky dweller on the planet. Nace doubted that star dwellers wore square-cut diamonds.

The alleged meteor was a tub-sized blob of metal. Its surface was bulbous, pocked, and vaguely remindful of distorted pictures of the moon. The scientists were uncertain just what kind of metal it was.

The meteor had been found in swanky Lincoln park. It had given off a great, white-hot light which had emblazoned the apartment houses facing the park. It was still red-hot when

"You four," said the man grimly, "are gonna
be another added attraction at the Fair."

they found it.

Some persons claimed they had seen it flash across the sky. These individuals became doubtful when pressed for details. Maybe it had not blazed through the heavens, they admitted.

The scientists, at the suggestion of the police, decided to drill in and get the diamond.

Nace stood and watched.

"So this is the way we're going to spend our time at the Century of Progress!" complained Julia.

Julia was Nace's read-headed assistant. She was stunning in gray sports frock and tiny hat. She carried a large pancake compact, the new type. She might have been a society deb.

"This may be something for us," Nace told her.

"Who's going to pay us?" Julia was highly commercial. "Since when did we start working for nothing?"

"Was anything said about you hanging around?" Nace demanded. "Drag your skirt out of here and look at the fair."

Julia hung around. She kept away from Nace, and pretended elaborately not to know him.

THEY CORE-DRILLED the diamond out about dark. The gem was taken into a private room to be put under microscopes. Three policemen accompanied the two experts who were to do the examining.

Nace tried to get in. The sergeant in charge of the cops apparently did not like private detectives. He refused to let Nace be present.

Nace went to a phone booth nearby and called the head of the Chicago police. That worthy requested that police sergeant be put on the wire, and he would damn well see that Nace was present at proceedings.

Nace started to get the sergeant.

Then things happened.

Over where the remnant of the meteor lay, there was a terrific, white-hot glare. Nace tried to stare at the spot. It was as if he had been in a darkened room, and had suddenly sought to peer into the eye of a powerful searchlight. He was blinded.

Men and women screeched in fright and agony. There was a panic-stricken rush from the spot.

Nace felt a wave of heat against his face. It was if a welding torch had been held a few inches from his features. He spun and ran with the others. But he veered to the right as he did so. The room where they were inspecting the diamond was over there.

The angle of a wall cut him off from the terrific glare. But even the reflected blaze of the hellish light ached his eyes.

He made small caverns over his eyes with his hands, peering through the thin flesh where his long, bony fingers rested together. So incredibly brilliant was the luminance that it went through his palms as though tablet paper. Sunlight never equaled it.

He reached the door of the room which held the diamond.

The door burst open. Behind it was another white-hot glare. It was as if the lid of Hades had been shoved ajar.

The three cops plunged out. The two scientists trailed them. They slammed the door.

Nace put a palm against the door, with the idea of shoving it open again. But it was so hot that he wrenched his hand away. The plywood began to smoke. Paint curled off.

Who-o-sh! The door burst into flame.

Nace retreated.

The other glare was subsiding rapidly. Nace approached it, eyes shaded.

The meteor was glowing with an awful heat. It lay in a pit it had melted in the floor. It had rested on a metal table. Molten metal from the table and liquidized sand from the concrete poured down the side of the pit.

It was impossible to approach within twenty feet of the spot. Modernistic fittings all about were smouldering or blazing. Smoke was filling the great exhibition buildings.

Backing away, Nace shook his head rapidly. On his forehead, a small patch of scarlet flushed out and rapidly assumed a definite form. The mark had been unnoticeable heretofore.

The crimson blotch had the shape of a coiled serpent—an adder. A Chinaman had once hit Nace on the forehead with the hilt of a dagger which bore the carving of a coiled snake. He was destined to carry the scar. It was garishly noticeable under the shock of blond hair. It came only when he was angry or puzzled.

He was puzzled now. He had never before seen such infernal heat as this.

There was another thing which worried him. Red-headed Julia was nowhere in sight.

EMERGENCY FIRE apparatus arrived and extinguished the blazing parts of the exhibition building. Great clouds of steam poured from the supposed meteor. It cooled enough that it could be examined.

It was put under the X-ray again. The human skull was no longer discernible. It had melted into nothingness by the amazing heat.

The diamond was found to be missing from the room where it had been taken for examination.

Nace collared one of the scientists who had been making the inspection.

"I don't know what happened!" the man groaned, and wiped his forehead. "We were just starting to inspect the stone, and there was a blinding light in the ceiling. We looked up. All hell seemed to be coming through the plaster. The light was so bright we couldn't tell what it was. We ran!"

Nace prowled a little. He found one of the strange meteor-like lumps of metal in a self-melted pit in the floor. Its heat, he concluded, had been terrific enough to dissolve the diamond!

Most of the ceiling was gone. The room above, he found, had been one used only for storage.

Nace said nothing. But he thought a lot. The skull in the meteor and the diamond had been evidence. By striking twice, the hellish heat, whatever it was, had wiped out both skull and diamond.

With a hammer, Nace knocked off a hunk of the strange, clinker-like metal. He borrowed a microscope from an optical concern exhibit, some chemicals from another display, and retired to a theatre where television shows were given periodically. It was not show hour and the theatre was empty.

Nace was something of a scientist himself. He set to work making an analysis, applying various acids and watching the resulting reactions.

The adder scar became even more pronounced on his forehead as he proceeded. The first half dozen tests had gotten him nowhere. The job was going to take some time.

He pocketed the bit of clinker, went out and circled for some minutes through the crowds. There was much excitement. Gaunt and blond, only a little under seven feet in height, Nace skirted the throng, threaded its center.

Red-headed Julia, his assistant, was still nowhere in evidence.

NACE RETURNED to the television theatre. He moved his microscope and chemicals to the projection booth behind the screen. There was more privacy in the booth. He turned out the other lights.

Before resuming his task, he crumpled twenty or thirty advertising pamphlets he found on a table and strewed them along the aisles of the darkened theatre.

He was back in the booth, applying a chemical mixture to the meteor fragment when he heard one of the paper balls crackle. Someone had stepped on it.

Nace had planted the paper in hopes it would give him just such a warning.

His eyes roved, came to rest on a spool of fine insulated wire. He seized the wire and tied the end to the neck of a small chemical bottle. This he placed in the glass bowl in which he was mixing ingredients.

He tweaked the wire. This caused the bottle to rattle in the bowl, giving off a tinkling sound, as if chemicals being mixed.

He eased out of the booth. From time to time, he tugged the wire, which he unspooled as he backed away. Glassy jingles came from the booth each time he yanked. From the noise, the prowler would think he was still at work.

Someone had spotted his lone-wolf investigations. He was not displeased. Such a possibility had been in his mind when he went about them so openly.

Nace circled warily in the darkness, found an aisle and eased down it, still unspooling his wire. He felt out the location of his crumpled paper balls and carefully avoided them.

From time to time, he gave the wire a gentle jerk. The bottle in the bowl tinkle-tinkled.

He listened carefully. No sound—except the bottle in the bowl.

He crept toward the door, ears aching from the strain of listening. At the entrance, the nearness of the light switch intrigued him. He considered, put a hand on the switch, hesitated, tinkled his bottle in the bowl. Nothing happened.

He turned on the lights.

No one was in the television theatre.

Absently, Nace fished a pipe out of a pocket. It was stubby, with a big bowl. He clamped it in his teeth. He liked to bite on something when the going got bewildering or tough.

He snapped at the pipe stem—surprise made his teeth set hard, so hard the tough Bakelite broke like gravel.

Something grisly, blinding was happening to the ceiling over the projection booth. It was dissolving, a white-hot, sudden flash, as if it were so much ignited flashlight powder.

He saw a great ball of incandescence swoop downward upon the booth. Heat that seared like flame washed against his face. His eyes pinched shut involuntarily. He heaved around, shouldered through the door.

The hell heat had struck at his life, coming from above, from one of the rooms overhead.

A thought struck him. He spun back, flat on the floor, eyes closed. He crawled a few feet. His hands, groping, gathered in balls of the crumpled paper. He carried them back outside.

The outer exhibit rooms, brilliantly lighted by electronic bulbs, seemed in a twilight after that terrific glare in the television theatre. He brought the paper wads close to his eyes, peered at them.

None were flattened, as they would have been had someone

had stepped on them.

A FRESH uproar seized the vast exhibit as the new blaze was discovered. Fire apparatus, still on hand from the other two fires, charged the spot.

Nace worked left, mounted stairs. Smoke rolled like living, smudged masses of cotton. He waded through it. The exhibit rooms upstairs were deserted, sucked clean of their throngs by the previous excitement below.

The room above the television theatre booth was occupied by an exhibit of surgical instruments. A vast hole in the center, over the booth, glowed with intense heat.

Nace tapped a coat pocket. The fragment he had chipped from the clinker of strange metal reposed there. He went downstairs again, ducking aside as a fire hose flung spray in his direction. He had an idea what they would find in the projection booth—another of those strange clinkers.

He circled through exhibition rooms, his pace rapid, uneasy. His unusual height enabled him to peer over heads.

He saw no trace of red-headed Julia.

He found a phone, put in a call to his hotel.

"Anyone left word there for Lee Nace?" he asked the girl on the phone board.

"A young lady telephoned a few minutes ago," he was told. "A young lady who gave her name as Julia."

"She leave a message?"

"Yes. She said she would be in the room which holds the diamond exhibit at the Century of Progress grounds."

Nace hung up. He produced a guide book, scraped a finger nail down the list of exhibitors, and found the location of the structure which held the diamond display. It was down the midway a short distance.

CHAPTER 11

The Scared Man

THE ROOM WAS big, done in modernistic metals and woods. The paint scheme was brilliant.

In the center stood a metallic looking block. It was several feet square, perhaps waist high. Atop it was a glass case—the diamond exhibit case.

There was a diamond in the case worth three hundred thousand dollars. There were others almost as valuable. The case was fitted with tear gas. The glass was bulletproof. The gem display would drop automatically into a safe the instant the bulletproof glass was assaulted. Or so a printed sign said.

People milled about, staring at the brilliants, pressing faces against the cases to read the identifying cards. The Century of Progress show was so vast that the three appearances of the mysterious and frightful white-hot flame had not drawn spectators from the diamond exhibit.

Nace lounged in, slouching so that his height would not draw attention.

Julia was across the room, showing interest in a sample of the blue ground from which diamonds were taken. She was very pretty. She was getting, from nearby men, more attention than the diamond exhibit.

Nace produced his stubby pipe. The stem was ruined where he had bitten it. He dug an extra stem from a flat case which held several. Ruining stems was a habit of his; he carried spares always.

He stoked the bowl with tobacco, applied a match. Smoke crawled from his lips. Long puffs; short ones! A close observer might have perceived they were spelling words in the Morse dot-and-dash code.

"What's up?" he asked with the smoke puffs.

The red-head lost interest in the sample of blue ground. She flipped open her flat pancake compact and went to work on her complexion. There was a bright light over the blue ground exhibit. The compact mirror caught this and tossed a reflected dab of luminance against the ceiling. It winked dots and dashes as the powder puff covered and uncovered the mirror.

"Over in the northeast corner—the man who looks scared," she transmitted.

Nace removed his pipe, pretended to inspect the bowl. His gaze went on to the scared man.

The fellow was somewhat taller than Nace, which made him not many inches under seven feet. He had a small face, an enormous gray moustache. His dwarf features seemed bunched back of the big moustache. The rest of him was a collection of bones in a well-tailored sack.

His eyes held fear. They roved. His hands strayed nervously. His gaze went frequently to the diamond case, but seemed interested not in the contents, but in the crowd around about.

"O. K.," Nace puffed, measuring smoke carefully through his lips. "What about him?"

"I saw him acting queer when the big blaze first hit in the other building," Julia heliographed with her compact mirror. "I tailed him here. He's got something on his mind."

"You've been watching him all the time?"

"Sure."

"He didn't have a try at scragging me in the television theater?"

"He hasn't been near any television theater!" Julia looked worried. "Has somebody been after you?"

"They've been messing around. Keep your eyes open."

Nace walked over to the man who was scared. He cupped a palm under the fellow's right elbow. The gesture looked friendly. Actually, it placed Nace in a position to block any effort the man might make at drawing a gun.

"Some trouble, brother?" Nace asked.

THE MAN looked around, down. His eye stuck out a little. He began to tremble. He said nothing.

Nace tugged gently. In a dazed way, the man let himself be guided out of the press around the diamond case. Nace stopped him near a stand that sold an orange drink.

A girl in an orange-colored dress operated the stand. She was big-boned, but not hard to look at. She wore orange-hued earrings.

She came up, asked, "Two?"

Nace nodded, dropped two dimes on the marble and she set out two glasses.

The bony man was studying Nace nervously. He did not touch the orange drink.

The girl in the stand withdrew to the far end. She was fully fifteen feet distant. There was noise in the exhibition room—the conglomerate jumble of voices, loudspeakers, music somewhere.

Only if Nace raised his voice, could the girl overhear.

Nace produced his agency badge, displayed it.

The man trembled more violently, muttered, "The police!"

"What're you worried about?" Nace questioned.

"I'm not worried!" the man retorted, and shivered. "I don't know what you're talking about!"

"Better spill it!"

The man swallowed rapidly, said nothing.

Nace, deciding the fellow was about to walk off, reached out and took him firmly by the elbow.

"I'm not a cop," he explained. "I'm a private detective."

The man braced himself, scowled. "Leggo me, or I'll hand you something for your jaw!"

"My business is helping people out of trouble," Nace told him. "You look like a customer."

"My looks deceived you, then!" snapped the man.

Jerking, he got loose. He spun and walked rapidly away, eyes staring straight ahead.

Nace glowered after him. On Nace's forehead, the serpentine scar came out like something faded in by a concealed color camera.

Across the room, red-headed Julia made an impish mouth over her compact.

Nace, drawing deeply on his pipe, let out smoke in dots and dashes.

"Follow that monkey," he directed.

Julia closed her compact, started away, then turned back abruptly and seemed to find something of renewed interest in the blue ground display.

The scared man had wheeled and was returning.

He stopped in front of Nace, looked about uneasily. No one was close. The girl with the orange dress and orange earrings was still at the other end of the stand. She seemed half asleep.

The frightened man's voice was a wispy whisper.

"Can I talk to you and be sure it won't get to the police?" he demanded.

NACE SUCKED deeply on his pipe. The bowl gurgled, hissed, popped faintly. "That depends."

The other wet his lips. "Depends on what?"

"On whether I think the cops ought to have you or not."

The man looked at the adder scar on Nace's forehead. "But how can I tell—"

"You can't!"

The other squirmed, swiped nervously at his big gray moustache. Facial expression said he was making up his mind.

"I've got to take the chance!" he gulped at last. "I've got to do something! I thought of going to the police! I really did! But after that—after what happened to that thing they thought was a meteor, I didn't dare. They might not have—well, er-r—"

"Quite understood, eh?"

"That's it."

"What mightn't they understand?"

"It's horrible! So very horrible!" The man was becoming excited. He came closer; his face was almost against Nace's. "Tell me, did they get a close enough look at that diamond to identify it? I mean—enough of a look that the jeweler who sold it would recognize the gem?"

"No."

The man was perspiring. "That's too bad! Too awfully bad! I was in hopes the police would get a clue to the man's identity!"

Nace nodded as if he understood everything. "What's this all about?"

The fellow peered narrowly at Nace. "Maybe I had better go to the police with this, after all! It's big! So very big! And ghastly!"

"You'd better let me be the judge about the police!"

The man glanced to right and left, behind him. "They may be around here! I think I saw two of them a minute ago!"

"Two of who?"

The bristling gray moustache came so close that it almost touched Nace's face.

"Would you believe me if I told you there was a gigantic plot underfoot?" the fellow demanded. "A plot to steal millions! A plot which even includes the theft of the diamonds in this very room! But it won't stop there! They have that devilish stuff—the hell heat! It will melt the strongest bank vault as a blow torch melts butter. It will consume the bodies of men, and leave not a trace!"

"It left a trace last night," Nace pointed out. "There was a human skull and a setting from a ring embedded in that supposed meteor."

The man squirmed. "They didn't use enough of it! They were inexperienced. But they know how much to use now. They are liable to be here any time, after these diamonds—"

The girl in the orange-drink stand had been watching—although she was certainly out of earshot. Now she came forward, with a cat speed and silently.

A pepper shaker stood beside a basket of oilpaper-wrapped sandwiches. She scooped this up, twisted it open, dumped the contents in the palm of her left hand.

Leaning far out, she gave Nace a swipe across the eyes with the hand which held the pepper.

NACE CLAPPED both hands over his eyes. The girl had been behind him; had taken him by surprise.

He bent double and lunged violently away from the spot. He heard the orange-stand girl rap excited words.

"C'mon, tall boy!" she called, evidently to the man to whom Nace had been talking. "You and me are going places!"

"I don't understand!" gulped the tall man's voice. "Who are—"

"Clam up! C'mon!"

That was all Nace heard. There was no pepper in his eyeballs; he had closed his lids in time. But flakes crammed the tiny wrinkles in his lids and clung to the skin. He dared not open his eyes, or they would begin smarting.

A drinking fountain stood down a passage and around a corner. He had spotted it on his way here. It was a tribute to his sense of direction when he bumped blindly into it.

The fountain, like many others about the Century of Progress grounds, was one which started flowing automatically when one bent over it. The mechanism held a photo-electric cell which caused the water to go on when blanketed by the head-shadow of a drinker.

Nace bent over it. Water gushed against his face, a chill stream. He brushed his face from side to side, washing off the pepper.

Back in the diamond exhibit room, he could hear no undue excitement. Perhaps the pepper throwing incident had passed unnoticed.

Nace washed violently. The delay irked him. But it was necessary. If he did not get all the pepper off, it would be minutes before he could see.

He debated. The girl in the orange stand—obviously she wasn't what she seemed. But how had she known he was about to get the tall man to tell what he knew?

The pepper all removed, Nace straightened, spun and barged back into the tall man with the moustache.

Nace roved his eyes.

Julia, his red-haired aide, was also gone.

The eerie flush of a serpent glowing redly on his forehead, Nace elbowed for the exit nearest the orange-drink stand. The case of diamonds was a scintillating blaze. A fat man, staring at them, jeered, "I wonder if anybody is sucker enough to think these are the McCoy?"

Nace went on. The gems were real enough. The fat man was fooled by the case. It was as near thief proof as science could make it, but it looked innocent as a cigar case in a corner drugstore.

Reaching an exit, Nace stopped. From where he stood, it was possible to see some several thousand people. Loudspeakers mouthed on poles along the midway, the announcer describing a boat race in the lagoon. No one seemed interested. To the south, an artificial dinosaur in an oil company exhibit was wagging its head and tail and emitting bizarre roars.

The tall man, the girl from the orange stand, red-headed Julia—none were in sight.

Nace, hearing faint movement behind him, stepped sidewise and pivoted. Two men who had been about to grasp his elbows from behind clutched empty air and looked foolish.

"What's the idea?" Nace demanded sharply.

BOTH MEN were stocky, thick. Their combined weight would total near four hundred pounds. The day was hot; not twenty men in sight wore coats. These two wore theirs.

Each dropped a hand to his right hip, under his coat tail.

"Behave yourself, and you won't get hurt!" one growled.

Nace jutted a long, scowling face at them. "You guys try to pull a circus on me and I'll make somebody think he got hurt! What's the idea?"

"We're the law!" grunted one.

"Police detectives!" echoed the other.

"So what?"

"We want to know what happened in there. What's up?"

"Search me!"

"Cough up! We saw you pullin' some kind of an act inside. You gotta explain that, or we'll throw your pants into the can on suspicion."

Moving slowly so as not to excite the pair into using their guns, Nace drew his agency badge and displayed it.

"Private shamus, huh?" one muttered. "What's your name?"

"Lee Nace."

The two swapped sharp glances. They had heard of Nace. That was not surprising. He was one of the most widely known private operatives in the country. Scotland Yard had even brought him to England for a time in a consulting capacity. Magazines of national circulation carried his articles on criminology.

"Well, Nace, what happened inside?"

"I was talking to a guy and a dame in an orange stand smeared pepper into my eyes. Then her and the guy went off together, I guess."

"Who was the guy?"

"I don't know."

"Why was you talkin' to 'im?"

"He looked scared."

The two again traded looks. They made displeased faces.

One grunted, "That sounds thin! You'd better come and tell it to the sarge!"

Nace gritted, "Now listen—"

"There ain't no use arguin' with us! We got orders to snap up any suspicious characters around the diamond exhibit. And you fit!"

"I haven't the slightest idea—"

"Nix!" One grasped Nace's arm on either side. "Let's ankle!"

Through his teeth, Nace said, "A cop—always my pal!" He let himself be led away.

They took the center of the midway. On either side, modernistic exhibit buildings reared. An autogyro pulling a long aerial advertising sign had joined the two dirigibles overhead. Barkers cried their wares, not in the old-time carnival style, but through vacuum tube amplifiers and loudspeakers. Two men, dressed exactly alike in white-trousered military uniforms and carrying small hand sprayers went past arm in arm—advertisement for a fly spray.

Nace started to veer right. The pair tugged him back.

"The Exposition police headquarters is over here," Nace objected.

"Sure it is! But we're takin' you to the city station!"

THEY WORKED through the crowds. Possibly half the men carried souvenir canes. Four out of every five walked gingerly, on tired feet. Parties of four and six were frequent—family groups.

Benches in the shade were crowded; those in the sun were deserted. The announcer at the loudspeaker had finished the boat race and was telling the throngs what a great thing the Century of Progress was. An old man and an old lady sat on a bench in the shade, both with their shoes off.

They came to the turnstiles at an exit, hipped their way through, Nace in the center. They dodged traffic across a street.

There was a parking lot ahead, long, rowed with thousands of cars.

"We've got an iron in here," offered one of the men.

Nace said nothing. His long face was placid, but the serpentine scar was like a design done with ocher.

A parking lot attendant took a check one of them presented, then guided them down an alley of cars. He came to a large coupe, snatched a duplicate tag off the radiator, then wheeled and walked away. He did not look back.

"Get in!"

Nace, opening the coupe door, kept his eyes downcast. He could see the shadows of his two companions on the ground.

One of them was lifting a hand above Nace's head. The fist gripped a gun.

Nace, from the shadow, calculated how the blow would fall. He shifted his gaunt frame slightly—took the smashing swing of the gun barrel directly atop his head.

He sprawled down on the running board, slid from there to the ground, and lay motionless.

CHAPTER III

The Heat

"THAT'S KISSIN' 'IM, Shack!" chuckled one of the two men.

Shack laughed fiercely. "Feel of his wrist, Tubby, and see if he needs another one!"

Stooping, Tubby laid the tips of stubby fingers against Nace's wrist. "Hell! He's still tickin'!"

Shack elbowed closer. "I'll hand him one alongside the temple! That'll do the job!"

"Hey, wait! Hadn't we better ask 'im some questions?"

"What for?"

"Hell! To find out how much he knows!"

"Nix!"

"But maybe the cops are wise! We can tromp this bozo until he tells us whether they are or not! Then we'll know whether it's safe to go ahead with the big idea!"

"Waste of time!" Shack jeered. "This Nace don't know nothin'! He just saw Canadan actin' jittery an' started to talk to 'im! Move over! I'll fix Nace!"

"But that dame who snatched Canadan after she throwed pepper in Nace's eyes! For cryin' out loud! Who was she? Where'd she take Canadan? What was her idea?"

"Will you move over an' let me swing this Roscoe?"

"But that orange-stand dame—"

"She ain't our worry! We had orders to get rid of Nace.

T'hell with the dame! She'll be taken care of!"

"Oh, all right!" Tubby sidestepped to give Shack room to swing his weapon. Suddenly his arms flew up. They wind-milled. Tilting over, he slammed into Shack. Off balance, they both sprawled down in the narrow space between the parked cars.

Nace came to his feet. He still held Tubby's ankles, which he had grasped. He lifted on the ankles, elbows braced close to his side. When he had Tubby dangling off the ground, he angled a leg around expertly and knocked a heel against the fellow's temple. Tubby became slack.

Grunting with the effort, Nace heaved Tubby atop Shack. He fell upon the pile the pair made, spearing expert blows with a bony fist.

Shack fired his gun. The bullet squealed off under cars and caused a tire to blow out somewhere with a bang almost as loud as the shot itself.

Nace grasped the gun hand, succeeded in gouging the bar-rel into the ground. It went off again. The earth closed the barrel end, and the powder gases, backed up, split the cylinder open, rendering the weapon useless.

Tubby began to squirm, reviving. His weight still held Shack down. Nace, braced atop the pair, burrowed teeth into his coat sleeve and yanked out his shirt cuff. A wrench of his teeth tore the cuff entirely off.

The links in the cuff were rather large, elongated. His fin-gers found a catch in one, opened it. A small lid flew up. Two tiny darts dropped out.

Scooping the darts up, Nace jabbed one into Shack, the other into Tubby.

The struggle went out of both men. They seemed to go soundly asleep. They would remain thus for perhaps two hours, thanks to the drug contained in the tips of the diminu-tive darts.

Nace heaved both men in the rear compartment of the

coupe and locked them in.

Getting behind the wheel, he used Shack's keys on the ignition and drove out of the parking lot. He saw the attendant peeking out of a sedan in which he had taken concealment at sound of the fight.

Nace turned down a side street, hit Michigan Avenue and wheeled right.

Reaching up, he removed his entire thatch of blond hair. It was attached to a rubber-padded steel skull cap. He wiped perspiration from his close-cropped natural hair, which was of a hue which exactly matched that of the wig.

He replaced the steel-lined wig. When Shack had struck him down, the thing had saved him, not only from unconsciousness, but from almost certain death.

NACE PARKED the coupe in front of a little hotel in the loop district. He did not examine the pair in the rear. To do so might attract attention. The streets were crowded. Cracks in the floor boards would admit air enough for the pair, anyway.

Entering the hotel, Nace got his key and went to his room on the ninth floor. Up until he entered the room, he moved as if in a great hurry; but once inside, all his bustle departed. He sat down by the telephone, stoked his pipe, waited.

Minutes dragged. Nace killed time by looking for the name of Canadan in the telephone directory. Canadan, of course, had been the name of the tall man with the enormous gray moustache. There was no Canadan listed.

The phone rang.

Nace swept up the instrument. "Shoot, baby!"

"My, oh my!" Julia said sarcastically. "By chance, you weren't camped there by phone pining away for my dulcet voice—"

"Cut it out!"

"Go ahead! Bite me!"

"I'll tear your arms and legs off if you don't start telling things! This is big! That Canadan was on the point of—"

"That the tall one who hides behind the gray cookie duster?"

"Sure. He was just opening up when that orange-stand girl pulled her act."

Julia's voice became businesslike. "I trailed that girl from the orange-drink stand. She took this Canadan along. He didn't seem to want to come. I think she put a gun in his back."

"What'd you learn?"

"Not much, except that they like to ride the taxicabs. They went up and down Lincoln Park. They stopped once and got out. They went over to where a little crowd stood, then came back and got in their hack."

"What was the crowd?"

"A bunch rubbering at the spot where that meteor fell last night. The thing melted a big hole in the ground where it hit."

"That wasn't any meteor."

"Well, I've guessed as much. But do you know of a better name to call it?"

"I'm not sure what the dang thing is," Nace admitted.

"They're in the Idyll House, now," Julia continued. "It's a little hotel in the loop." She gave an address.

"That's only half a dozen blocks from here," Nace told her. "What're they doing?"

"Sitting here in the lobby talking. They've been talking every time they left the Century of Progress grounds."

"Then she isn't holding a gun on him now?"

"Nope. They seem to have come to an agreement. At least, they're mighty sociable."

"Have they seen you?"

"Just here in the hotel. I had to show myself. There was no other phone near. The girl has looked me over two or three times, but I don't think she smells anything."

"Can she see your lips?"

"Sure."

Nace groaned deeply. "Turn around so she can't see your

face! She's a lip reader. She must be! At that orange-drink stand, she wasn't close enough to hear what I was saying to Canadan, but she knew I had him on the point of talking. A lip-reader is the only way to explain it."

"For the love of mud!" Julia said sharply.

"What now?"

"You were right, Lee! She's wise! She's up on her feet and coming over here!"

"See what you can get out of her!" Nace rapped.

"Can you tell me something, so I can make a play that I know more than I do?"

"You know as much about it as I do—except that two plugs named Shack and Tubby tried to sashay me. And the diamond exhibit out at the Century grounds must be a part of it."

"A lot of help you are!" Julia's voice changed—evidently she was addressing the girl from the orange-drink stand. "I say now, honey—are you an old friend or something? The way you're staring—"

There was a short, sharp racket. Scuffling! The phone went dead.

Nace jammed his pipe stem between his teeth, strained his ears. The receiver at the other end must have been hung up. There was no sound. The pipe stem made crunching sounds as his teeth worried it.

He ran out of the room, paced circles in the elevator cage as it lowered him, and dived into his car. He headed toward the Idyll House.

THE IDYLL HOUSE proved to be a wedge of brick between department stores which were closed at this hour.

Nace saw two running policeman before he saw the hostelry. The officers were headed for the hotel. Angling his car in to the curb, Nace sauntered in behind them.

The two cops were getting the story from the desk clerk. Voices were loud. Nace heard what was said without appearing to show interest in proceedings.

"A man and a woman grabbed another woman out of a telephone booth and made off with her," announced the clerk.

"Which way'd they go?"

"South. They got in a taxicab."

One cop dashed out to spread an alarm.

"Who were they?" the other officer asked the clerk.

"I didn't know any of them. The woman they grabbed was red-headed—a peach of a looker. The other woman wore an orange-colored dress and one orange-colored earring. She wasn't so hard to look at, either. I don't know the man's name, but I've seen him before."

"Seen him when?"

"Oh, he came in a time or two with one of our guests, a Mister Osterfelt."

"Osterfelt here now?" demanded the officer.

"No. He didn't come in last night. Hasn't been in all day."

"Why didn't you notify the police he was missing?"

The clerk shrugged. "We don't usually rush into things like that. He might have put up with a friend for the night."

UNNOTICED, NACE glided over to the desk. Instead of the old-fashioned registration book, this hostelry used a card index system. He opened the card drawer surreptitiously and thumbed through it.

Mel. G. Osterfelt, from Berlin, Germany, had registered for 1103.

Without attracting attention, Nace went to the bank of pigeon holes which held keys. Then he rode the elevator up.

The door of 1103 was locked. The key he had taken from the pigeon hole downstairs fitted. He let himself in.

The room was plain, like most of the other hotel rooms Nace had seen. A big traveling bag, plastered with steamship stickers, stood near the bed. Osterfelt must have traveled a lot. There were stickers from most of the big steamship lines.

Nace opened the bag. It was empty. There was clothing in the closet, neat business suits. Osterfelt had evidently unpacked for a stay.

Measuring the suits against his own gaunt height, Nace concluded Osterfelt had been a stocky man, very fat. He had been a dresser; there was silk underwear in the dresser drawers.

The dresser had two half-drawers at the top. One of these held a brief case. It was stuffed. Nace dumped the contents.

Papers showed Mel. G. Osterfelt to be a research chemist for a Berlin firm specializing in the manufacture of welding equipment.

There was a black bag, leather-padded, perhaps two inches square. Nace opened it. It was a ring box, empty.

The padded satin of the lid carried the indentation made by the setting of a ring which must have been placed there often. Nace calculated. The impression was about the size and shape of the diamond which had been found in the alleged meteor.

Nace replaced the box. It had about convinced him that the man who died—murdered, probably—in the hellish blaze which many had thought was a meteor, was Osterfelt. At least, the victim had been wearing Osterfelt's ring.

Pushing his search, Nace found one more item of interest. It was a receipt for the shipment of a package from New York by serial express.

NACE LEFT the room, locking the door. The policeman and the clerk were just entering an elevator, enroute up to Osterfelt's room, no doubt, when he reached the lobby.

He entered a booth which was one of a bank. From one of these, Julia must have been dragged.

Nace thumbed through a directory, found the number of the local office at which aerial express arrived. He described the package designated in the receipt and asked if it was being held.

"It was called for yesterday," he was told.

"How many men came after it?" he queried.

"Three," was the reply. "I remember the occasion because one of them, a short, fat fellow, was some kind of a foreigner. He couldn't speak much English."

That would be Osterfelt, Nace reflected.

"What about the other two?"

"I don't remember much about them."

Nace described the two men unconscious in his car—Shack and Tubby. "That sound like them?"

"Sure. That's the pair. I remember now."

"Any idea what was in the package?"

"Hell no!"

Nace hung up. Shack and Tubby had gone with Osterfelt to get his package. Then Osterfelt had been murdered. Or so it seemed.

A squad car filled with police moaned up in front. Officers blocked the door.

Nace started to leave.

"Sorry, buddy," he was told. "Something just happened here. A kidnapping, or something. We've got to find out what it's about before anybody leaves."

Nace nodded meekly, entered an elevator, got off at the second floor, let himself through a window onto the bottom landing of a fire escape and managed it from there to an alley.

He walked around in front, kept parked cars between himself and the police, and entered the coupe. He got away without being discovered.

He drove to his hotel. For the moment, there was nothing else to do.

It would be—he consulted his watch—thirty minutes before Shack and Tubby awakened. Not until then could they be questioned.

As for Julia, no telling where she had been taken. If she got a chance, she would give Nace a call at his hotel. It was the

242 • THE WEIRD ADVENTURES OF THE BLOND ADDER

only spot where she could be sure of finding him.

He parked the machine and rode up to his room. He did not wait idly this time. Out of a closet, he dug a zipper-closed canvas bag. This container held tools of his trade. It was his sack of magic.

His clothing was a bit rumpled. He changed to a neat dark blue linen suit. A white Panama came out of a suitcase. He examined it carefully, put it back on.

He extracted a small flask of rubbing alcohol from his bag. Then he went downstairs.

"The room next to mine don't happen to be vacant?" he queried.

The clerk consulted his record. "The connecting room on the right is unoccupied."

"I'll take it," Nace told him. "A couple of friends of mine have been foolish enough to take on a little bigger load than they can stand. They're both—well, pretty tight. I don't like to take them home in that condition. I'll just put them up there and let them sleep it off."

The clerk smiled knowingly.

CHAPTER IV

Tricks

n **ACE SIGNED FOR** the room, paid the tariff, then went out to his car. He waited until no one was near, then unlocked the rear compartment and dragged out both prisoners.

On each man, he sprinkled a quantity of the rubbing alcohol. The stuff evaporated, but left the strong scent of liquor.

An arm about the waist of each, he lugged them inside.

"Passed plumb out," he told the clerk.

"I'll help you," the clerk offered.

Together, they got the pair up to the room Nace had rented. Nace gave the clerk a dollar for his trouble, and watched the fellow depart.

Nace now used sheets and towels to bind each man. He did not apply the lashings any too tightly. He dumped them on the bed.

He unlocked the connecting door.

He was standing there when the pair on the bed began to squirm with returning consciousness. They rolled their eyes at him, glared. One opened his mouth.

"Go ahead—squawk!" Nace invited. "Cops will be up here thicker'n flies!"

The man changed his mind about yelling.

"Whatcha want?" he snarled.

"Your company is all for the present," Nace said dryly.

"Huh?" They seemed surprised.

"Sure," Nace chuckled fiercely. "You see, I've sort of got a line on you two punks. We'll wait around a bit and see what happens."

He said nothing more, but watched them. They squirmed, testing their bonds. Then they exchanged looks and remained quiet. Each had discovered he could slip the lashings in a very few minutes.

After a bit, Nace went into his own room. He closed the door. Instantly, he could hear the pair struggling with their tyings.

Nace lifted the receiver quietly off his phone, got the operator and asked for the adjoining room.

An instant later, the phone in the next room began shrilling.

He left the receiver off the prong of his own instrument and walked through the connecting door.

Shack and Tubby instantly became quiescent. Their bindings were markedly looser.

Nace picked up the ringing telephone. "Yeah? Oh, it's you, kid?"

He listened intently for a moment.

"That's swell," he declared, pretending the call was genuine. "Canadan spilled the works, did he? Now, let me get this straight! Canadan knew Shack and Tubby had lifted the secret of that infernal heat from Osterfelt. Shack and Tubby killed Osterfelt. They promised to kill Canadan if he told anybody they intended to pull a series of big robberies, the first of which was the theft of the diamond exhibit at the Century of Progress? That it…"

Shack and Tubby were swapping pop-eyed looks.

"You say Canadan has offered to produce proof that Shack and Tubby killed Osterfelt after they got the ingredients for making the infernal heat from the aerial express office?" Nace continued. "That's swell!… He can prove they destroyed the diamond and Osterfelt's skull, too? And that they tried to get me in that television theatre?… He will! That's even better!"

Nace went through the motions of listening intently. "O. K. They'll be here when you come up with the cops."

Hanging up, Nace went over and gagged Shack and Tubby. He did not touch their bindings.

"You monkeys are bad actors!" he said in a blustering tone. "I'm going down and see if I can raise a gun. I'll need it, maybe, with two mugs like you on my hands."

He went out, locked both doors, and hurried downstairs. He grinned at the clerk, said, "My two pals are coming along all hunky," and went out.

He circled to an alley in the rear and watched the hotel fire escape. He wore his Panama, and carried his canvas zipper bag.

Not more than four minutes later, both Shack and Tubby came out of the hotel window. They piled down the fire escape in great haste.

NACE WITHDREW from view. From his bag, he took a delicate periscope. The stem of this was not much larger than a match, but so perfectly ground were the tiny mirrors and lenses that it functioned with the efficiency of a much larger instrument. It was possible to thrust the thing through a keyhole and survey an entire room.

Using this around the angle of a brick wall, Nace watched Shack and Tubby. When they ran toward him, he withdrew and hailed a taxi.

He was seated on the floorboards in the rear of the taxi when Shack and Tubby came out of the alley. For a moment, he thought they were going to attempt to hail the hack in which he crouched. They did not notice the tiny stick of the periscope.

Another cab came along and they piled in.

The trail led over to Michigan Avenue, then south past hotels which faced the lake, past expensive shops. The twin towers of the Sky Ride in the Century of Progress grounds hove into view ahead. The towers were like girders standing on end.

Long rods of light striped their sides.

The two men did not stop at the Century of Progress, but went on southward, dismissing their conveyance at the Twenty Third Street entrance. They paid a fifty-cent admission apiece and passed through a turnstile.

Nace, carrying his zipper bag, trailed them. He kept under cover as much as he could.

A prominent radio broadcast band was blaring music from the loudspeakers mounted on poles along the midway. The crowds were thicker. The cool of the night had drawn them out. Overhead, one of the little dirigibles was pulling a long streamer of illuminated letters.

Shack and Tubby walked swiftly.

Nace got in a ricksha pulled by a college boy. He made the boy trot, kept his quarry in sight.

The two crossed the semi-circular bridge over the lagoon, passed the Spectaculum, passed a moored whaling ship, a Norwegian ship. They swung out on the steamer landing.

Nace dismissed his college boy.

Shack and Tubby entered a lake steamer moored to the landing. It was a small craft as such vessels go, obviously old, in need of a paint job. No smoke came from the funnels. The steamer apparently was not being used.

A sign, hung on a chain across the gangplank, said, "No admittance."

On the other side of the landing, another steamer, clean, neat, was taking on passengers for a night ride on the lake.

Nace, walking back a few yards, paid twenty-five cents admission and went aboard the whaling ship. From the far rail, he could see a speed boat tied to the lakeward side of the old steamer.

He quitted the whaler and approached the old boat. Posting himself near the stern, in the shelter of a piling, he watched the boat which was taking on passengers. It was loaded. They were hauling in the gangplank. A moment later, the whistle blared out, a signal prepatory to departing.

Under cover of the great roar, Nace ran lightly, leaped. He landed on the steamer rail. A twist, and he was aboard the old boat.

HE CROUCHED there for a time. There was no light, no sound. He sidled over and saw the speed boat still tied to the lakeward rail.

Working forward, he found, in the engine room, the explanation of why the old steamer was inoperable. Something had gone wrong with the engine. A boiler was partially dismantled.

He went on, ears alert, entering narrow passages which were shabbily carpeted. Stateroom doors crowded either side. One of these, well down the corridor, showed a bar of light at the bottom.

He stopped before this, stooped, put an ear to the keyhole.

"So this guy Nace was pulling a fast one!" growled Shack's voice. "You sure?"

"I had not told him a thing," Canadan's voice quavered.

"He talked like somebody had put a bug in his ear!" Tubby put in. "He knew about Osterfelt—how Osterfelt brought the secret of the big heat and the ingredients for making it to this country. He also knowed we lifted it from Osterfelt, then scragged 'im!"

Shack swore violently. "He knew we had planned to take a whack at the diamond exhibit here! How'd he figure that out?"

"Plain as your nose!" Tubby jeered. "He found Canadan hangin' around the diamond exhibit. That told him. He's a dick. He can deduce things!"

"I'll deduce things too, if I get my hands on that shamus!" Shack gritted savagely. "Say, d'you reckon he could've let us loose so he could follow us? Them sheets and things he tied us with were mighty loose. He might've trailed us—"

A feminine voice behind Nace said grimly, "And I presume that's exactly what he did!"

Nace erected, spun. Simultaneously, a flashlight sprayed him with white.

The girl from the orange-drink stand stood just out of reach. A tiny automatic poked a black snout out of her fist.

She waved the gun. "You know the motions! Go through 'em!"

Nace carefully lowered his zipper bag and lifted his hands.

SHE CAME forward, patted his armpits, his hips, his coat pockets. "Well, for the love of Mabel! Don't you carry a gun?"

Nace, keeping his arms up, said, "No!"

Inside the stateroom, silence had suddenly fallen.

Canadan's shaky voice called, "What's happened?"

"I've got our friend Nace," retorted the orange-stand girl. "He was using his ears out here."

"Bring him in," suggested Canadan, after the briefest of pauses.

"In a minute!"

Nace scowled at the girl. She still wore her one orange colored earring. "So you're one of the gang?"

She laughed shortly. "The great Lee Nace! I always did figure they had you overrated!"

"Yeah?"

"You said it! You've got this gloriously balled up. Your redhead wasn't so hot, either."

"Where is Julia?" Nace asked sharply.

"She's all right."

"Where is she?"

"Down in the hold, cuffed to a hull brace, and chewing on a mouthful of her own nifty frock."

Nace rocked slowly on his heels, hands still high. "She'd better be okay!"

The orange-stand girl laughed again. "I wouldn't hurt her!"

"Yes you wouldn't!"

"Cross my heart, I wouldn't. I told you that you had this all balled. I haven't anything against you and the red-head, except that I thought it'd be swell to put it over on you. The great Lee Nace, who went to England to show Scotland Yard how it was done! Ha! Either you're lousy, or we're pretty good here in Chicago."

"You talk like a cop!" Nace jeered.

"I used to be on the city detective force," confided the orange-stand girl. "Just now, I'm an agency dick like yourself. I was one of several assigned to guard that diamond exhibit."

Nace lowered his hands. "So you thought you'd put one over on me?"

"You said it! I got wise when you started to talk to Canadan. I can read lips. So I got Canadan away from you and persuaded him to talk. When your red-head came nosing around, I just collared her to keep her out of the way. Then we came here to the gang hangout and waited for Shack and Tubby to turn up."

Nace looked at the stateroom door. "You've got Shack and Tubby?"

"Sure. They're handcuffed in there. Canadan is watchin' 'em! You see, Canadan was a friend of Osterfelt. Shack and Tubby approached Osterfelt with the plan for a series of robberies with the infernal heat. He refused to have anything to do with it, told Canadan about it, and they decided to go to the cops. Osterfelt was killed. Canadan was wandering around, scared to talk, when you collared him. I persuaded him it would be all right to spill the works."

Nace glowered. "You might have told me you were a private cop in the first place!"

"Don't be silly! There's a standing reward of five thousand to anybody who thwarts an attempt to steal that diamond exhibit. Do you think I wanted to cut you in on that jack?"

Nace shrugged. "You win!" He adjusted his Panama, picked up his bag. "Go ahead and grab the glory!"

The girl shoved the door open, backed inside. She was barely across the threshold when a fist flashed into view. It held a revolver; the weapon cracked against her gun hand.

She dropped her automatic.

Shack leaped into view and grabbed her by the throat.

Tubby, jumping around the pair, pointed another gun at Nace.

"Walk in!" he snarled. "And be plenty careful!"

Nace walked in.

CANADAN, TALL and bony, his dwarf face more than ever seeming to seek concealment behind his big gray moustache, stood against the opposite bulkhead. Handcuffs were on his wrists.

Tubby, jerking open Nace's zipper bag, brought to light several pairs of handcuffs. He slapped a set of these on Nace's wrists, others on his ankles.

Shack ceased choking the orange-stand girl. They put Nace's handcuffs on her, ankle and wrist.

Nace looked at her, snorted, "So you had 'em!"

The girl glared, then stared in bewilderment at Canadan.

The tall man wiped his forehead with his manacled hands. "It's too bad! They sprang upon me when I was not looking!"

"You as much as decoyed me in here!" the girl snapped.

Canadan squirmed. "I couldn't help it! They threatened to kill me if I didn't pretend everything was all right!"

Shack eyed the orange-stand girl. "Where's Nace's redhead?"

"Go jump in the lake!" she spat at him.

"C'mon, sister! Where is she?"

"I don't know!"

Shack spun on Canadan. He cocked the revolver he held. "Where is she? Spit it out quick!"

Canadan rolled his eyes, blew a groan through his big moustache, and moved his limbs as if he were being tortured.

He began, "I don't—"

"Out with it!" Shack snarled. He shoved his gun muzzle against Canadan's temple.

Canadan shrank from the weapon as if the blued steel were a burning iron.

"She's down in the hold, handcuffed to a brace!" he wailed.

Shack looked at Nace, at the orange-stand girl, jeered, "You private dicks trying to stem each other out of a reward made it easy on us!" He went out.

Three or four minutes passed. Tubby, juggling his gun, admonished fiercely, "You could yell, and people outside wouldn't pay no attention, on account of so much yelling around the fair grounds. But I wouldn't try it!"

Shack came back. Ahead of him, he propelled red-headed Julia. She was disheveled. A two-inch strip off the hem of her sports frock was balled in her teeth, held there with twine. Handcuffs clinked on her wrists.

She eyed Nace, made buzzing noises through her nose. The sounds—long and short dashes and dots—transmitted a diguised message.

"So this is the way you rescue me?"

Nace snorted.

CHAPTER V

Horror in
the Sky Ride

USING MORE HANDCUFFS from Nace's zipper bag, Shack secured the prisoners to the metal posts of the stateroom bunks. Sheets from the bunks were converted into gags.

Shack spent approximately ten minutes in the tying process. He did a thorough job.

Only Nace and the two girls were fastened. Canadan was not touched.

"What're you gonna do with me?" Canadan whimpered.

Shack leered at him. "We're taking you along, brother. We've got a little job to do! And if the cops are wise to us, there may be some lead fly. In that case, it'll be just too bad for you. It was your loose mouth that made us all this trouble!"

Canadan moaned. "I will be seen on the robbery scene! The police will think I am equally guilty with you fellows!"

"Ain't that too bad!" Tubby jeered.

"Who said anything about a robbery?" Shack rapped.

"You're going after the diamonds?" Nace interposed.

Shack came over, leaned down and rasped the rough cylinder of his revolver across Nace's face. The steel tore flesh. Four or five scarlet strings sprawled down Nace's cheeks and off his jaw.

"Don't ask goofy questions!" Shack advised.

Nace, saying no more, held his head to one side so the crimson would not soil his dark linen suit. His white Panama lay to one side.

Tubby kicked the hat under a bunk, waved his gun at Canadan. "C'mon, tall stuff! We're taking the cuffs off you. But if you start to run, say your prayers first!"

The bracelets were removed from Canadan's wrists. He stumbled out of the stateroom.

Shack stopped in the door to glower at Nace. "It may interest you, shamus, to know we're comin' back!" He chuckled nastily. "This old boat would make a swell meteor, wouldn't it?

He pulled the door shut behind him, locked it.

Nace listened. He lost track of footsteps. There was a monotonous roar of sound—loudspeakers, bands, concession barkers, the bawling of paper-mache dinosaurs in prehistoric world exhibits. The mumble penetrated even to the innards of the ancient lake boat, blanketing the footsteps.

He heard the speed boat start. Shack, Tubby and Canadan had departed by water.

Nace braced a wristband of his handcuffs against the edge of the berth. He pressed, apparently endeavoring to force the wrist circlet tighter. There was a click.

The cuff dropped away from his wrist.

The orange-stand girl stared, wide-eyed.

"I've had my own handcuffs put on me before," Nace told her. "I had a special brand made up. You have to turn the key into a certain position when you lock them, or they won't hold."

Working rapidly, Nace freed the girls. He ungagged them. Julia, manacled with cuffs which had belonged to the orange-stand girl, proved more of a problem.

Nace took a small metal spike of a probe from his zipper bag. Two minutes work was enough to pick the lock on Julia's manacles.

Nace crawled under the bunk and got his white Panama hat. He jammed it on his head, scooped up his bag.

"You two had better beat it somewhere!" he told Julia and the orange-stand girl.

"I'm seeing it through!" said the girl in the orange dress. "I'll take back what I said, Nace. I'm just a bum!"

Red-headed Julia gave her a mean look. "You said it, honey!"

THEY SCRAMBLED out of the old boat, ran down the gangplank, vaulting the chain on which hung the "No Admittance" sign.

"Where to?" Julia demanded.

"The building which holds the diamond exhibit!" Nace rapped.

They ran. That was quickest. The semi-circular bridge over the lagoon with its numerous concession stands was crowded. They took the right rail, where the throng was thinnest.

Nace pointed. "Look! Half way down the lagoon—directly under the cables of the sky ride!"

"Their speed boat!" Julia gasped. "They're leading us!"

They left the bridge, passed the hump of an exhibit known as "The World A Million Years Ago." A gigantic ape stood in front of the exhibit, wagging its head slowly, mechanically. The ape was wood, cloth, artificial hair and paint. The Hall of Religion bulked gigantic on their right.

"Not much farther!" Nace grunted, and took the center of the midway.

Purposefully, he increased his pace. The two girls were left behind.

Ahead, a sudden bedlam of yelling arose. Shots snapped. Somewhere, a siren shrilled. The sounds mounted, became a thunderous babble.

"Too late!" Nace gritted.

The uproar was coming from the exhibit building which held the diamond display.

Smoke poured from ventilating rifts in the ceiling of the vast structure. People were milling about the doors. Others, inside, were struggling to get out.

Nace took an entrance marked, "Employees." Down a brilliantly lighted passage, he plunged. There was smoke, acrid with the tang of scorched paint and varnish.

Police and special Century of Congress officers had already thrown a cordon around the diamond exhibit. Nace struggled close enough to glimpse the display. Tear gas smarted his eyes.

The robbery had been successful. The much-advertised burglar-proof diamond case had yielded its contents. The metallic block of a safe below the case, into which the diamond display dropped when the case was molested, had an enormous hole eaten in its side.

Edges of the hole glowed red-hot.

To the left, the wall of the exhibit booth was in flames.

"They got our attention with that fire over there," a cop was yelling. "Then they wiped out the side of the safe and grabbed the sparkler. We couldn't do much in the smoke and excitement."

The officer fell to coughing from the effects of the tear gas.

Nace backed out, rubbing his eyes. The special police on guard wore gas masks. The thieves must have worn them, too.

Julia was at Nace's elbow. How she had kept track of him was a miracle.

"The boat in the lagoon—"

"I know!" Nace cut in. "Listen, you clear out! These birds are bad actors! Snatching them jewels like that took nerve! They won't stop at anything! You may get hurt!"

As he spoke, he was running toward the lagoon.

"In your hat!" Julia told him.

Nace, as if reminded of something, felt of his white Panama. It was still on his head.

The girl from the orange stand pounded up, moving fast, skirts gathered above her knees.

"You're a better runner than you are detective!" Julia told her nastily.

"You dry up!" retorted the other. "Or I'll pull me some red hair!"

NACE RAN past the tower on the Sky Ride. Spidery, streaked with lights, it reared more than six hundred feet. From a point slightly less than half way up, the manifold cables on which the cars ran stretched their great span across the lagoon to the other tower. Elevators lifted to that point, and to the observation platform at the top.

Around the north wing of the Hall of Science, Nace soon located the launch. It bounced up and down on the small waves within the lagoon, moored by the bow to the railing along the lagoon edge.

Shack, Tubby—Canadan—none of the three were in sight.

Vaulting the railing, Nace landed lightly on the speedboat deck. He wrenched up the engine cover, dived in a hand, grasped a fistful of ignition wires and tore them out.

He threw the wires into the lagoon. The boat would not start soon.

Julia and the girl in orange came up.

"They either haven't reached the launch yet, or have taken another way out!" Nace told them.

"Let's go up in the car landing of the sky ride!" Julia suggested. "We may be able to spot them from here."

"O. K." Nace ran to one of the nickel-in-a-slot telescopes, many of which were mounted along the lagoon edge to catch sightseer's coins.

He grasped the glass, wrenched. The mounting resisted. He tried again. It snapped off.

They sprinted for the Sky Ride tower. Nace, holding his hat on with one hand, carried the telescope with the other. He had lost his zipper bag somewhere. It was clumsy to carry, anyway.

Julia demanded, "Nace—do you know what that infernal heat is?"

"I can't tell you exactly what's in it," he threw over his shoulder. "I didn't get to make a full analysis. But it's some kind of highly perfected thermit."

"What's thermit?" demanded the orange-stand girl.

"A metallic powder which burns with terrible heat. It was used in incendiary bombs in the war. It's used in welding. Osterfelt, the bird who perfected this stuff, worked for a manufacturer of welding equipment. He must have developed it in the course of his chemical research work. Probably brought it to the Century of Progress for exhibition."

They reached the tower of the Sky Ride. An elevator was waiting. Nace chucked a dollar bill and two dimes in the window—admission for three. The lift raced them upward.

The cage halted at the car landing. The doors whispered back.

Nace stared, made a sudden gesture to get the doors shut again. He was too late.

Shack and Tubby stood on the car landing, menacing them with drawn revolvers. Behind them stood Canadan. He was handcuffed.

"SWEET, THIS!" Shack jeered.

He stepped into the cage and rapped the elevator operator viciously over the head with his gun. The uniformed operator dropped. Shack hauled him out bodily.

The operator of another cage—evidently the one which had brought the three men up—lay in a slack pile on the landing, scarlet trickling from a welt on his head.

Shack dumped both elevator attendants in a waiting car.

"Now you get in!" He gestured meaningly at Nace and the two young women.

Julia looked at Nace. Her eyes were wide, scared.

"Just string along with them!" Nace advised her.

She nodded. They entered the car. The big box of an affair had two levels for passengers. They were on the lower. Apparently, there was no one above.

Nace sat down on one of the seats which ran lengthwise of the car. The earth, not quite three hundred feet below, looked very distant.

Canadan got inside. Then came Tubby. He had his arms full of squarish cloth packets from which webbing straps dangled. Parachutes—three of them. He also carried tear gas masks, obviously those used in the raid of the gem exhibit. He tossed the latter carelessly aside.

Shack came in with a large bag. It made a gravel-like rattle when he dropped it on the floor. The diamonds!

It was Shack who got the car in motion.

"We found out how this thing operates earlier today!" he chuckled. "We figured we might have to use this thing for a getaway. Lookit—see that boat?"

Nace followed his pointing arm. On the opposite side of the lagoon, nearly under the point over which the Sky Ride cables passed, another speed boat was moored. It was, as near as Nace could tell by the glow of electric lights, a twin to the one from which he had just torn the ignition cables.

The car was moving. Machinery made a dull moan. The vehicle gave a somewhat unnerving lurch when suspension points on the tracks were passed.

Nace lifted his hands and grasped the brim of his Panama, as if to hold the hat on.

Shack gave him an ugly look. "In case you ain't guessed it, we're gonna step in the door when we get over that speed boat, pull the ripcord on our chutes and go down. There's enough wind to open the chutes before we take off, so we won't have to run the chance of the drop openin' them!"

He fumbled in the bag which held the diamonds, brought out a metallic looking egg of an object somewhat larger than a football. "I'm gonna be the last guy out! And I'll leave this egg for you! You know what it is?"

"Thermit bomb?" Nace guessed dryly.

"Right," Shack grinned. "A new kind of thermit. There's

enough of the stuff in here to melt the middle out of a battleship. You'll be cooked so quick you'll never see the thing let loose!"

"You're going to kill us?"

"What the hell'd you think?" Shack demanded.

Nace looked at tall, moustached Canadan. "In that case, there's no need of Canadan playing prisoner any longer!"

Canadan started violently. "Huh?"

"You're not fooling anybody," Nace growled. "I've had it figured for some time that you were giving Shack and Tubby their orders."

CANADAN'S DWARF face seemed to swell behind his moustache. He blurted, "That is ridiculous—"

"Oh, cut it out!" Nace snapped. "You claimed Shack and Tubby overpowered you back there in the lake steamer, but there wasn't a mark of a struggle on you. That alone was enough to give you away. You turned them loose. And their taking you along when they went to commit the diamond robbery. That's a laugh! You went along to supervise the job. They'd never take a prisoner with 'em to look on!"

"You're crazy!" Canadan sputtered indignantly.

"Your yarn about being scared was intended to interest me until you could get me off some place and dispose of me, but you made it stick with the girl here."

The girl in the orange dress groaned. "What a bright one I was!"

Canadan gave his handcuffs a tug. They had not been locked. They came off. He threw them the length of the car.

"O. K.!" he snapped. "What're you going to do about it?"

Nace took off his Panama.

"*This!*" he rapped, and gave the hat band a tug.

There was a loud ripping sound. Sparks flew as the hat band, turned by the force of the wrench, ground against a friction igniter.

Like a stricken match, the hat burst into flame. It blazed brilliantly, gave off a tremendous cloud of billious yellow smoke.

Nace flung the headgear at Canadan. The man ducked. Nace twisted sidewise.

He had clamped one hand tightly over his mouth and nostrils. His eyes were closed.

He found a window. With his free fist, he beat madly against it. The glass was the non-shattering type. It gave like cardboard under the furiously-driven blows. When he had a sufficient aperture, he thrust out his head.

Even then, Nace did not breathe in air until his lungs were throbbing. He drew in tentatively, made a face, began to cough violently. He hung in the window, limp, features distorted, until the car reached the other tower.

For a time, he was entirely unconscious.

THE JAR as the car arrived at the landing stage aroused him. He stumbled to the mechanism, got it stopped before the car had rounded the horseshoe turn-track and started back. He gained the door, stumbled out on the platform, then wheeled dizzily and stared.

Everyone in the car was unconscious.

It required ten minutes to get police on the spot, turn Shack, Tubby and Canadan over to them, together with the sack containing, at a conservative estimate, some millions in gems.

Nace got a receipt for the stones. Then he set about reviving Julia and the girl detective from the orange-drink stand. That took another five minutes.

The girl in orange took her head in both hands and rocked. "Do I feel awful! What'd you do, anyway?"

"My hat was painted inside with a chemical mixture which, when burned, produces a gas that'll knock you instantly," Nace explained. "The hat itself is whitened with a highly inflammable paint, a mixture of celluloid and some other stuff." He coughed. "I got a dose of the gas myself."

The orange-drink girl scowled. "You might have told me in advance what was coming off!"

Red-headed Julia laughed spitefully. "After the way you clowned around, you should squawk, honey!"

(1)

L E E   N A C E

HIS CHARACTER TRAITS

(This Thing Started May 1, 1933)

Lester Dent's complete "Bible" for the Lee Nace series.

(2)

LEE COURTNEY NACE

"NACE"

KNOBBY HEIGHT---Is the thing which characterizes Nace upon first
    glance. He is tall enough to tower over everyone near him.
    He is bony, muscular. A "bony Viking."

PHYSICAL ASPECTS

HEIGHT---6 feet, 7 inches.
WEIGHT--180 pounds.
BUILD---Knobby, big-boned, big-fisted.
SHOULDERS---Might have been made out of a 6x6 timber slightly less
    than three feet long.
HAIR---Blonde, touseled always. Shaggy at temples.
EYES---Pale. They are blue when the going is okay, but get pale
    when things are tough.
SKIN---Light, and subject to sunburn, windubrn, etc., so as to
    mirror any weather to which Nace has been exposed.
FOREHEAD---Is high, with scar on the center, which flushes red when
    he is mad, and is shaped like a coiled snake. This scar came from
    being struck on the forehead once by the handle of a dagger which
    bore a snake carving.
MOUTH---Nace's mouth is thin-lipped, the lips suitable to untying
    things if necessary. His lips have a thin, grim aspect.
TEETH---Average in size, even, white.
CHEEKS---Flat, paper-like, giving the impression of thin covers over
    working machinery, because of the prominent bones and muscles
    under them.
EARS---Nace's ears are rather large. One has a slight crop from a
    bullet. This one is the upper left, and Nace's blonde hair
    is combed so as to hide it. He wears his hair shaggy at temples
    to hide this bullet cropped ear.
NOSE---Nace's nose is shapely, but often broken. He has a plastic
    surgeon who does the work on his nose when necessary. This
    plastic surgeon, Doctor Fidel Halligan by name, is a source of
    occasional wise cracks about Nace's snozzle.
TONGUE.--An amazingly flat, ribbonglike tongue, capable of making
    strange sounds.
ARMS---Big-boned, corded with muscle; the same size all the way up,
    except for knobby joints.
CHEST---Flat, deep, something like a triangular box set under the
    cross beam of his shoulders. He has excellent lunts, and
    is almost tireless.

(3)

LUNGS.--Nace has good lung capacity, and takes care that he never
has a cold. He had "a friend who went west---clear west" from
t.b., and he takes medicine the instant he feels a cold
coming on.
STOMACH.--Nace can and does eat any kind of food. He is a firm
believer in variety, and will eat one night in a German restaurant
the next night in a Japanese, and the next in an Italian, and
so on. This is a strong point of his character, this eating at
different restaurants.
HIPS---Somewhat bony, prominent. He's certainly not thin-hipped; he
had good underpinning.
FEET---Big feet, like all swedes.

. . . .

NACE'S EARLY TRAINING.

Lee Courtney Nace was born in 1905 at Elmer, Missouri, in the
Chariton river brakes. He was born during a cyclone which killed
his parents. Nace became something of a drifter. He has been a
stage magician, acrobat, farmer, cowboy, moonshiner, worked his way
through college as a pro ahtlete, played pro baseball, basketball,
hockey, tennis, golf, and been a commercial chemist. He has become
a cynic by nature; a private detective by choice. His avowed
purpose in life is to show up the police, who have been his enemies.

NACE'S LATER TRAINING.

Nace became a detective after an intensive course of study, in
which he determined to put to use every modern device, as well as the
magic, chemistry and so forth, that he knew.

OFFICE.

Is situated in the Globe Theater Building, with a flashing Neon
sign over the window. This is on Broadway, the main stem of the
town. It consists of an inner reception room, and an office proper.
From the window of the latter, Nace can reach a sign with a rope
and swing to another floor, thus leaving his sanctum secretly.

HABITS:

SMOKING-- Nace smokes a stubby pipe. He has a habit of biting through
his pipe stems, so he carries surplus stems in a pocket case.

PANAMA HAT---Nace wears a panama hat, winter or summer, rain or
shine, because, when burned, this hat produces a blinding gas,
the fabric of the weave being impregnated with a solidified form
of tear gas.

DARK CLOTHES---Nace's clothing is always dark, priestly, almost.

(4)

GUNS---One in heel of shoe, which he can fire in an emergency.

HANDBAG---Canvas, closed by zipper fastener. It holds many things,
    amplifier-listener, hand-contact odor powder, etc.

Lester Dent
8904 34th Avenue
Jackson Heights, L.I., N.Y.
Phone NEwton 9-4729

15,000 words.
First North American
Serial Rights.

HOT OIL

By Lester Dent

She was tall, blonde, streamlined. The roadster was long, cream-colored, and also streamlined.

She was making motions at powdering her nose, using a pancake compact with a mirror only four inches across. She held it braced against the steering wheel. Utter concentration rode her long, beautiful face.

The big, flat powder puff dabbed the compact with strangely erratic frequency. It only slapped the mirror——never the powder cake.

Oklahoma sunlight, white hot, sprayed blonde and roadster. To the right, it cooked overgrown stucco buildings of the Tulsa Municipal Airport. To the left, it toasted flat classroom and barrack structures of a school of aeronautics.

In spasms, the sun leaped from the blonde's compact mirror. Her powder puff, whipping systematically, was dividing the beam into dots and dashes.

A fragment of an early draft of "The Tank of Terror" (then known as "Hot Oil"); these pages contain Lester Dent's hand-written corrections.

On hands and knees beside the airport waiting room, Lee
Nace crawled. He was very long, and bony, and blue-eyed. He was
gathering together the wind-scattered sheets of a letter.

Standing and staring at Nace were six or seven people who
had been his fellow passengers on the recently arrived New York
plane. They were fascinated by the scar on Nace's forehead. It
was a perfect likeness of a small coiled snake—an adder. A
Chinaman had once hit Nace on the forehead with a knife hilt which
bore a serpent carving, and he was destined to forever carry the scar. Ordinarily the scar was unnoticeable, but it flushed out redly when he was angry or worried.

He was worried now.

Inside the ornate, modernisitic waiting room, a male voice
was shouting: "Telegram! Wire for Lee Nace, private Detective!
Telegram!"

Nace continued picking up the sheets of his letter. He pretended
to read each. When he had spilled the sheets, he had taken pains to
make it seem an accident.

Slyly, over the paper, he read the heliograph message being
flashed by the blonde's compact mirror. Three of them, Mac

"A reception committee," she sun-flashed. One with the
telegram is one. The other two are wearing coveralls
to hide bullet proof vests."

Nace captured two more sheets of his letter, pretended to read, but kept his eyes on the mirror.

"The one with the telegram is 'Robinhood' Lloyd," the girl
continued. "He's Oklahoma's bad boy."

~~She is the only thing to be found.~~

~~The Blonde~~ ended her transmission.

Mace arose and barged in under a striped canopy ~~curb~~ ~~that~~.

telescoped out to meet arriving planes. He entered the flashy

ACE waiting room.

"Telegram for Lee Mace," droned ~~a bell-hop~~ Lloyd. The

Robinhood was a lean, ~~young-old~~ wolf. His chin bore ~~scars~~

irregular, wavy lines _mobs_ ~~of an ancient~~ beating with knucks.

Two men sat side by side on a modernistic divan. They were

Chunky. ~~Aloof.~~ Their faces might have been _meaty_ ~~chunky~~ blocks covered with

a good grade of brown saddle leather. Both wore khaki coveralls.

Both had newspapers spread open on their laps.

Headlines on the papers read:

OIL SCANDAL GROWING!

There was a ~~particular~~ picture of a man with a flowing white

beard. He looked like Santa Claus. _Under_ ~~After~~ that, ~~there~~ was another

black-faced type line.

~~EDITOR APP LEADS IN OIL INVESTIGATION~~
Stubby
EDITOR APP LEADS ~~NEW~~ OIL INVESTIGATION.

Mace sidled, long-legged, for the seated pair. These men did not know him, or they would not be using the telegram ruse to spot him.

He was still moving when his long arms shot out. His hands, lean, long-fingered, bony, swung hard against the right ear of one man, and the left ear of the other. Their heads, driven together, made a bonk.

Each man gave one convulsive quiver as he became unconscious. The newspapers slid off their laps, revealing frontier six-shooters. They lay back on the modernistic divan, mouths agape, eyes pinched.

Robinhood Lloyd stood motionless, a yellow telegram envelope dangling from his right hand. Suddenly he dropped the envelope and began to shake his right hand madly.

A small revolver, dislodged from an armpit, dropped out of the sleeve and hung swinging on a string.

Before Robin Hood could seize his hideout weapon, Mace's fist landed. It hit the handiest spot, the undershot jaw which gave Robin Hood his wolf look.

Oklahoma's bad boy flopped his hands convulsively. He was not entirely out, and feeling himself going down, wheeled in an effort to land on all fours. He failed, hit the floor all spread out.

The sound as he came down was a metallic clank, as of a pile of scrap iron dumped on the tile floor, rather than a man.

Mace had read about this Oklahoma cut-up in the New York papers. The fellow went around armored like a knight of old, not only with bullet vest, but with steel leg and arm shields.

The Robin Hood rolled on his back, made a tent over his face with his hands, and moaned loudly.

"The wild and woolly west," Mace said through his teeth. "I'll show you how we handle men, where the lights are shining bright."

He rushed, bent low, long arms hanging down.

He never did know exactly what happened next. One of the men on the modernistic divan unlimbered a gun. Maybe it was both of them. A bullet slammed against Mace's right side. It spun him just enough so that the second slug got him in the stomach. The Robin Hood drew back both feet and kicked him in the head.

Mace's eyes became two gory bonfires of pain. His insides felt as if they were torn out.

He started to cave. It soaked through his dazed brain that he would die if he did. He hauled up, swayed around, and ran blindly for the white blur he knew was the sunlit door.

When he *got* outside, he knew it only because he seemed to be in a white-hot snow storm. He pawed his kicked face, beat his body where the bullets had hit. *He wore a* ~~The~~ bullet proof jacket, *which* had saved his life, but the slugs had mauled him horribly. Flaying his tortured brain, he managed to remember where they had stacked the baggage from the plane.

He veered for the luggage heap. His canvas zipper bag was there. He wanted it. ~~It~~ was his war sack, his bag of tricks, his life preserver.

He was ~~too~~ drunk with pain ~~to realize~~ to realize he could *come* get the bag before the trio in the waiting room ~~could come~~ him. ~~...~~ face never carried a gun. He subscribed to a theory that toting a ~~gun~~ firearm tended to make a man helpless, *ever* he was caught without it. ~~...~~

Finally he snapped out of the daze ~~...~~ *He* ~~"..."~~ he ~~...~~ and swiveled around drunkenly on a ~~heel...~~

His hand, clawing inside his coat, fished out a little metal firing cylinder ~~...~~. He exploded it into the waiting room door. On the *opposite* side of the building the roadster engine was moaning anxiously. ~~...~~ the blonde *waited tense at the*

~~"..."~~

The Robin Hood and his two followers floundered out into the *sunlight* ~~...~~ blinded by the tear gas, they were holding *hands* to keep track of each other. They acted like three small boys trying not to get lost.

"Come on, guys, ~~...~~" rapped the blonde. "*Boss!*

~~...~~

~~"..."~~ the blinded Robin Hood ~~...~~ *tried* to *roadster, bride*

the back seat ~~xxxxxxxxxxxxxxxxxxxxxxxx~~ He hauled
out a single action gun, jabbed it above his head, fanned out its
~~slugs~~ then ~~found~~ the car door and piled in. "O.K. ~~xxx~~
~~xxx~~ hold em! Blow!,"

The roadster seemed to snug its oilpan belly to the ground,
then jump. ~~It~~ *Shooting* *It left* away, ~~xxx~~ a rain of gravel.
"Did ~~they~~ get the ~~dirty~~ so-and-so" the blonde ~~xxxxxx~~ *demanded*

"Hell no!" The Robin Hood held his jaw with a clench so tight
that ~~the~~ tendons on his hands whitened out like chalk ~~xxxxx~~ *rods* x

"Damn!Did he hang one on ~~my~~ *your* kisser?" x

"My ~~xxxxx~~" ~~the~~ *girls* ~~xxxxxxxxxxxxx~~. But her eyes were
brightly glad.

As if it were clawing ~~xxxx~~ *cats* the wind tore her blonde hair
about. It was so very very blonde, that hair, that it was *plainly*
~~xxxxxxxxx~~ dyed.

Mace staggered around the airport waiting-room, covering as much
ground ~~to~~ right and left as he did ahead.

The field operation office was in the same building, with the
waiting room but there were doors, probably closed, *through which* ~~xxx~~ the tear
gas had not yet penetrated.

Like a dude out of a bandbox, a man popped from an office
window. He wore striped trousers *and* a gray lap-over tea vest, x *the*
pearl grip of a derringer protruded, charm-like, from his watch pockt.

He ~~xxxxxxxxxxxxxx~~ *pulled his* tiny gun, ~~xxx~~ levelled it. The thing made a

6917058R0

Made in the USA
Charleston, SC
23 December 2010